The Desert Healer

The Desert Healer

E.M. Hull

MINT EDITIONS

The Desert Healer was first published in 1922.

This edition published by Mint Editions 2021.

ISBN 9781513277448 | E-ISBN 9781513277851

Published by Mint Editions®

 MINT
EDITIONS

minteditionbooks.com

Publishing Director: Jennifer Newens
Design & Production: Rachel Lopez Metzger
Project Manager: Micaela Clark
Typesetting: Westchester Publishing Services

Contents

I

The slanting rays of the afternoon sun, unusually powerful for the time of year, lay warmly on the southern slopes of a tiny spur of the Little Atlas Mountains, glowing redly on the patches of bare earth and naked rock cropping out between the scrubby undergrowth that straggled sparsely up the hill-side, and flickering through the leaves of a clump of olive trees huddled at its base where three horses stood tethered, lazily switching at the troublesome flies with their long tails and shifting their feet uneasily from time to time.

Ten miles away to the westward lay Blidah, Europeanised and noisy, but here was the deep stillness and solitude—though not the arid desolation—of the open desert. The silence was broken only by the monotonous cooing of pigeons and the low murmur of voices.

At a little distance from the picketed horses, out in the full sunshine, a man lay on his back on the soft ground apparently asleep, his hands clasped under his head, his face almost hidden by a sun helmet beneath the brim of which protruded grotesquely a disreputable age-black pipe which even in sleep his teeth held firmly. There were amongst William Chalmers' patients and intimate acquaintances those who affirmed positively that that foul old meerschaum—treasured relic of his hospital days—ranked second in his affections only to the adored wife who was sitting now near his recumbent figure. Alert and youthful looking in spite of her grey hairs, she lounged comfortably against a sun warmed rock talking animatedly yet softly to the third member of the party, a well set up man of soldierly appearance who sprawled full length at her feet. There was a certain definite resemblance between the two, a similarity of speech and gesture, that proclaimed a near relationship.

Mrs. Chalmers broke off in the middle of a sentence to flap her gauntlet gloves at a swarm of persistent flies. "All the same, I think it's perfectly disgraceful that you are still a bachelor, Micky," she said, with emphatic cousinly candour, resuming an argument which had raged for the last half hour. Major Meredith grinned with perfect good humour.

"Haven't time for matrimony," he answered lazily, "too busy watching our wily brothers over the Border. And besides," with a provocative sidelong glance, "marriage is a lottery. We can't all expect to have Bill's luck."

Mrs. Chalmers wrinkled her nose at him disgustedly. "That's a *cliché*," she said with fine scorn, ignoring the implied compliment, "it merely means that you haven't yet met the right woman. However—" she laughed mischievously—"there's still hope for you. A year at home after nearly ten years of exile will probably make you change your mind. It's a pity you didn't take your leave sooner, there were some charming girls here last winter. Unfortunately this year's sample is not recommendable, there is scarcely a really nice girl in the place—always excepting Marny Geradine, and she's married already—poor child."

"Why 'poor child?'" asked the soldier, his cousin's sudden change of tone seeming to call for some comment. "Because—" Mrs. Chalmers paused frowningly, "oh, well, you haven't seen Lord Geradine or you wouldn't ask," she went on soberly, "he's been away on a shooting trip since you've been here—and the air of Algiers has been consequently cleaner," she added with a little shiver.

Major Meredith hoisted his long limbs up into a sitting position. "A case of a misfit marriage?" he suggested.

"Marriage!" echoed Mrs. Chalmers scornfully, "it isn't a marriage, it's a crime. It makes my blood boil to think of it. And yet I hardly know them. He's impossible, and she is the shyest, most reserved young woman I have ever met. I'd give a great deal to be able to help her, she seems so lonely and there is tragedy staring at you out of her eyes. But of course one can't do anything. She isn't the kind of person who makes confidants. I've blundered in pretty often during my life when it hasn't been my business, but I simply shouldn't dare to speak to Lady Geradine of her affairs—though I am old enough to be her mother. Ugh! let's talk of something less revolting," she said hastily, a trace of huskiness in her voice. And for a time she sat silent, staring absently in front of her with eyes that had become very wistful and tender. Then with a shrug and a half sigh she turned again eagerly to her companion. "There is a great deal that wants putting right in the world, Micky," she said with ungrammatical decisiveness, "but I'm not going to spoil a perfect afternoon by moralising. It has been jolly, hasn't it? I thought you would like this little valley. So few people seem to know of it, no special inducement to bring them here except peace and quietness which most of the folk wintering in Algiers don't seem particularly to hanker after. We found it years ago and have camped here often, a haven of refuge when life was especially strenuous or perplexing. It is sad to think that it is our last visit and that in a few weeks we shall have shaken the dust of Algeria off our feet. Five years, Micky, five years that Bill has been marking time in this Back of Beyond because of my stupid lungs. But they are all right now, thank God, and we are off to America as soon as may be to investigate some new nerve treatment Bill is interested in. And when he has picked the brains of his transatlantic *confrères* we shall come home to end our days in Harley Street in an odour of sanctity and general stuffiness. Won't London be simply horrid after years of fresh air and open spaces? So, you see, you only just caught us in time. If your leave had been delayed you would have missed us, and I did want you to see our Algerian home. It's been a hectic fortnight, but I've enjoyed every minute of it, and I think we've managed to show you all the sights of Algiers and its immediate surroundings. But I do regret one thing—I wish you could have seen our Mystery-man. He is quite a feature of the place. An Englishman who lives like an Arab—you needn't pull a face, Micky, I don't mean that he has 'gone native' or anything horrid of that kind, he is *much* too dignified. But he lives in a sort of splendid isolation in the loveliest villa in Mustapha, with a retinue like a Chief's. And though he is tremendously popular with the French officers and all the important Sheiks who come into Algiers he pointedly avoids his fellow countrymen. And he won't speak to or even look at a woman! He wears Arab dress most of the time and would pass for a native anywhere. He lives for months together in the desert and descends on Algiers at irregular intervals. One hears that he is in the town, and glimpses him occasionally stalking along with his head in the air rather like a supercilious camel, or riding like a hurricane through the streets in approved Arab style, but that is all that the English community ever see of him. And he has obviously heaps of money—and it's a gorgeous villa. He might be such an acquisition to the place, but, as it is, he is merely an intriguing personality who is 'wropt in mystery,' as old Nannie used to say. Needless to add that in a place like this, where we all discuss our neighbours, he is the subject of endless speculation. But nobody really knows anything about him."

A faint chuckle came from behind Doctor Chalmers' big helmet. "I'm sorry to contradict you, Mollie, but that is not strictly accurate," he said sleepily. His wife sat up with a jerk. "Who knows?" she challenged.

"Well—I do, for one," replied Doctor Chalmers coolly.

"*You* know, Bill—and you've never said. How like a man! Really, you are the most exasperating creatures on earth. Fancy having that pearl of information up your sleeve—I'm getting mixed up in my metaphors, but never mind—and withholding it from the partner of your joys and sorrows. I shouldn't have passed it on if it was a confidence, you know that very well. But since you have admitted so much you can soothe my outraged feelings by imparting a little more."

Doctor Chalmers laughed and stretched lazily. "Can't be done," he replied succinctly.

"Why not? I wouldn't tell a soul, and Micky is only a bird of passage so it can't possibly matter what he hears. Don't be tiresome, Bill, expound."

But the doctor shook his head. "My dear Mollie," he expostulated, fingering the old pipe tenderly, "a confidence is a confidence and I can't break it simply to satisfy your curiosity, natural though it may be. And hasn't the poor devil been discussed enough? How he lives and what he chooses to do in the desert is, after all, entirely his own affair—nobody else's business."

"But, Bill, one hears such queer stories—"

"Queer stories be hanged, m'dear. A silly lot of idiotic gossip, this place is rotten with it. Some fool of a busybody starts a rumour without a tithe of foundation to it and it's all over the town as gospel truth the next day. Carew's mode of life, his antipathy to women, and his obvious sympathy with the Arabs make him a bit peculiar. Just because the poor chap has the bad taste to ignore your charming sex all the women have got their knives into him. I bet the queer stories you speak of emanate from your blessed feminine tea parties. Trust a woman to invent a mystery—"

"But, Bill, he *is* mysterious."

"Rubbish, Mollie. He prefers to make his friends amongst the French and he hates women—that's the sum total of his crimes as far as I'm aware. Peculiar, if you like, but certainly not mysterious. And as to the last indictment—" the doctor laughed and winked unblushingly at Major Meredith, "—personally I call him a sensible chap to mix only with his own broader minded and more enlightened sex—*ouch!*" he grunted, as his wife's helmet landed with a thud on his chest.

"Bill, you're horrid. Men gossip just as much as women."

Doctor Chalmers returned her helmet with an ironical bow. "They may do, my dear," he said with sudden gravity, "but in Algiers it is not the men who gossip about Carew. And for the short time we remain in this hot-bed of intrigue you will oblige me by contradicting, on my authority, any silly stories you may hear about him. He's a friend of mine. I value his friendship, and I won't have him adversely discussed in my house."

Mrs. Chalmers bowed her head to the unexpected storm she had raised. "I'm sorry, dear," she said contritely, "I didn't know he was really a friend. In all the years we've lived here you've hardly ever mentioned him. I do think men are the queerest things," she added in a puzzled voice that made her companions laugh. Her husband rolled over and began to fill his pipe. "There are still a few little secrets I keep from the wife of my bosom," he murmured teasingly, "but, seriously, Mollie, hands off Carew."

"Very well, dear," she replied with surprising meekness. And for some time she sat silent with knitted brows, poking the sand absently with the handle of her whip. Then she spoke abruptly—"But there's no smoke without fire, Bill. There must be some foundation for the stories that are told about him. He was divorced or something unpleasant of the kind, wasn't he?"

"He may have been," replied the doctor indifferently, pressing the tobacco down into the bowl of his pipe with a blunt thumb, "I don't know—and I'm afraid I don't care. I take people as I find them, and Gervas Carew is one of the whitest, cleanest men I have ever met."

Major Meredith looked up with a sudden start.

"Gervas Carew," he said quickly, "*Sir* Gervas Carew?"

The doctor shrugged. "I believe so," he said guardedly, "though he doesn't seem to have any use for the title. He drops it here in Algeria. And if you have anything detrimental to say about him I'd rather not hear it," he added shortly, with a sudden flicker of anger in his sleepy blue eyes.

But Major Meredith was obviously not listening.

"Gervas Carew—after all these years!" he exclaimed, "so your Mystery-man, Mollie, turns out to be Gervas Carew. Gad, what a small place the world is! Poor old Gervas—of all people!"

Mrs. Chalmers' eyes danced with excitement. She laid an impatient hand on her cousin's shoulder, and shook him vigorously. "If you don't say something more explicit in a minute, Micky, I shall scream. It's no good sitting there looking as if you had seen a ghost and murmuring tragically 'poor old Gervas,' you've simply got to explain. And if Bill doesn't want to listen he can go and saddle the horses. It's time we made a move anyhow."

Meredith turned slowly and looked at her through narrowing eyelids. "Give a dog a bad name, and hang him," he said with a touch of contempt in his voice. "From what you say, Mollie, Algiers appears to have been hanging Gervas Carew pretty thoroughly and, as he was my best friend once, I think it is up to me to explain. You needn't go, Bill," he added hastily as the doctor heaved himself on to his feet with a smothered word of profanity. "You're seldom wrong in a diagnosis, old man, and you haven't made a mistake this time. It's not a long story, nor, unfortunately, an uncommon one. Carew and I were chums at Rugby, and until I got my commission and went to India. When he was about twenty-five, shortly after his father's death and he had succeeded to the title, he married. The girl, who was a few years younger than himself, was the worst kind of Society production, artificial to her finger tips. I stayed with them on my first home leave and hated her at sight. But poor old Gervas was blindly in love. He worshipped the ground she walked on. She was beautiful, of course, one of those pale-complexioned, copper-haired women who are liable to sudden and tremendous passion—but Gervas hadn't touched her. Mentally and morally he was miles above her. She was as incapable of appreciating the fineness of his character as he was of suspecting the falseness of hers. His love didn't content her and, though she was clever enough to hide it from him, she flirted shamelessly with every man who came to the house. She craved for adulation. Anybody was fair game to her. She tried it on with me before I'd been there half a day—but I hadn't served five years' apprenticeship in India for nothing and she ended by hating me as thoroughly as I hated her. Then the South African war broke out and I did all I could to get to the front but they sent me back to the Frontier. And Gervas, who had always wanted to be a soldier and had had to content himself with the Yeomanry, was in the seventh heaven, poor devil, and took a troop out to the Cape, largely composed of men off his own estate. He was invalided back to England after nine months to find that his wife had consoled herself in his absence with an Austrian Count, of sorts, and had cleared out with the blighter, leaving a delicate baby behind her. The child died the night Gervas reached home. I heard what happened from a mutual friend. For a few weeks he was to all intents and purposes out of his mind. He was in a very weak state from his wound, and the double shock of his wife's faithlessness and the baby's death—he was devoted to the little chap—was too much for him. Then he took up life again, but he was utterly changed. He divorced the woman that she might marry the man she had gone off with and six months afterwards he disappeared.

"That's ten or twelve years ago and I've never been able to get into communication with him since. That's Gervas Carew's story, Mollie.

"I can't give any explanation of his avoidance of English people except that he was always a sensitive sort of chap. But I think that his present attitude towards women, at any rate, is understandable. There was one woman in the world for him—and she let him down."

There was a long silence after the soldier stopped speaking. Mrs. Chalmers sat very subdued, blinking away the tears that had risen in her eyes.

"I wish I'd known before, Micky. I feel a beast," she said at last with regretful fervour.

"You might well," growled her husband unsympathetically, and stalked away to the horses.

Major Meredith prepared to follow, but lingered for a moment beside his cousin who had also risen to her feet.

"I need hardly add that what I've told you is entirely between ourselves, Mollie. I only wanted to put Carew right with you and Bill. What the rest of Algiers chooses to think doesn't matter a tinker's curse. I wish I could have seen the poor old chap, but as I'm off tomorrow that is hardly probable. Still, I've located him, which is more than I ever expected to do."

Mrs. Chalmers followed him thoughtfully to the clump of olive trees where the doctor with recovered good temper was busily saddling the horses.

They mounted and moved off leisurely down the steep side of the hill, picking a careful way between rocks and scrub and cactus bushes until they reached a narrow track winding in and out at the foot of the mountain a few feet above the bed of the tiny ravine that separated it from the adjoining range.

The track was wide enough only for two to ride abreast and the doctor forged ahead leaving his wife to follow with her cousin.

MRS. CHALMERS MADE NO FURTHER REFERENCE to the story she had heard, guessing that Meredith would not care to speak of it again, but chatted instead of the neighbourhood through which they were passing.

"These hills are a maze," she explained with a sweeping gesture of her whip that effectually upset the hitherto irreproachable behaviour of the horse she was riding. She reined him back with difficulty.

"I forgot I mustn't do that. Captain André told me he couldn't bear to have a whip whiffled about his ears," she said laughingly. "Some of the gorges are wider than this, perfect camping grounds," she continued, after she had soothed her mount's ruffled sensibilities. "Very often a Sheik will camp here on his way to Algiers. Extraordinarily interesting they are, especially the ones who come from the far south—the wildest creatures, with hordes of fierce retainers who look as if they would think nothing of murdering one just for the sheer fun of it. But they are always very nice to us—they like the English. I am ashamed to say I have learned very little Arabic but when we meet them I smile and say 'Anglaise' and they get quite excited and salaam and grin and chatter like magpies. Then, again, we come here and may ride for miles and never see a soul for days together."

"That is what one thinks on the Frontier but the beggars are there all the time, right enough," said Meredith with a quick smile. "You will be riding over a bit of country that you wouldn't think could afford cover for a cat and *ping* goes a bullet past your head. If they weren't such thundering bad shots I, for one, should have been a goner years ago." He laughed light-heartedly, and Mrs. Chalmers glanced at him curiously, marvelling, as she had marvelled frequently in the last fortnight, at the hazardous life that is some men's portion and the fatalistic indifference it usually engenders. During his short visit she had listened with wonder and amazement to her cousin's reluctant account of his work on the Border.

To Meredith it was the Great Game. Now, quite suddenly, she wondered what it would mean to the woman he might make his wife.

"I don't believe, after all, Micky, that men like you ought to marry," she said pensively. Meredith laughed at the patently regretful tone of her voice, for her matchmaking proclivities were notorious.

"I'm quite sure of it," he replied promptly, and unwillingly Mrs. Chalmers was obliged to laugh with him.

But further conversation became for the time impossible. The rough track they were following grew narrower and less perceptible until it suddenly vanished altogether and the horses slithered and slipped down to the rocky bed of the dry watercourse at the bottom of the defile. The pass was bearing steadily towards the south and Doctor Chalmers who was some little distance ahead of them had already disappeared from sight behind a jutting angle of rock where the hill curved abruptly. Following in single file they reached the sharp bend and rounding it close under the stark cliff face, emerged into a wider, less rugged valley that stretched on the one hand far up into the mountains and on the other led to open country. A quarter of a mile away, at the entrance of the valley, Doctor Chalmers was waiting for them. Scrambling out of the river bed they spurred their horses, racing to join him, and as they neared he turned in the saddle beckoning vigorously. "You're in luck, Micky," he shouted, "there's your man." And following his pointing finger they saw a small party of horsemen galloping towards the mountains. The leader, who was riding slightly in advance of his escort, was distinguished from his white-clad followers by an embroidered blue cloth burnous that billowed round him in swelling folds. With a little thrill of excitement Mrs. Chalmers glanced quickly at her cousin, and decided for the second time that day that men were queer creatures. They never did what one expected them to do. A little more than half-an-hour ago Micky had expressed a great wish to meet again the friend of his youth. The wish unexpectedly fulfilled, it was to be supposed that his inward gratification would take some outward and visible form. He sat instead motionless on his fretting horse, scowling at the approaching horsemen, his underlip sucked in beneath his trim brown moustache, in very obvious hesitation.

It was Doctor Chalmers who rode forward and waved his hand with a welcoming shout. And for a moment it seemed as if his greeting was going to pass unrecognised. The horsemen were nearly abreast of them, riding at a tremendous pace, another moment they would have swept past. Then, with a powerful jerk that sent the bright bay straight up into the air spinning high on his hind legs, the leader checked his mount suddenly. It was a common trick among the Arabs which Mrs. Chalmers had often witnessed, but she never watched it without a quickening heartbeat, and she gave a little sigh of relief now as the horse came down without the ugly backward tremble she had seen once and dreaded to see again. She was conscious of a feeling of extreme embarrassment at the near presence of the man whose mysterious personality she had discussed freely with her circle of acquaintances during the last five years, but who now appeared to her in a new and totally different light. Her warm impulsive heart had been touched by Micky Meredith's story and a hot wave of discomfort passed over her as she recollected the idle gossip she had both countenanced and participated in. She determined to delay the inevitable meeting with the much criticised Mystery-man until the first greeting and explanations between the two old friends were over. Leaving Meredith to go alone, she lingered behind under pretext of re-arranging her habit, and for some minutes she bent over her perfectly adjusted safety skirt pulling and patting it into further order while her fidgety horse wheeled and backed impatiently at the forced stand. Then she rode forward with unusual diffidence to join the three men who, dismounted, were deep in conversation. They drew apart at her coming and Meredith effected the necessary introduction.

In response to Mrs. Chalmers' murmured greeting the tall picturesque-looking man who had turned almost reluctantly towards her replied briefly and bowed with grave, unsmiling aloofness that seemed consistent with the Arab robes he wore so naturally. She had a swift glimpse of a lean brown clean-shaven face, of a pair of dark blue sombre eyes that did not quite meet her own, and then her husband's genial voice broke the threatening silence.

"Sir Gervas is camping in the neighborhood, Mollie. He wants Micky to wait over until the later train. We shall have to push on as I promised to be in Algiers early this evening," he explained, preparing to remount. "Your train leaves Blidah at eleven, Micky," he added. "And, Carew, the horse is André's. See that he gets back all right to the cavalry barracks, will you? Ready, Mollie? Then take hold of that beast of yours. We shall have to run for it."

As the Doctor and his wife cantered off, Meredith looked after their retreating figures with a gleam of amusement in his eyes. Bill's diplomacy had been worthy of a greater cause. Then he turned to his companion.

"That's a dam' good fellow," he said emphatically, "one in a billion."

But the silent man beside him did not at the moment seem inclined to discuss Doctor Chalmers' merits.

Nodding briefly he signed to his servants to bring up the spirited bay that had been removed from the proximity of the other horses.

And as they rode along together Meredith tried in vain to trace in this grave, taciturn individual some resemblance to the gay, happy-go-lucky Gervas Carew of long ago. He wondered, if alone, he would have even known him. Carew had apparently recognised him at once, but the recognition was easy, for the passing years had made no great alteration in him; while to Meredith the face of his old friend had become the face of a stranger, hardened, remoulded almost, until even the contour seemed different. Other changes too became gradually evident. The restless impatience that Meredith remembered had given place to a calm imperturbability that was more oriental than occidental. There was a dignity and stateliness in his bearing that contrasted forcibly with his former boyish impulsiveness. Of the old Gervas Carew there was clearly nothing left, and the new Gervas seemed reluctant to reveal himself. The threads, too, of the early acquaintance, broken for so long, were curiously difficult to pick up but Micky Meredith, trained to waiting, was content to let the matter take its course. Enough that a desire had been shown for his company, the rest would follow.

Once only during the half-hour ride did Carew open his mouth. He turned and looked critically at Meredith's mount. "Shall we let them out?" he said slowly, with a certain hesitation in his voice as if his mother-tongue came unnaturally. "André's horses have a reputation."

And as they raced neck and neck towards the north over the broken country that bordered the foothills they were skirting, Meredith found a certain measure of satisfaction in the fact that one interest, at least, had survived the general upheaval. Carew had always been a horseman and a lover of horses. More than ever did he seem so now. And as the soldier looked at the magnificent creature his companion was riding, and, glancing behind him, found the escort thundering close at their heels, he decided that it was not only the courteous cavalry captain at Blidah whose stud must have a reputation in the country. It was one bond of sympathy remaining, he reflected, and sat down to ride as he had rarely ridden in his life.

His borrowed horse responded gallantly to the effort demanded of him, but the pace was punishing and the animal's satiny neck grew dark and seamed with sweat as he strained to keep up with the bay that showed no sign of distress and seemed to be rather checked than urged by his rider. And with the perspiration pouring down his own face Meredith was not sorry when a sudden curve in the hillside revealed a deserted fruit farm with Carew's camp scattered amongst the orange trees.

The big double tent of the owner was pitched at some distance from those of its followers, lying in an open clearing where once the farm buildings must have stood. And all about were horses and camels, tethered or wandering at will, and a small army of Arabs languidly fulfilling the various duties of the camp or squatting idly on their heels engaged in endless argument.

But the return of the master roused his retainers to sudden and spontaneous activity, and Meredith noted with a smile of approval the evident signs of discipline and authority. Waiting grooms who had been lounging near the big tent sprang to the horses' heads and the soldier slid out of the saddle with a grunt of relief and mopped his forehead with a gaudy silk handkerchief. "Do you usually ride at that pace?" he enquired, laughing.

Carew turned from fondling the big bay that was nozzling him affectionately. "Pretty usually," he answered, "it's a bad habit one catches in the desert. But I've always wanted to try Suliman against that grey of André's. He had him beaten from the start," he added with a faint smile, "come have a drink." And he led the way under the lance-propped awning into the cool dimness of the tent.

Meredith glanced about with interest. The costly but sparse furnishings were almost entirely of the country; a small camp table and a solitary deck chair, the sole concessions to European taste, looked incongruous in conjunction with the low inlaid stools and gay brocaded silk mats that were purely Arab. A wide divan, heaped with heavy cushions and covered with a couple of leopard skins, stood in the centre of the room. Looped back curtains of gold-embroidered silk hung before the entrance to the sleeping apartment.

At first sight Meredith thought the tent empty. But as his eyes grew accustomed to the soft light he saw, in a far corner, the slender figure of a child sitting on the ground swaying gently to and fro, his handsome little face upturned in rapt devotion as he crooned softly to himself while the beads of a long rosary slipped through his small brown fingers. The thick rugs on the floor deadened the sound of their footsteps and for a moment the entrance of the two men passed unnoticed. Then Carew moved and his foot struck sharply against a small brass bowl that had fallen from a nearby stool. At the sound the lad stopped swaying and sat rigid as if listening intently, his face turned eagerly towards them. Then with a glad cry he tossed the rosary away and scrambling to his feet came flying across the tent with outstretched hands. A thick cushion that in its bright-hued covering appeared perfectly obvious against the dark rug lay directly in his path but he blundered straight into it and fell headlong before Carew could catch him. And as Meredith watched the big man bending over the little white-clad figure and saw the stern lines of his face change into a wonderful tenderness, and heard the sudden gentleness of his voice as he murmured in soft quick Arabic, he recollected with a feeling of acute dismay the "queer stories" that Mollie Chalmers had referred to. Was this, then, the solution of Carew's protracted sojourns in the desert? To the Anglo-Indian with his deep-rooted prejudices the supposition was repulsive. It was to him little short of a crime. And yet was there not perhaps an excuse? Sudden pity contended with repulsion as he remembered Carew's devotion to his tiny son, and the tragedy that had robbed him of his child. Had the ardent desire for parenthood that had formerly been so strong in him risen even against racial restrictions and the misogyny with which he was now accredited?

Meredith was relieved when his disturbing thoughts were interrupted. The boy was on his feet again, talking excitedly, but Carew silenced him with a hand on his shoulder.

"There is a guest, Saba," he said in French, "salute the English lord, and go bid Hosein hasten with the cooling drink."

Suddenly shy the boy moved forward, bending his supple little figure in a deep salaam. Then drawing himself erect, he lifted his face to Meredith's with a curiously uncertain movement. And looking down into the beautiful dark eyes raised to his the soldier saw the reason for that hasty tumble and an involuntary exclamation escaped him. He looked enquiringly at his host.

Carew nodded. "Yes, he's blind," he said in English, "but you needn't pity him. He has never known anything different and he is a thoroughly happy little imp." And drawing the boy to him with a quick caress he set him with his face towards the door and watched him grope his way from the tent.

Then, pulling forward the deck chair, he placed cigarettes beside his guest. From behind a cloud of smoke Meredith spoke with obvious constraint. "I'm awfully sorry—" he began awkwardly, and something in his voice made Carew turn quickly to look at him. For a moment his sombre eyes rested on the soldier's embarrassed face, then he shook his head with a grave smile that had in it a trace of bitterness.

"It's not what you think," he said evenly, "though I admit the thought is natural. He is not mine—sometimes I wish to God he were. He's only a waif picked up in the desert, five or six hundred miles away in the south, there. I found him six years ago, when I was helping to clean up an Arab raid, lying across his dead mother's body and whimpering like a hungry kitten. He wasn't more than a year old. I've had him ever since. I don't think I could get on without the little chap now. He's an interest, and fills up my time when I'm not otherwise occupied—fills it pretty completely, too, for he is as sharp as a needle and, when the mood takes him, as keen on mischief as any boy with the full use of his eyes. But tell me about yourself. Are you still on the Frontier?"

And Meredith, keenly anxious to renew the old intimacy, let himself be drawn and talked of his life on the Indian Border as he had never talked of it before. Baldly and jerkily at first and then with increasing ease he spoke of the years of arduous work that had claimed his whole time and thought; of perilous journeys and months passed in disguise amongst the savage northern tribes, of hairbreadth escapes and strange experiences, of periods of so-called leave which to the man intent on his job and absorbed in his occupation had only meant work in another form.

For an hour or more his quiet voice went on until the lengthening shadows deepened into blackness and the tent grew dark and obscure, until Carew, sitting Arab fashion on the divan, was almost invisible and only the glowing end of his cigarette revealed his presence. And Meredith—the first plunge made—found him curiously easy to talk to, curiously knowledgeable too. From one or two comments he let fall Meredith was inclined to believe that the Watching Game was no new one to him and the knowledge made his own tale less difficult to tell.

He stopped at last and groped for the matches on the stool beside him. "That about lets me out," he said, as he lit a cigarette. Carew rose and going to the tent door clapped his hands. "You're doing a big work, Micky," he said as he came slowly through the gloom. "You'll end on the Indian Council if you don't take care," he added with almost the old bantering note in his voice.

"If I don't end with a bullet through my head, which is much more probable," replied Meredith with a quick laugh, blinking at the lighted lamps that were being brought into the tent.

During the dinner that followed the conversation was mainly of Algeria. But though Carew discussed the country and its conditions, its people and the sport it afforded, of his own life there he said nothing. Neither did he refer to the old days when their friendship had meant so much to each. The past was evidently a sealed book that he had no intention of reopening. A tentative remark hazarded by Meredith met with no response and it was not until later when they were sitting out in the darkness under the awning that the soldier put the question he had been trying to ask all evening. They had sat for some time in silence, smoking, looking across the moonlit plain, listening to the subdued noises of the camp behind them and to the faint rhythmical thump of a tom-tom far off amongst the orange trees. A tiny breeze drifting, perfume laden, across their faces made Meredith think suddenly of the scented gardens of Kashmere. He twisted in his chair to get a better view of the starry heavens, and blurted out his question.

"Why didn't you write, old man?"

For a long time there was no answer and he mentally kicked himself for a blundering fool. Then Carew's deep voice, deeper even than usual, came out of the darkness. "I couldn't. I tried once—but there seemed nothing to say. I hoped you would understand."

Meredith moved uncomfortably. "I was—damned sorry," he muttered gruffly. Carew lit a fresh cigarette slowly.

"You needn't waste any sympathy on me, Micky," he said with a sudden hard laugh. "I was a fool once—but I learnt my lesson—thoroughly." There was another long silence. Then Meredith asked abruptly: "Why Algeria?"

Carew shrugged. "I had to go somewhere. The house—its associations were a hell I wasn't strong enough to stand. So I played the coward's part and ran away. My people used to winter in Algiers when I was a boy. I liked the country. It seemed the natural place to come to, somehow." He paused. When he spoke again it was in a voice that was new to Meredith. "It's a wonderful place, the desert, Micky," he said dreamily, "it gets you in the end—if you go far enough, and stay long enough. It's got me all right. I don't suppose I shall ever leave it now. I come into Algiers sometimes, but never for very long. Always I go back to it. It holds me as nothing else has ever held me. The mystery of it, the charm of it—always new, never the same, changing from day to day. And its moods, my God, Micky, its moods! The peace of heaven one moment and the fury of hell let loose the next. Cruel but beautiful, pitiless but fascinating. And, somehow, one forgets the cruelty and only the beauty remains—the beauty of its wonderful solitudes, its marvellous emptiness."

"And being there—what do you do?" Meredith had no wish to appear inquisitive but for the last few minutes he had been trying, unsuccessfully, to fit his old friend into the new setting that seemed so incongruous. Gervas and solitude! To Meredith, remembering the perpetual house parties at Royal Carew, the crowds of pleasure-seeking, sport-loving men and women with whom the genial host of those old days had surrounded himself, it appeared a thing incredible. And again he asked with growing perplexity: "What do you do?" and wondered if Carew would consign him to the devil. But the retort he half expected did not ensue. "What do I do?" repeated Carew slowly. "That was the question I asked myself when I came to Algeria, when I seemed to have come to the end of everything—'what shall I do.' My first trip into the desert settled that quickly enough. I had always been interested in the Arabs—I spoke the language as early as I spoke English—but I only knew the Arabs of the towns. So I went down into the south to see the real life of the desert. I met some of the old Sheiks who used to come into Algiers when I was a boy and who still remembered my father. They made it easy for me and passed me on into districts where otherwise I could never have penetrated, and I saw more than I had ever hoped to see. I started my wanderings with no higher motive than curiosity—and a desire to get away from my own thoughts. It had never occurred to me that up till then I had led an utterly purposeless life, that not a soul in the world was the better for my being in it. But out there in the desert the crying need I found forced me to think, for the reckless waste of life and the ghastly unnecessary suffering I saw appalled me. I knew that one man alone could not do much—but he could do something. It didn't take me long to make up my mind. The old life was over. I wanted a new life that wouldn't give me time to think, that would give me opportunity to help the people I had professed to be interested in. I went to Paris and studied medicine, specializing in surgery, and took my degree. Afterwards I put in six months with a man in Switzerland, a brute—but a wizard with the knife, and then came back to Algeria. That's what I do, Micky."

Meredith drew a deep breath. "And a dam' fine thing, too," he said heartily. And reaching out a long arm he gripped the other's shoulder for a moment with a pressure that was painful. "So that's what you do in the desert when you vanish for months at a time, is it?" he said slowly, with a curious expression of relief in his voice and a feeling of self-disgust as he thought of the suspicions that had been forced upon him earlier in the evening.

"It isn't all plain sailing, I suppose?" he suggested.

"Far from it," replied Carew, "but it depends on the district, of course. Usually the beggars are grateful enough and I go pretty much where I please. But they are a naturally suspicious people and there are some places I can't get into at any price. They think my work is a pretext and that I am a spy of the Government."

"And are you?"

"Officially, no. But sometimes I see and hear things I think the Government should know—it's a difficult country to administer—and at times the Government make use of my knowledge. I have acted as intermediary more than once in negotiations with some of the outlying tribes where it would be impossible to send a regularly accredited Agent without a regiment to back him up—and that usually ends in fighting which the Government try to avoid. There's unrest enough in the south without stirring up any more trouble," he added, turning to speak to a tall, saturnine-looking Arab who had suddenly approached with a soft murmur of apology.

The shrill sequel of a stallion and the trampling of hoofs made Meredith realise the reason for the interruption.

"Time up?" he said regretfully, following Carew into the tent. "By jove, it's late!" he added, glancing at his watch, "can we get into Blidah by eleven?"

"Not by the way the Chalmers brought you," replied Carew with a faint smile, buckling the clasp of the heavy burnous his servant folded about his shoulders. The same escort that had ridden with him earlier in the day was waiting but he dismissed them and alone the two men rode out into the moonlit night. For a time they did not speak. Carew had apparently reached the limit of his confidences and Meredith was in no mood to break the silence. It had been a curious meeting, a curious renewal of an old friendship, but the soldier was left with an uncomfortable feeling of doubt whether it would not have been kinder if no reminder of his early life had been brought to disturb the peace that, seemingly, his old friend had found in the desert. His presence must have vividly awakened in Carew memories of the past. For how much did the past still count with him? Did he never regret the fine old property in England where generations of Carews had lived since the days of the Virgin Queen whose visit during a royal progress had given the house its name? Meredith had many pleasant recollections of Royal Carew and the thought of the stately house he had known so full of life and happiness standing now empty and forlorn in the midst of its beautiful park gave him a feeling of sadness.

"Will you never go back, Gervas?" he asked involuntarily.

"Go back—where?"

"To Royal Carew."

Carew shook his head. "I told you I had done with the old life," he said rather wearily. "Royal Carew belongs to the past—and the past is dead. And I couldn't very well go back now, if I wanted to. I let my cousin have the place. He is my heir, it would have come to him eventually. It was better he should go there while he was still young enough to enjoy it. It's a damned poor game waiting for dead men's shoes," he added with a short laugh.

They were galloping now over undulating country where the crests of the gently swelling hillocks were almost as light as day and the tiny intervening valleys lay like pools of dark, still water. As they reached the summit of a rather larger hill than they had yet encountered, Carew slackened speed with a word of warning.

"There is a deserted village in the valley," he said, pointing down into the darkness, "be careful how you go, it's a confusing place at night. And if anything happens—sit tight and leave the talking to me," he added significantly. And as he spurred the bay a half length in advance Meredith saw his hand go to the silk shawl that was swathed about his waist. A deserted village—but Carew was reaching for his revolver. With a grin Meredith took a firmer grip of Captain André's grey. He had passed through similar deserted villages in India.

"Heave ahead," he said cheerily, and followed his companion closely down the long slope.

The valley was shallower than others they had traversed and here and there a shaft of moonlight cut through the murky gloom. They were on the village before Meredith realised its nearness, and as they threaded the empty streets at a slow canter he looked keenly about him with a slight feeling of pleasurable excitement. But no sound broke the stillness and no furtive figures lurking among the ruined huts appeared to justify Carew's warning. Then the grey stumbled badly on a heap of rubble lying across the road and until they were clear of the village he gave his whole attention to his borrowed horse. But when they were speeding across the plain once more with the lights of Blidah faint in the distance he turned to Carew with a look of enquiry. "What might have happened?" he asked curiously.

"Anything—murder, probably, if you had been alone."

Meredith chuckled at the casual tone. "Healthy spot for a midnight ride!"

"It saves three miles," replied Carew calmly.

And Meredith flung back his head and laughed like a boy.

II

For a few moments after the train that was carrying Major Meredith back to Algiers had pulled jerkily out of the station, Carew lingered on the deserted ill-lit platform. Then, acknowledging with a curt nod the half-caste stationmaster's obsequious greeting, he strode leisurely to where the horses were waiting in the care of a Kabyle lad he had picked out from among the heterogeneous collection of loafers lounging before the station entrance. He signed to the boy to follow him with Captain André's horse and trotted Suliman slowly towards the town. Entering by the Es-Sebt Gate he turned in the direction of the cavalry barracks. Despite the late hour the numberless cafés with their flaring gas lamps and tawdry garishness were at their busiest. The pavements were thronged, a ceaseless stream of cosmopolitan humanity; slow-moving, dignified Arabs, servile and furtive-eyed Jews meekly giving place to all who elbowed them, and eager, chattering Frenchmen—all jostling, indiscriminately. Even the roadway was invaded, and bands of Zouaves with interlocked arms reeled along regardless of the traffic, roaring out the latest musical song with unmelodious vigour and shouting questionable jibes at the passers by.

Tonight Blidah seemed to be *en fête*, noisier and more blatant than usual. And to Carew, fresh from nearly a year in the desert, the scene was distasteful. It was not new to him, years spent in Algeria had familiarised him with the nightly aspect of the garrison towns, and he was in no mood to be either interested or amused by what he saw. He had no love for Blidah at the best of times and he had already been there once before that day.

At the cavalry barracks he handed over Captain André's grey to the sleepy groom who was waiting and, dismissing the Kabyle lad, turned with a sigh of relief in the direction of the Bab-el-Rabah. Passing through the gateway he headed towards the east, intending to return by the same route by which he had brought Major Meredith. Once clear of the town Suliman broke of his own accord into the long, swinging gallop to which he was accustomed and for a time Carew let him take his own pace. But soon he checked him, drawing him into a reluctant walk. And as the bay sidled and reared, snorting impatiently, his master bent forward in the saddle and ran his hand caressingly over the glossy arched neck. "Gently, gently, core of my heart," he murmured in the language that came more readily to his lips than his own, "there is no need for haste. Tomorrow is also a day." And pacing slowly forward through the quiet night he set himself at last to face the torturing recollections of the past that for years he had put resolutely out of his mind but which had been cruelly awakened by the wholly unexpected advent of his old friend. Inscrutable as the Arabs amongst whom he lived, he exhibited no outward sign of agitation, but under the passivity that had become second nature with him there was raging a bitter storm of anger and revolt against fate that had thrown Micky Meredith across his path to shatter the hard-won peace that had come to him in the desert. Meredith was bound up with all he wished to forget, was the living reminder of the home and happiness he had lost. His coming had reopened the wound that Carew had thought healed forever. Memories, like stabs of actual pain, crowded in upon him. The old struggle, the old bitterness he had conquered once was overwhelming him again, shaking him to the very depths of his being. The past he had resolved to forget rose up anew with terrible distinctness. Royal Carew—and the woman he had loved! With the sweat of agony thick on his forehead he lived again through the horror of that ghastly homecoming. He saw again, clearly as though they stood before him, the pitying, terrified faces of the old servants from whom he learned the sordid story of his betrayal. He passed once more through the hours of anguish when he had knelt in dumb, helpless misery beside the tiny cot in the luxurious nursery and watched the death struggle of the child whom, worse than motherless, he loved so passionately. The dark waters of despair had closed over his head that night. Weak from the terrible wound that had brought him back to England, crushed by the double tragedy, he had longed and prayed for death. And when he had at last found courage to go forward with what remained to him of life, it was as a changed man, embittered out of any semblance to his former self. He had divorced his wife that she might marry the man for whom she had left him, and with grim justice, because she had been the mother of his son, he had settled upon her an adequate fortune. But for the woman herself he had no feeling left but loathing and contempt. She had deceived him, lied to him. She had destroyed his faith, his trust. She had opened his eyes at last to the unworthiness that had been patent to all but the husband who worshipped her. She had killed his love—and with it had died esteem and belief in the sex she represented. With her his ideal of womanhood, pinnacled high with chivalrous regard, had shattered into nothingness.

E.M. HULL

Because of her he had become the cynical misogynist he was, seeing in all women the one woman whose falseness had poisoned his life. The thought of her stirred him now to nothing but a sense of cold disgust.

But the memory of the little son who had died was a living force within him. It had gone with him through all the years of loneliness and disillusion, a grief as bitter now as on that first night of his bereavement. Not for the woman, but for the child his starved heart still yearned with passionate intensity. The tiny face was present with him always, even yet he could remember the clinging touch of the fragile baby fingers closing convulsively on his in that last moment of terrible struggle. It was to try and deaden the pain of memory, to ease the burden of his solitude, that he had kept the little waif of the desert. And the blind boy in his helplessness and dependence had in some measure filled the blank in his life. But tonight the remembrance of his loss was heavy upon him. Even with the child Meredith was connected, for his visit to Royal Carew had been made a few months after the birth of the heir who had been born to such high hopes. Together the two men had discussed in all solemnity the probable career of the sleepy scrap of pink humanity who at that time had shown no sign of the delicacy which had developed later.

And Royal Carew! For the first time in years he let his thoughts turn to the beautiful property he had voluntarily surrendered and a wave of intense home sickness passed over him. He crushed it down with a feeling of contempt for his own weakness. Once it had seemed to him the fairest place on God's earth, he had loved every stick and stone of it. He loved it still, but with his love was the remembrance of bitter pain that made him shrink from ever seeing it again. Childless, it was for him purposeless. If the child had lived—but the child was dead, and things were better as they were. Regrets were useless. There was nothing to be gained by harking back to what might have been. Carew's lips tightened and he forced his mind into another channel of thought. After all, it had been no fault of Meredith's. Carew had guessed the reason of the soldier's restrained manner at the moment of meeting and the knowledge had added warmth to his own greeting. Pride had stirred him, that and a vague idea of testing his own command over himself. Naturally long-sighted he had seen and known Meredith even before Doctor Chalmers had hailed him. Almost he had been tempted to pass by with no sign of recognition. Then he had cursed himself for a coward and had reined in Suliman with that sudden jerk that had made

Mrs. Chalmers' heart stand still. And now was he glad or sorry for Meredith's coming? It was a question that in his present mood he found himself unable to answer. He had no wish to further analyse his feelings. He had become unaccustomed to self-consideration. For once he had relaxed the rigid control he exercised over his own thoughts—and once was enough. During the years of strenuous work in the desert he had succeeded in suppressing self, and in that work he would endeavour to regain the contentment that was all he had to hope for.

With a powerful effort of will he put away all thoughts of Meredith and the memories he had awakened and, touching Suliman with his heel, concentrated on the results of the difficult mission from which he was now returning to Algiers.

It had been a delicate business, attended with considerable danger that had not disturbed him, and subtle oriental intrigue, in dealing with which Hosein's help had been invaluable. The man had been Carew's body-servant and faithful companion for all the years he had lived in Algeria. The son of his father's old dragoman, Carew remembered him as a singularly intelligent urchin, a year or two older than himself, employed about the villa on Mustapha Superieur where the winters of his own boyhood had been spent, and he had sought him out on his first return to the country. He had never regretted it. Devoted and singleminded in his service the Arab had been friend as well as servant and a loyal cooperator in Carew's chosen work. A wanderer by instinct, it was not only in Algeria that Hosein had travelled and the green band of the Mecca pilgrim that he wore gave him a prestige which had carried his master and himself through some sufficiently awkward situations. Carew had owed his life to him not once nor twice, and he knew that but for Hosein's watchfulness he would never have returned alive from this last dangerous undertaking. The report he was carrying back to the Governor in Algiers was due as much to Hosein as to himself. And the Arab should not be the loser if he could help it, he thought with a sudden rare smile.

Immersed in his thoughts he had taken little notice of his surroundings and had not realised how far he had come on his homeward journey. A whistling snort from Suliman and a sudden wild swerve that would have unseated a less practised horseman brought him back abruptly to the immediate present, and looking round sharply he saw that they had arrived at the outskirts of the deserted village. Dragging his horse to a standstill he looked keenly about him, but in spite of the brilliant moonlight, he could see nothing moving. Yet Suliman was accustomed to night work and it was unlike him to shy at shadows. The deserted village had a bad reputation in the neighbourhood but Carew had never avoided it on that account, he had a reputation himself that was sufficiently widely known.

He glanced perfunctorily to right and left as he rode through the winding, grass-grown street, but to all appearances, the place seemed empty as it had been when he passed through it earlier in the evening. He was nearing the last group of tumbled-down huts when the sound of a piercing shriek breaking weirdly on the silence of the night sent Suliman high on his heels in furious protest. Hauling him down, Carew twisted in the saddle, listening intently. It came again, echoing from a little lane that straggled from the main street, the wail of a woman's voice crying wildly in French for help. A woman—in such a place and at such an hour! Carew's compressed lips parted in a mirthless grin and he relaxed his strained attention. What was a woman doing at midnight in that village of ill repute? Some little fool, doubtless, who had tempted providence too highly, paying the price of her folly! Well, let her pay. In all probability she had brought it on herself—she could abide by the consequences. It was no business of his, anyhow. Why should he, of all men, interfere to help a woman in her need—what was a woman's suffering to him? His face was set and grimly hard as he soothed his plunging horse and prepared to ride on. But as Suliman started forward the cry was repeated with words that made Carew check him with an iron hand and bring him, quivering to his haunches. Clear and distinct they came to him—words of frenzied entreaty to a higher power than his, words in a language he least expected to hear.

"Help, help! oh, God, send help!"

An Englishwoman! For a moment he battled with himself. Then with a terrible oath he wrenched his horse's head round savagely and drove him down the little lane at a headlong gallop.

The lane was a cul-de-sac, the house he sought at the far end of it, for there only did a dim light filtering through an unshuttered window show any sign of habitation. Deep shadows masked the entrance and a few feet short of it, in a patch of vivid moonlight, he pulled up and, leaping to the ground, raced towards the hidden doorway. His foot was on the crumbling step when out of the gloom three figures rose up to bar his entrance and hurled themselves upon him. The attack was silent, and in silence he met it. There was no time to reach for the revolver he had neglected to draw. Straining, heaving, he wrestled in the darkness with opponents whose faces he could not see, whose arms encircled him and whose clutching sinewy hands tore murderously at his throat. A knife pricked him and with a blind instinct he caught at and held the hand that brandished it, crushing it in his strong fingers till he felt the yielding bones crack and the weapon slipped to the ground with a faint tinkle. In perfect physical condition, with steely muscles toughened by years of strenuous and active life, he knew that singly he could have matched any one of the men who were hemming him in, but against three even his great strength was unavailing. Struggling to free his arms, he gave back step by step as they pressed him closer in a continued silence that was menacing by its very unusualness. Even the man whose hand he had maimed had made no sound beyond a muffled growl. Only the shuffling of feet on the dry ground, the panting, animal-like grunts of exertion as they grappled with him, were audible. The rank stench of filthy, sweat-drenched garments was pungent in his nostrils; hot, fetid breath fanning his face gave him—accustomed though he was to the dirt and squalor of the Arabs—a feeling of nausea that sent a shiver of disgust through him. At last with a tremendous effort he wrenched himself free and reeled back, gasping, into the patch of moonlight, his heart pounding against his ribs, perspiration pouring from him. And as the bright light struck across his face the men who had followed him swiftly drew back with sudden indetermination, muttering amongst themselves. He caught the words "El Hakim," the title he bore amongst the desert people, and almost before he realised it they had vanished into the shadows of the neighbouring houses and he was alone. For a moment he fought for breath, wiping the blinding moisture from his dripping face, fumbling for the revolver in his waistcloth. Then another strangled cry from within the lighted hut spurred him into action and he sprang forward, flinging back the heavy burnous from his shoulders as he ran. The rotting door crashed open under the sudden impact of his weight and in the entrance he halted with levelled revolver. For a second only. His eyes sweeping the tiny room met those of a gigantic, evil-faced Arab who, startled at his appearance, had flung to the ground the woman who struggled in his arms and turned to meet the intruder with a scowl of murderous ferocity. A grim smile of recognition flickered across Carew's stern face. "*Thou*—dog?" he thundered, and leaped at him. For a moment the Arab wavered, then a knife flashed in his hand. But with a quick feint Carew dodged the sweeping blow and caught the upraised wrist in a vice-like grip. With his revolver pressing into the man's stomach he forced him back slowly against the wall of the hut, his fingers tightening their hold until the paralysed hand unclenched and the knife clattered to the floor. Kicking it beyond reach, Carew backed a few paces and, still keeping the Arab covered, turned his attention for the first time to the woman he had come reluctantly to aid. Only a girl apparently, her face almost childish in its strained, white piteousness, she had dragged herself up from the floor and was standing rocking on her feet in the middle of the room. He looked with a kind of cruel deliberation on the slender, shaking limbs which, clothed in boyish riding dress that intimately revealed their delicate beauty, would have been the joy of an artist, but which filled him only with an acute feeling of antagonism. The folly of it, the shameless, senseless folly of it! A woman must be a fool and worse than a fool to expose herself thus in a land of veiled femininity. His antagonism augmented and he viewed unmoved the signs of terrible struggle through which she had passed. That she had fought desperately was evidenced in the marks of violent handling she bore, in the unbound hair that lay in curling chestnut waves about her shoulders, in the tattered silk shirt that, ripped from throat to waist, bared the soft whiteness of her heaving breasts to the austere gaze bent so pitilessly on her. She seemed unaware of Carew's nearness. Panting for breath, her hands clenching and unclenching mechanically, she stood like a driven animal at bay, her eyes fixed on the Arab in a wild, unblinking stare. Carew broke the silence abruptly with a blunt question addressed to her that was brutally direct. He spoke in French that both could understand and because he had no wish tonight to pass as other than an Arab himself. The harsh voice roused her to a realisation of his presence. She started violently, her hunted eyes turning slowly to him as if she dared not lose sight of the sinister figure by the wall. For a few seconds she stared at him uncomprehendingly, then her cheeks flamed suddenly as the meaning of his words penetrated. Her lips quivered and she shrank back, dragging the tangle of soft hair over her uncovered bosom with an instinctive gesture of modesty. She tried to speak, but for some time no words would come, then a wail of entreaty burst from her. "Take me away, oh, for God's sake take me away!" she cried, and buried her face in her hands with a convulsive shudder.

He jerked his head impatiently. The life he had led for the last twelve years had made him intolerant of convention, he had no intention of allowing it to interfere now with the rough and ready justice he was fully prepared to administer. He had no reason to hesitate. The Arab was a well-known criminal, the abduction of an English visitor an offence the Algerian Government could not in any sense condone.

"I will take you away when you have answered my question, Madame," he said coldly. "This is no time or place for false modesty. Does he go free or—" he raised his revolver with a gesture that was unmistakable. But the sharp cry of protest arrested him, and shuddering again she drew further from him till she leant against the opposite wall, clinging to it and hiding her face like a child fearful of some impending horror. "No—no—not that," she gasped, "let him go. You came—in time." The last words trailed into an almost inaudible whisper and with a little moan she slipped to the floor as if the last remnant of her strength had left her.

Indifferent to her distress he turned from her to the more pressing matter of the Arab.

"What shame is this, O Abdul?" he said sternly, relapsing into Arabic. Shuffling his feet the man glanced past him towards the open doorway from which Carew's tall figure effectually barred him. He knew that in the few minutes that had passed he had been nearer to death than was comfortable to contemplate. He had no desire to enter into a detailed history of his offence, his sole wish at the moment was to remove himself as speedily as might be from the proximity of the accusing eyes fixed on him. True, a reprieve had been granted—but for how long? Memories of past dealings with the man who stood before him made him keep a wary eye on the revolver that Carew still held with unpleasant suggestiveness.

"Shame indeed, O Sidi," he whined with a cringing salaam, "had I known that the *lalla* was under thy protection. But is not my lord known throughout all Algeria as one who deigns not to stoop his eyes to the face of a woman?"

There was cunning mixed with curiosity in the swift upward glance that met Carew's frowning stare for an instant and then wavered to earth again. The scowl on the Englishman's face deepened.

"Yet would I have killed thee for what thou hast done tonight," he said quickly, "be very sure of that, O Abdul. But the *lalla* has given thee thy life. Give thanks—and go."

He cut short the Arab's glib protestations and hustled him towards the door. But on the threshold the man paused irresolutely, with another obsequious salaam.

"I have served my lord in the past," he muttered sullenly, "for the sake of that service will not my lord forget—tonight?"

Carew looked at him through narrowing eyelids.

"To suit thine own ends hast thou served me," he said pointedly, "and forgetfulness comes not readily to those who live with a sharp reminder—as I shall live," he added, stooping swiftly and catching up the knife that lay near his foot. With a cold smile he thrust it into his waistcloth and turned slowly back into the room. He did not trouble to wait and watch the man off the premises. He had known Abdul el Dhib for years and his knowledge made him confident that in the meantime he was safe from any form of revenge from the human jackal on whose head the Algerian Government had set a price. Usually his activities were confined to more remote districts and Carew had been surprised to see him so near to civilisation. But it was no part of his business to act as a common police spy and he knew that Abdul had counted on the fact when he had endeavoured to make terms with him. Remained the more perplexing problem of the woman thrust, wholly undesired, on his hands. She was still crouched on the dusty mud floor where she had fallen and he went to her reluctantly.

She shivered at his touch, staggering to her feet with a swift glance of apprehension round the room. Clutching the screening mass of curls about her she passed a hand over her eyes as though clearing away the remembrance of some horrible vision. She showed no fear of the tall Arab-clad figure standing beside her, by some curious instinct she seemed sensible that his presence constituted a protection and not a menace. But equally she displayed no haste to explain the predicament in which he had found her or to disclose her identity. Stunned by the terrible experience through which she had passed, she appeared to be only half conscious and incapable of any initiative. Carew, passionately anxious to be quit of the whole business, was not inclined to beat about the bush, but came to the point with characteristic directness.

"You come from Blidah, Madame?"

She looked at him blankly, her puzzled eyes still shadowy with pain, and he repeated the question slower and more distinctly.

"Blidah—" she echoed vaguely. "Blidah? No—Algiers."

A look of dismay crossed Carew's face. Algiers was thirty miles away. He could have taken her back to Blidah easily enough, but Algiers with Suliman, who had already done a hard day's work, carrying double—it was out of the question. He jerked his head with a gesture of annoyance and scowled thoughtfully, mentally cursing Abdul el Dhib and the woman beside him with fine impartiality.

"Where in Algiers?" he asked shortly, by way of gaining time to think out the awkward situation. But the girl was past all explanations. "Algiers—" she repeated weakly and, reeling, would have fallen but for the strong arm slipped round her. That settled it. Half fainting and wholly unable to express herself she could give him no assistance and he realised there was nothing for it but the expedient he least desired— that of taking her to his own camp. His own camp—good God! Antagonism grew into actual dislike as he glanced down at the slender boyish figure leaning against him. With a grunt of disgust he half led, half carried her out of the hut.

Suliman, trained to stand, was waiting in the patch of moonlight, jerking the dangling bridle impatiently. Unhooking his heavy burnous Carew rolled it into a long, soft pad and flung it across the horse's neck in front of the high-peaked saddle. Then he swung the girl up with a curt "Hold on to his mane" and leaped up behind her, wondering what would be the result of Suliman's first excited plunge. But with instinctive good grace the horse refrained from his usual display of light-hearted exuberance and set off soberly at a slow canter to which Carew held him. There were no signs of Abdul and his band of cut-throats, no lurking shadows in the vicinity of the silent houses and in a few minutes the village was behind them.

Carew rode with a tight rein and a watchful eye on the drooping little figure in front of him. His own tall, muscular form was drawn up in the saddle taut and rigid with repugnance at her nearness, every fibre in his being revolting from the proximity of her woman's body. The subtle torture of it made him grit his teeth and thick, cold drops of moisture gathered on his forehead. He raged at the necessity that had forced him to a step that an hour ago he would have thought beyond the bounds of possibility. And tonight of all nights, when his senses were already raw and aching with the recollections of the past that had racked him almost beyond bearing.

The calm to which he had schooled himself through years of self-discipline and self-suppression had been swept away and he was aghast at the tumult within him which seemed to be tearing down every defence and barrier he had raised so strenuously.

The need of one fragile girl had caused him to break a resolution from which he had sworn never to turn. And at the moment he could cheerfully have thrown the fragile girl behind the clump of rocks they were passing and washed his hands of the whole affair. Because she was English—it was the sole reason for the action that had so surprised himself. Race loyalty had, in an extreme moment, proved stronger than his determination and her sex had been swamped in her nationality. But for those few words in English he would have ridden on. The appeal coming in another language had left him unmoved, but repeated in the mother-tongue that had become almost foreign to him had stirred him powerfully, even against his own inclination. But the call of the blood that had triumphed so unexpectedly over him did not in any way mitigate the constraint of his present situation. It was an embarrassment that grew momentarily more acute and distasteful. He was impatient of every little circumstance that augmented his discomfiture. His nerves on edge he found cause for annoyance even in the slow pace at which he was compelled to ride. It irked him as badly as it was irking Suliman who, with his nose turned towards home, was snatching at his bit and endeavouring to break into the usual gallop. The girl herself settled the last problem. She had been drooping more and more over the horse's neck, clutching instinctively at the thick mane in which her fingers were twined, but now without a word or sound she collapsed and fell back in a dead faint.

With his face gone suddenly ghastly Carew lifted her until she lay across his thighs, his left arm crooked about her shoulders, her dishevelled little head pressing against his breast. God in heaven, it only wanted this! Cursing savagely he drove his spurs with unwonted cruelty into his horse's sides and gave him his head. And in the wild rush through the cool night that followed he tried to forget that he carried a woman in his arms. But the slender little body, warm and yielding against his own, was a reminder that obtruded too powerfully to allow of forgetfulness. So had he carried his wife once after a minor accident in the hunting field, and then, as now, a thick strand of scented hair had blown across his face blinding him with its soft fragrance. He tore it away with shaking fingers.

Impossible now to stem the flood of recollection. It was stronger than his will to put it from him. More painful, more crushing even than before it swept him with a force he was powerless to resist and he made no further effort, surrendering his mind to its bitter memories while he urged Suliman recklessly, careless whether he broke his neck and the girl's or not. And with a madness almost equal to his own, goaded by the sharp spurs that Carew used so seldom the bay tore on at racing speed, breasting the tiny hillocks and thundering down their gentle declivities, taking rocks and pitfalls in his stride, as if tireless. And when at last the open plain was reached he turned of his own accord in the direction of the camp, hardly slackening his pace until he arrived with a great slithering rush before the tent door. A couple of grooms sprang forward, but the last spurt had been his final effort and he made no attempt to evade them, standing with down-drooping head and widely planted feet, breathing heavily and trembling with exhaustion.

Gathering the girl closer in his arms Carew slipped to the ground. To Hosein, imperturbable even in the face of this unprecedented spectacle, he vouchsafed only the curt explanation "Abdul el Dhib" and ordering coffee to be brought to him carried his slight burden into the tent.

Prejudiced and angry he scowled down at her with fierce resentment as he laid her among the silk cushions on the divan. That he had himself been compelled to bring her here did not in any way lessen his anger or make his task easier. But since she was here, helpless and dependent on him, common humanity demanded that he should do all in his power to aid her. Striving to sink the man in the doctor he endeavoured to regard her only as a case and set to work to combat the prolonged fainting fit that seemed to argue something more than a mere collapse from fear and fatigue. And as his sombre eyes dwelt on her he found himself reluctantly admitting the uncommon beauty of her face and form. But her beauty made him no more kindly disposed towards her. A woman's beauty—the transient snare that lured trusting fools to their undoing— what was it to him who had learned the vileness and hypocrisy that lay beneath seeming outward loveliness? With a shrug of disdain he raised her higher on the cushions.

And at last she stirred, the long, dark lashes that lay like a dusky fringe on her pale cheek fluttering tremulously. And, as he bent over her, two deep blue eyes looked suddenly into his, blankly at first, then with quick apprehension that in turn gave place to dawning recognition.

The colour crept back slowly into her face and with a whispered enquiry she struggled to sit up. But he pressed her back, slipping another cushion under her head. "Lie still for a little while," he said slowly, "you fainted. I had to bring you to my camp. You are quite safe."

The curious trust she had shown earlier was manifested again for she obeyed him without protest, her rigid limbs relaxing against the soft cushions. But the colour in her cheeks deepened as she glanced wonderingly about the room and then at her own disordered appearance.

"I've never fainted before in my life," she murmured, "I'm sorry to have been so stupid—to have given so much trouble." Then, all at once, her lips quivered and with a sharp, dry sob she flung her arm across her face. But the natural outburst of womanly weeping that Carew expected did not follow, only, watching her, he saw from time to time spasms of terrible shuddering shake her from head to foot.

The coffee that Hosein brought a few minutes later steadied her, and when Carew turned to her again after giving his servant further orders she staggered unsteadily to her feet with a half shy, half nervous glance about the tent.

"You have been very kind—I don't know how to thank you," she said hurriedly, "but I can't trespass on your hospitality any longer. I—my husband—oh, I *must* get back—if—if you could lend me a horse—" But even as she spoke she swayed giddily and caught at the divan for support. Carew looked at her narrowly. "When did you eat last?" he asked abruptly, ignoring her request. Her eyes closed wearily. "I don't know," she faltered, "this morning, I think. A cup of coffee—before I left home. Oh, it seems ten years ago!" she burst out shuddering.

It was a simple explanation of her exhaustion that had already occurred to him, and for which he had provided. Want of food, combined with reaction following a nerve-racking experience—small wonder she had collapsed, he reflected.

"Algiers is thirty miles away," he explained gravely, "you are not fit to ride now. You must eat, and rest for a few hours before you attempt to return."

But she shook her head vehemently. "I couldn't eat," she panted, a desperate urgency in her voice, "I couldn't rest, I *mustn't* rest. I've got to get back home. Oh, you don't understand—but I must get back to Algiers." She was shaking with nervousness but Carew felt instinctively that it was not of him she was afraid. And consequently who or what inspired her fear was no business of his, though as he watched her restlessly twisting the golden circlet that gleamed so incongruously on her slim, boyish hand he made a shrewd guess at the cause of her agitation. But that was her affair. He was concerned only with the need of the moment.

"Be reasonable, Madame," he said sharply, "I do not keep you to amuse myself, but because you are not in a fit state at the moment to ride thirty miles. Eat what my servant is bringing, rest for a couple of hours, and then I will take you back to Algiers. If your—your friends are anxious about you they must be anxious for a few hours longer."

He spoke almost brutally and though she flinched from his tone she seemed to realise the necessity of submitting to his decision. But her distress was still obvious and he could see that she was fighting hard to maintain the restraint she imposed upon herself. And grudgingly he conceded admiration he was loath to accord. Usually courage of any kind appealed to him, but, morbidly prejudiced, he was irritated now by the unexpected moral courage she displayed. He did not want to admit it, did not want to be forced to admire where he preferred to condemn, and he turned away with a sudden rush of unreasonable anger. The entrance of Hosein with the food he had ordered put a period to an awkward silence. And when the man withdrew, Carew followed him out under the awning leaving the girl alone, for it seemed to him that his presence must be as distasteful to her as her own was to him. He detained the Arab for a few moments to explain his further requirements, and then subsided into the deck chair with a stifled yawn. Like Suliman, he had already put in a hard day's work and there were still thirty miles to ride before sunrise. But he was used to turning night into day and inured to fatigue, and it was mental rather than physical weariness that made him relax in his chair with a heavy sigh. In spite of his efforts to control his thoughts, his mind was in a ferment, and brain and body alike were in a state of nervous tension that sapped his strength and left him at the mercy of an overwhelming tide of long forgotten emotions. The strain of the meeting with Micky Meredith had weakened him for the further developments of the evening. He could still feel the soft weight of the girl's limp body in his arms, he brushed his hand across his face as though the thick strand of hair was again smothering him with its soft fragrance. Angry with himself, angry with her, he tried to forget her—and found himself suddenly wondering who she was. Good Lord, as if it mattered! Cursing under his breath he pitched his cigarette away and went back into the tent.

The girl met his glance with a shy smile. "I was hungry, after all," she said, pointing to the empty tray, "and I'm so sleepy I can hardly keep my eyes open."

But determined to go no further than bare courtesy demanded he vouchsafed only a brief nod to her tentative advance and led the way to the inner room. She paused on the threshold, looking curiously at the little sleeping apartment, then turned to him with a swift imploring glance. "You won't let me sleep too long?"

For a moment Carew's gloomy eyes looked deeply into the troubled depths of the blue ones fixed so earnestly on his, then: "The horses will be ready in two hours," he said curtly, and dropped the portiere into place. For some time he paced the big tent restlessly, a prey to violent agitation. He swore at himself angrily. What in God's name was the matter with him! Why did his thoughts, despite himself, keep turning to the woman in the adjoining room? Woman! She was only a girl, little more than a child in spite of the wedding ring that seemed to lie so uneasily on her slim finger. Any woman or child, what did she matter to him. Once safely back in Algiers she could go to the devil for all he cared.

Swinging on his heel he crossed the room and taking a medical book from a small case by the door, flung himself on the divan to read until the waiting time was over.

He was still reading when Hosein came back two hours later.

Laying the book aside with no particular haste he took a white burnous his servant tendered him and went slowly towards the inner room, scowling with annoyance and disinclination. Yet somebody had to wake the girl and he could hardly relegate the job to Hosein. He swept the curtains aside with an impatient jerk. She was still asleep, lying in an attitude of unconscious grace, her face hidden in the mass of tangled curls spread over the pillow. And from her his frowning gaze went swiftly round the room as if the alien presence made him see it with new eyes. His stern lips set more rigidly as he touched her shoulder. She woke with a start and leaped to her feet with a sharp cry that changed quickly to a nervous little laugh of embarrassment. "I was dreaming—I—is it time?" she stammered, stifling a yawn and blinking like a sleepy child. Sparing of speech he held out the white cloak. "The night is cool," he said briefly, and turned away too quickly to notice the vivid blush that suffused her face.

At the door of the tent, under the awning, he found Hosein, who was to accompany them, waiting for him and together they watched the three black horses Carew had selected for the journey being walked to and fro in the moonlight by the grooms.

And in an incredibly short space of time the girl joined them. The enveloping burnous was clasped securely, hiding her tattered clothing, and she seemed to have regained her self-possession for she was quite at ease and looked about with eager curiosity at the scattered camp, and then with even greater interest at the waiting horses. The stallion Carew was to ride was almost unapproachable, wild-eyed and savage, held with difficulty by the two men who clung to his head. But the mount he had chosen for his unwelcome guest was a steadier, friendly beast that nozzled her inquisitively as she went to him. She caught at his velvety nose with a little cry of delight, "Oh, what a darling!" and rubbed her cheek against his muzzle, crooning to him softly. Then before Carew could aid her she was in the saddle, backing to make room for the screaming fury that was demonstrating his own reluctance to be mounted by every device known to his equine intelligence. But his rage was futile and Carew was up in a flash. And for five minutes Marny Geradine, who had ridden from babyhood, watched with breathless interest the sharpest tussle she had ever seen between a horse and its rider, and marvelled at the infinite patience of the man who sat the plunging, frenzied brute like a centaur, handling him perfectly without exhibiting the smallest trace of annoyance. His methods were not the cruel ones which, for five miserable years, she had been compelled to witness, she thought with sudden bitterness. And yet this man was an Arab in whom cruelty might be excused.

Then as Carew wheeled alongside of her she put away the painful thoughts that had risen in her mind and gave herself up to the delights of this strange ride with this equally strange companion.

It was all like a dream, fantastic and unreal, but a dream that gave her more happiness than she had known for years. The swift gallop through the night, the cool wind blowing against her face, the easy movements of the horse between her knees, were all sheer joy to her. She had no wish to talk, even if the taciturn manner of the man beside her had not made speech difficult. She wanted nothing but the pleasure of the moment, the beauty of the moonlit scene and the charm of the wonderful solitude. For her Algeria had been Algiers, she had not been asked to accompany her husband on his occasional shooting expeditions, and she had wearied of the town and its immediate surroundings. She had longed to go further afield, to get right out into the desert, but she had been given no opportunity and she had long since learned to suppress inclinations that were ridiculed and never gratified. She craved for open spaces and the lonely places of the earth, and she had been chained to towns or crowded country houses and forced into a company whose society nauseated her; she had dreamt of nights like this, of the silence and peace of the wilderness, of solitary camps where she would sleep in happy dreamlessness under the radiant stars—and the nights that were her portion had been her chiefest torment. But this one night she could revel in her dream come true and rejoice in the freedom that might never again be hers. That she might have to pay, and perhaps pay hideously, for what had occurred did not matter, almost she did not care. She had suffered so much already that further suffering seemed almost inevitable and she would not spoil the rare joy of this wonderful ride by anticipating trouble. But even as she argued bravely with herself, she blanched at the possible consequences of the terrible adventure that had been no fault of her own. If when she reached the villa at Mustapha, Clyde had already returned! She clenched her teeth on her quivering lip. He had gone for a fortnight's shooting and the fortnight would be up tomorrow—today, she remembered with a sudden glance of apprehension at the sky, where the pinky flush of dawn was already showing. He might be back now! And if he were—what would her punishment be, what would she have to endure from one who knew his strength and used it brutally, who was cruel and merciless by nature as if he, too, were an Arab. Her mind leapt to the man who had abducted her. When, at the close of an appalling day, she had been brought to the hut in the deserted village, when she had finally realised the sinister purpose intended against her, the ghastly fear that had come to her, the paralysing sense of helplessness she had felt as she struggled against the crushing arms that held her, the horror of the relentless face thrust close to hers quivering with lust and desire, was no new thing. So did Clyde look at her, so did she shrink and sicken when he touched her. Were all men alike—sensual brutes with no consideration or pity? One, at least, had shown himself to be different—and he was an Arab! She turned and looked at him curiously. By the light of the brilliant moon she studied the lean, tanned face, wondering at its grave austerity. And as her gaze lingered on the white seam of an old scar that ran diagonally across his cheek above the curve of his square-cut jaw, she remembered suddenly that the stern, sombre eyes that had looked into hers were blue. Were there, then, blue-eyed Arabs, as there were blue-eyed Afghans? Who was he? A personage of importance, obviously—the rich appointments of the camp to which he had taken her, proved it. The embroidered cloth burnous, the wide silk scarf swathed about the haick that shaded his face, the scarlet leather boots he wore was the dress of a Chief. One of the wealthy Sheiks from the far south, perhaps, coming into Algiers for the Governor's annual ball. Whoever he was, he had saved her honour, had saved her from worse than death. And a sudden inexplicable desire came to her to explain to this strange, taciturn Arab the situation in which he had found her. She swung her horse nearer. "I oughtn't to have ridden alone," she began jerkily. "I know that, but I was quite close to Algiers—it seemed safe enough—and I had a reason for what I did. One has to—be alone—sometimes. I didn't think there could be any danger. It all happened so suddenly—" she broke off, chilled with his silence, wondering how she had found courage to speak to him at all, for his frigid manner did not invite confidence. And his brief answer did not tend to put her more at ease.

"It is always dangerous for a woman to ride alone in Algeria," he said gravely. It was his tone rather than the actual words that sent the hot blood rushing to her face and reduced her to a silence that lasted until they sighted the outskirts of Algiers. The dawn was brightening, already the stars were paling and dying, one by one, and the red glow of the rising sun was warming in the east.

With a sign to Hosein, Carew drew rein. "My servant will attend you, Madame. I can go no further," he said, abruptly, his eyes fixed on the distant city. She sat for a moment without answering, then she looked up quickly, her lips quivering, uncontrollably. "I don't know what to say—how to thank you—" He cut her short almost rudely. "I need no thanks, Madame. Put the one deed against the other—and do not judge the Arabs too harshly. They are as other men—no better, and perhaps no worse." She shook her head with a tremulous little smile, and for a time she seemed to be struggling with herself. Then she flung her hand out with an odd gesture of appeal. "If you won't let me thank you, will you let me be still further in your debt?" she said, unsteadily.

"As how?"

"The horse I rode," she faltered, "I—I——my husband values him. Can you help me get him back—and soon?"

Surprised that she should seek his aid in what was clearly a police matter, Carew glanced at her with a gathering frown, but what he saw in her eyes made him look away quickly.

"You shall have your horse, Madame. I pledge you my word," he said, shortly. A look of curious relief swept over her tense face.

"Then I shan't worry about him—any more," she said, with a shaky laugh. And reigning her horse nearer, again she held out her hand.

E.M. HULL

"Won't you tell me your name? I should like to know it, to remember it in—in—" she choked back a rising sob. "*Please*," she whispered.

He turned to her slowly, his eyes almost black in their sombre intensity. "I have many names," he replied, unwillingly, as though he were forcing himself to speak.

"Then tell me one," she pleaded, wistfully.

Still he hesitated, his square chin thrust out obstinately.

"I am called—El Hakim," he said at last, reluctantly. And touching his forehead in a perfunctory salaam, he wheeled his impatient horse and spurred him into a headlong gallop.

III

For a few moments, Marny Geradine, fighting to keep her own mount to a standstill, watched the fast retreating horseman until his tall, upright figure was blurred by the rush of hot tears that filled her eyes. She forced them back before they fell, the relief of tears was a luxury she had learned to deny herself, and turning once more towards Algiers cantered forward as slowly as her eager horse would permit. After all, what was the use of hurrying, she thought with a kind of dreary fatalism. If Clyde had already returned he would have arrived last night, a few minutes extra delay now would make no difference. The mischief would have been done. Nothing she could do would lessen his anger, nothing she could say would convince him against his own inclination. The true story of her terrible experience would find no credence with him. And even all the truth she dare not tell him. The latter part of the night's adventure could never be divulged. The strange Arab who rescued her, his hospitality, his chivalrous regard and consideration would be beyond her husband's comprehension. He was incapable of understanding a temperament other than his own, he would believe only the vile conclusion his own foul mind would leap at and hold in spite of all denials. She could never tell him. Enough that his return had found her absent, that she had lost a valuable horse for which he had recently paid a large figure. True, she had been promised that the horse would be returned, and the curious unaccountable faith she had in the man who had made that promise did not waver in spite of the seeming improbability of its fulfillment, but would his return even satisfy Clyde for his temporary loss? A cold feeling of fear ran through her, and then a wave of contemptuous anger at her own cowardice. She could make no explanations and offer no excuses. She would have to be silent as she always was silent rather than lie to shield herself from his imputations. Whatever she did was wrong, no matter how hard she tried to please him she always failed. She wondered, sometimes, how she found courage to go on trying. It all seemed so utterly useless. She pushed the heavy hair off her forehead with a bitter sigh. There wasn't much courage about her this morning, she thought. The exultation of that wild swift gallop through the night had passed, the new strength that had come to her had evaporated, leaving her utterly weary and sick at heart. It would have settled so many difficulties if the Arab who had abducted her had used with purpose the knife with which he had threatened her the previous day. Death would mean release from a life that was unbearable, and she was not afraid to die. Death was life— and the life she led was death. All whom she loved, all who had ever loved her—for Clyde's gross passion was not love—were dead. All except Ann—and how much longer would Ann be left to her? Clyde had so often threatened that she must go. For Ann's sake she must try and struggle on. But if Ann was taken from her—the beautiful, tired little face grew suddenly cold and set like a piece of carved white ivory and the slender, drooping figure drew straighter in the saddle as she wrenched her thoughts to the present. To get it over as soon as might be—to take her medicine like a man. Despite her unhappiness, she smiled at the recollection of the well remembered formula that in her childhood had been her father's invariable prelude to any correction he administered. And the father who had died so long ago, who had idolised her as she had idolised him, had never punished without reason. Clyde punished without either reason or provocation. The thought goaded her. No matter what form his anger took she would not give him the satisfaction he always hoped for. She would not let him see the physical fear he inspired that even her courageous spirit could not conquer. It would be worse for her in the end for her apparent callousness infuriated him, but she would rather break than bend, rather die than grovel at his feet which she knew was his desire. Avoiding the main road which she was approaching, she struck into a narrow bridle path that wound upward to the woods behind Mustapha, from where she had easy access to the little door that half hidden by flowering shrubs lay at the far end of the villa garden. The courage she still clung to did not extend to braving the curiosity of the gatekeeper at the main entrance. A turn in the track brought her to the path that led down to the garden gate. She reined in and slid to the ground. For a moment she stood still by the horse that had carried her so well, her face pressed against his neck, her fingers caressing the black muzzle thrust affectionately against her arm. Then she turned and handed the bridle to Hosein who was waiting stolidly beside her.

"That is the villa," she said, pointing downward, "will you tell your master that he may know where to send my horse? It is called the Villa des Ombres. You will not forget?"

The Arab's dark eyes followed the direction of her hand. "It is known to my lord," he said gravely, "it is the villa of the Vicomte de Granier, who is his friend."

She smiled at the little piece of gratuitous information.

"Go, with God," she murmured shyly in his own tongue. It was one of the few sentences she had learned and as the man heard the stumbling words his gloomy face lit up suddenly and he replied with a flow of soft quick Arabic she could not understand. She watched him mount and, leading the horse she had ridden, move slowly away, not, to her surprise, in the direction from which they had come but along the winding bridle road that led further up the hillside. The trees soon hid him from sight, and with another weary sigh she turned and looked again on the Villa des Ombres. White and dainty as a doll's house, set in the loveliest garden she had ever seen, surrounded by a high wall washed with palest yellow, the name seemed singularly inappropriate, yet as she looked at it now the significance of it struck her forcibly. For her it was indeed a villa of shadows, dark, menacing shadows that crept nearer to her as she hesitated beside the little path her feet had trodden so often. With a quickening heart-beat she pulled herself together and went down to the tiny doorway. Thick fronds of jasmine trailed across it and she put them aside carefully while she hunted for the key. The door opened inwards and she slipped through, closing it gently behind her, and stood for a moment with all the length of the garden between her and the villa, clutching the burnous closer round her, staring fixedly in the direction of the house. The garden was deserted, it was too early even for the gardeners who were not allowed to disturb by their chattering the protracted slumbers of the English *milor* who usually lay like a log for hours after the sun had risen. There was no sign of life within the villa. Everything was hushed and still, a brooding silence that oppressed her overwrought nerves. The heavy cloying perfume of the flowering shrubs brought a feeling of nausea that made her choke with sudden breathlessness. Her heart was beating suffocatingly as she started forward, moving slowly from tree to tree, instinctively taking what cover they afforded. At first she hardly realised what she was doing, then a blaze of anger went through her. She flung her shoulders back defiantly. She was not a thief to creep stealthily into her own house; whatever horrible construction Clyde might choose to put upon what had happened, she had done nothing to be ashamed of. With head held high and lips firmly compressed, she flung out from among the sheltering wealth of foliage into the open and walked steadily towards the house. It was a modern villa built in the French style, with all the rooms communicating. The bedrooms were at the back, opening on to a veranda which led to the garden. And to her own bedroom, the room she shared with the brute who owned her, she went with dragging feet. Before the open French window that gave access to the room, she came to a sudden halt and her eyes swept the cool dim interior with one swift glance of apprehension. Then she fell weakly against the window frame with a strangled gasp of relief, trembling violently, conscious for the first time of an overwhelming weariness that seemed to take from her every atom of strength. The room appeared to be empty; the massive bed, its silken curtains hanging from a gilt coronet fixed in the ceiling had not been slept in.

But as she looked again, too tired to move, she saw what she had overlooked at first, the tall gaunt figure of a woman, clothed in black, kneeling beside a big armchair, her neat grey head bowed on her folded arms. And as Marny bent forward eagerly there came to her ears the low soft murmur of a voice raised in passionate prayer.

A faint smile flitted across her pale face.

"Ann," she whispered.

With a wild cry the woman scrambled to her feet and rushed at her, catching her in her arms with hungry fierceness.

"My lamb—my lamb—" she sobbed, and held her as if she never meant to let her go. And yielding to the weakness that was growing on her, almost happy for the moment in the shelter of the tender arms wrapped around her, Marny laid her aching head on the shoulder of the woman who had nursed her from babyhood. But the transient happiness passed quickly and she freed herself with a single word of interrogation.

"Clyde?"

The old woman's face hardened suddenly. "His lordship's not back—thank God," she said, grimly. With an inward prayer of thankfulness Marny dropped into a chair. The relief was tremendous, the respite more than she had dared to hope for. As Clyde was not yet back then there was no possibility of his arriving before the evening when she would have strength again to meet him. But there was still one thing that had to be arranged before he came. She put aside the trembling hands that were fumbling at the clasp of the enveloping cloak.

"Tanner," she said, hoarsely, "fetch Tanner. I must speak to him at once."

The woman made a gesture of protest. "Never mind Tanner, Miss Marny dear," she said, soothingly. "Tanner can wait. Let me put you cosily into bed first and then I'll tell him you are safe home. He's close by and won't take any finding. Give him his due, he's been nearly as anxious as me, backwards and forwards between the house and the stables since yesterday morning—and worrying more about you, my precious, I'm bound to admit, than that nasty, vicious horse he's so partic'lar about," she added, trying again to unfasten the burnous. Marny guessed at the unspoken anxiety that made Ann's fingers so unusually clumsy and smiled reassuringly.

"You don't understand," she said, with gentle insistence, "I must see him. Don't fuss, Ann dear. I'm not hurt or damaged in any way, I'm only desperately tired. But I can't rest until I've spoken to Tanner. Bring him here, and then you can coddle me to your heart's content. But I won't move from this chair until I've seen him."

"But, Miss Marny, it's your bedroom," exclaimed Ann in horrified accents, "and you in that outlandish cloak and all, and your hair—"

"Oh, never mind my hair, you dear old propriety, and Tanner won't trouble his head about it being my bedroom. Do as I ask you, Ann, if you love me," said Marny, wearily. And muttering to herself Ann departed grudgingly.

She returned almost immediately followed by an undersized, sharp-faced man, who bore the marks of his calling stamped plainly upon him. Half jockey, half groom, Cockney from the top of his bullet head to the tips of his neat feet, he accepted the situation with the aplomb of his kind.

Saluting smartly, he waited for Lady Geradine to speak. And Marny who liked and trusted the little man did not hesitate.

"I've lost The Caid, Tanner," she said, bluntly. For a moment his coolness forsook him. "*My Gawd!*" he breathed and stared at her in frank dismay. Then he recovered himself quickly. "Did you take a toss, m'lady, did 'e 'arm you, the vicious devil—begging your ladyship's pardon. Mrs. Ann and me, we've been cruel anxious," he added with the suspicion of a shake in his rasping voice. Marny smiled at him and shook her head.

"I'm not hurt, thank you, Tanner. The chestnut was stolen. I ought not to have taken him so far from Algiers. I forgot that he might be known, might be a temptation to any Arab who knew his value—there are a lot of desert men coming into the town just now. Anyhow he's gone. I couldn't do anything alone. But I—I've given information about it and I'm almost certain that he will be sent back. So you needn't worry,

E.M. HULL

Tanner. I'm sure it will be all right. It was my fault entirely, it probably wouldn't have happened if I had taken you with me. But there is no good in going back to that. I'll explain to his lordship and—and please keep near the stables, Tanner, in case the horse comes back today," she added, hastily, struggling to keep her voice steady. For a moment the man hesitated, then with a quiet, "Very good, m'lady," he jerked his hand to his forehead and tip-toed from the room. Outside in the hall he looked back over his shoulder at the closed door, his face working oddly. "You'll explain to 'is blooming lordship, will you m'lady? Gawd almighty, we all know what that'll mean! I'd a deal rather take the blame meself—blast 'im!" he muttered, and strode off very far from sharing his mistress's optimism with regard to the stolen horse.

In the bedroom, Marny leant back wearily in the deep armchair, too tired to move, wondering at her own confidence in the promise that had been made to her, wondering at the man himself and at the strange feeling of security she had felt in his presence.

Ann's anxious voice roused her and rising with an effort she submitted without further protest to the ministrations of her old nurse who stripped the tattered clothing from her with exclamations of horror at the sight of the bruises marring the whiteness of the delicate body she worshipped.

She had seen, with almost murder in her heart, similar bruises before on those slim young arms and knew them for what they were, the marks of a man's merciless fingers. But she made no comment while she bathed the aching limbs, and brushed the tangled mop of curly hair, and finally tucked up her charge in bed as if she were a child again. And until the last drop of strong soup she brought was finished, and she had drawn the jalousies over the open window, she refrained from asking the questions that kept rising to her lips. But when everything she could think of for her mistress's comfort was done she slipped on to her knees by the bedside and caught the girl's hands in hers.

"Tell me, Miss Marny dear," she pleaded, tremulously, "you can't go bottling things up inside of you forever. It will ease your mind to speak—for once. There's a lot more than you let out to Tanner, you that came home in rags and bruised fit to break my heart. What did they do to you, my precious? Where have you been all these weary hours that I've been nearly out of my senses with fright—thinking you dead, or worse, and dreading his lordship'd come back and find you gone, and all."

And thankful for the opportunity of confiding fully once more in the faithful old nurse who, until five years ago, had shared her every secret, Marny told her. And Ann listened, as she had listened long ago to the frank recital of childish escapades, in silence. Only the trembling of her thin lips, the occasional tightening of her worn old hand, betrayed the agitation she would not allow herself to voice. Miss Marny had been through enough, had suffered enough for one day, she wouldn't want any more "scenes" now it was all safely over. She brushed the hair tenderly from the damp white forehead and rose to her feet with a long drawn breath. "It was bad enough—God be thanked it wasn't worse," she said, softly. "I'd never have believed the day would come when I'd feel a particle of gratitude toward an Arab—nasty, slinking, treacherous creatures I've always thought them. That man of his lordship's— Malec—fair gives me the creeps. But I suppose there's good as well as bad amongst them, there must be by what you've told me. A Christian gentleman couldn't have done more, and there's many who'd have done less. What did you say his name was, Miss Marny?"

Marny turned drowsily, settling more comfortably into the pillows.

"He didn't tell me his name," she said, sleepily, "he said he was called El Hakim."

"And what might that mean?"

"It means a doctor, I think, but I didn't know Arabs had doctors. Perhaps he has something to do with the Spahis—he talked French very well—perhaps he—" a big yawn swallowed the end of the sentence, and Ann drew up the coverlet with a little admonishing pat. "Never you bother your pretty head about him now, my lamb. Just go to sleep and forget all about it. And heaven send the man's as good as his word and gets that dratted horse back," she added, anxiously to herself as she left the room.

It was late in the afternoon when she reluctantly aroused her mistress and set down a dainty tea tray by the bedside.

"It's four o'clock, Miss Marny, and there's two eggs to your tea. I'll see you eat every bit of it," she announced cheerfully, bustling about the room and flinging back the shutters. Lady Geradine stretched luxuriously and then sat up, rubbing the sleep out of her eyes. "Oh, Ann, what fun," she said with a laugh the old woman had not heard for years. "It's like nursery days. Put heaps of cushions behind me and cut off the tops of the eggs. I'm simply famishing." Then she paused with a square of toast half way to her mouth and the laughter died out of her eyes.

E.M. HULL

"Has The Caid come back?"

Ann splashed the tea into the saucer at the sudden question.

"Not yet, dearie, but its only four o'clock—and the train doesn't get in until seven," she said, inconsequently. Marny understood very well the meaning of her somewhat obscure sentence, but she gave no sign of understanding. It was part of the pitiful game she played that even Ann received no confidences and was allowed to make no comment on the treatment her husband meted out to her. Angry with herself for the words that had escaped unintentionally, the old woman stole a penitent glance at the girl who was her idol. But Marny was apparently only concerned with the salting of her egg.

"The poor dear isn't likely to come back by train," she said lightly, as if the horse alone occupied her mind.

Finishing her tea she slipped out of bed and into the wrapper Ann held for her. Stretching out her arms she patted them tenderly, and then raising them high above her head bent forward easily, sweeping her finger-tips to the ground, and straightened again slowly with a laugh of satisfaction.

"I'm as right as rain, Ann," she said, reassuringly, "not a bit stiff. I'll dress for dinner now. I can't be bothered to change again so soon. Bring me that white teagown thing I got in Paris, it's loose and cool."

Too loose and too cool, thought Ann as she went with primly folded lips to fetch the diaphanous little garment that had been made to Lord Geradine's order and which she herself considered neither fit nor decent for her mistress to wear. A dress suitable in its sensuous appeal to the women with whom the Viscount chose to associate, but degrading to the innocent girl whom he had married. And when the final touches to Lady Geradine's toilet were completed, Ann stood back and surveyed her handiwork with grim disapproval. And Marny, staring absently into the long mirror, caught the expression in the stern old eyes fixed on her and moved abruptly with a smothered sigh, the colour deepening in her face. The dress was hateful and she loathed it, but in this as in everything else, loyalty to her husband kept her lips closed. Even his questionable taste must pass undiscussed. And discussion would make it no easier to bear. She had to submit to it as she had to submit to the man himself. She was not a free agent. Legally she was his wife, actually she was a slave to be and do at the whim of a capricious and tyrannical master.

In the early days of her married life, she had tried to rebel, and the memory of those futile struggles was like a horrible nightmare, but the passing years had taught her wisdom and given her strength to accept what she revolted from and detested.

Slipping a long chain of uncut emeralds round her neck she went silently out of the room. The drawing room she entered was more English than French in its appointments, bright with gay coloured chintzes and fragrant with masses of flowers banked in every available space. She lingered by a tall basket filled with giant roses, inhaling their delicate perfume and gathering the cool petals against her hot cheeks. Then she moved slowly to glance at a porcelain clock ticking noisily on the mantelpiece. Little more than an hour before Clyde might come and her brief holiday would be over. He rarely left her for so long and the days of respite had flown. With a shiver she lit a cigarette and began to pace the narrow room, her thoughts travelling back over the last five years of bitter misery to the day when, barely seventeen years of age, a child in every sense, she had grown suddenly in the space of a few agonising hours into womanhood, cruelly awakened to what it meant to be Clyde Geradine's wife. As he determined to continue so had he begun. The disgust and loathing he inspired in her had never lessened. Herself innately chaste, his gross coarseness and frank sensuality appalled her. If he had even once shown that he had been moved by any higher sentiment, had had any nobler thought beyond the purely physical attraction she had for him she would have tried to make allowances. But for him she was merely a perfectly made vigorous young animal by whom he hoped, as he candidly told her, to get the heir on whom he had set his heart. And with nothing to cling to, nothing to hope for, she felt only degradation in her association with him. His moods were variable as his temper was uncertain. He was made up of contradictions. Despite his own infidelities, infidelities of which she was fully aware, despite the fact that he deliberately paraded her beauty on every possible occasion, he was possessed with an insensate jealousy. Faithless himself he placed no trust in her faithfulness, and was suspicious of every mark of admiration shown her. She was his, he insisted, as much his property as any horse or dog in his stable, his to use as he would. His also, it seemed, to abuse and torture by every subtle mental torment his cruel nature could devise. And not mental only. It pleased him to know her powerless against his strength, it pleased him when the mood was on him to subject her to physical violence that his warped mind held to be within his right. He had bought her, body and soul he had bought her, and brutally he allowed her no possibility of ever forgetting the fact.

Motherless before she was old enough to know her loss, she had grown up in a big rambling house in an isolated part of the west coast of Ireland. The father she adored had died when she was twelve, leaving her in care of her brother Denis, who was ten years her senior. Neighbours were few and far between, their visits long since discouraged by the lonely, broken-hearted man who had lived a life of seclusion since his wife's death. With no companions of her own age, with almost no associates of her own rank, she had spent her days in the open, riding and fishing, content with the limited life she led. Ann's had been the only womanly influence she had known, Ann who had been her mother's nurse and then her own.

And Denis, a ne'er-do-well with tastes and inclinations studiously hidden during his father's lifetime, had, on succeeding to his inheritance, shaken the dust of Ireland off his feet to seek a more exhilarating sphere of activity where he had successfully dissipated his patrimony, and incidentally fallen under the influence and into the power of Lord Geradine who was a past master in all the vices the younger man emulated. Marny had never known the real truth of the whole sordid story. She only knew that after years of absence Denis had returned, changed almost beyond recognition, bringing with him a stranger who had stayed for a fortnight in the house. She had hated the big domineering Englishman at sight, instinctively repelled, and the attention that almost from the first he had shown had terrified her. Then he had gone, and a couple of months later Denis had reappeared, more haggard, more careworn than before. He had told her a long rambling tale, most of which she had not understood, and had ended with a wild appeal to her to save his honour and the honour of the family she had been taught from childhood to reverence. Only by her marriage with Lord Geradine, it seemed, could the family name escape disgrace. And, ignorant of what she did, carried away by Denis' eloquence, passionately jealous for the name that had gone untarnished for generations, she had consented. She had been given no time for further reflection, and in spite of Ann's horrified remonstrances and pleadings she had been married almost at once. That was five years ago. And for five years she had endured a life of misery, in an alien environment, disillusioned and shocked. Her husband's hold over her brother—a hold she had never comprehended and which had never been explained to her—was the means by which he compelled her submission in everything. And consistently she had done what she thought to be her duty, had striven to please him as far as she was able and had been loyal to him who had never shown loyalty to her.

Five years—only five years!

With a bitter sigh she sank wearily into a big chintz covered Chesterfield. For a long time she lay thinking, almost dreaming, until at last she awoke with a sudden sense of shock to the import of her thoughts. The Arab who had saved her! She could see distinctly every line of his tall, graceful figure, every feature of his grave, bronzed face. She found herself wondering again at the cold austerity of his expression, so different from the appraising glances of admiration usually accorded her and which made her hate the beauty that inspired them. He had not even appeared to know that she was beautiful. His sombre eyes had rested on her with complete indifference, almost, so it seemed to her, with dislike. Hyper-sensitive, she had been conscious that his aid, his hospitality had been given unwillingly. She remembered the curt impatient voice, "I do not keep you to please myself—" and wondered why the fact of his indifference seemed so suddenly to hurt her. If he had not been indifferent, if he had looked on her as other men did, what would have been her fate? She would have escaped one horrible peril only to fall into another as horrible. She had been utterly in his power, utterly at his mercy—the mercy of an Arab. She owed her honour to an Arab—and she did not even know his name! Why had he evaded what was a perfectly natural question, why hidden his identity under a sobriquet? Was he afraid that she would try to trace him, try to force on him some tangible proof of the gratitude he had refused to listen to? Her cheeks burned. What he had done was beyond payment. In all probability she would never see him again. She would have to be content with the meagre information he had given her, content with the memory of a wonderful chivalry she had never thought to experience and which had been a revelation. It was as though some healing power had touched her, like the clean, wholesome breath of some purifying wind penetrating the defiling atmosphere that surrounded her, opening her eyes to a new conception of man's attitude towards woman. The men she had hitherto met had been uniformly alike in taste and inclination to the husband who forced their society upon her. She shrank from them as she shrank from him with a sense of shame that was unendurable. Compelled to participate in a life she abhorred, she seemed to be on the brink of some loathsome pit, choked with the fetid fumes of its foul putrescence, steadily sinking downward into an abyss of horrible and terrible darkness, her whole soul recoiling from the moral destruction that appeared to loom inevitably ahead of her. What did her soul matter to Clyde? It was only her body he wanted. It was only physical admiration she saw in the eyes of his friends. Yesterday for the first time she had met a man who had ignored her sex, whose gaze had not lingered desirously on the fair exterior compelling a remembrance of her womanhood, whose proximity had not moved her to hot discomfort, but had given instead a sense of security and trust. With him she had felt safe—safe and curiously unstrange. The hours spent in his tent, the long ride through the night at his side, would never be effaced from her memory. He had given her a glimpse of a finer, cleaner manhood than in her unhappy experience she had ever known. In some undefinable way he seemed to have restored the self-respect that year by year she had felt being torn from her. And he was an Arab! An Arab. She whispered it again, lying very still on the sofa, her fingers twining and untwining restlessly about the emerald chain. What did his nationality matter—it was the man himself who counted. The man who had shown her a nobler type than she had ever met with, the man who had shown her that all strength was not merciless, that all men did not look on women merely as their natural prey. And as with this desert man, so must it be with many men of her own race. Her brooding eyes darkened with sudden anguish, and she flung on to her face burying her head in the silken cushions, fighting the agony of misery and revolt that swept over her. Why had she been destined for such a fate? Why had it been her lot to be thrown only amongst those whose vileness debased the sacred image in which they were made? Why had she been given no chance of the happiness that must be the portion of luckier women than she? If it had been otherwise, if for her marriage had meant not only physical union but a higher, holier companionship of mind and spirit, how gladly would she have yielded to a passion hallowed by love, to possession tempered by consideration. If she could have loved and respected where now she only obeyed and endured! A marriage such as hers was ignoble, degrading, horrible beyond all thought. If she had known what it would mean, would she have had the courage to face what she had done in ignorance? She sat up, pushing the heavy hair off her forehead, staring into space with pain-filled eyes. Yes, she would have done it again in spite of everything. Not for love of Denis, she had never loved him—in childhood he had bullied her, in girlhood he had neglected her, and on the threshold of her womanhood he had made her pay the price of his infamy—but for love of the name and family that meant so much to her. And because of that, because her wretchedness was the result of her own willing sacrifice she must struggle on as she had struggled all these five terrible years, beaten and hopeless, but striving to fulfill her part of the marriage vows her husband treated so lightly. But, oh, dear God, she had never known it would be so hard! Harder now than ever. Why did her thoughts turn so persistently to the man who had saved her? Why did the recollection of his chivalry and generosity seem to make her feel so much more acutely the misery of her life? Was it only the contrast to the man whose wife she was? She hid her face in her hands with a sharp little cry of fear. It was more than that. Quite suddenly she realised it—the full meaning of what had happened to her, the full significance of the thoughts that were crowding in her brain. She shivered, clasping her hands closer over her eyes. Why, oh why had this come to her—had she not already enough to bear! And if she had not been bound, if she were free, it would make no difference. He was an Arab! Then her self-control gave way and she fell back among the cushions, dry-eyed but shaking with emotion. "I wouldn't have cared," she wailed, "I wouldn't care what he was."

But his indifference had been complete—and she was married! She wrung her hands in an agony of shame and horror. She was married. She was Clyde's wife. To even think of another man was sin. She must tear from her heart the image that in a few short hours had become so deeply implanted. She would never see him again. With quivering lips she whispered it, and writhed at the strange new sense of desolation that came upon her. A companionship that had been so brief, a passing stranger of an alien race whose name she did not even know—and yet the world seemed suddenly empty. She pondered it, ashamed and vaguely frightened. It was because she had trusted him, she thought with a pitiful attempt at self-justification, and because she was tired and overwrought. Unnerved, she had allowed his kindness to make too deep an impression.

Later, when strength was given her again, she would forget—not him—but the wickedness that filled her heart tonight. She moved listlessly on the sofa, mentally exhausted, too tired almost to care that The Caid was still missing, that very soon her husband might be returning and she would have to make her lame explanation and face his inevitable wrath. And for once, honesty compelled her to admit it, he would have good cause for anger. The horse was valuable, and she had had no right to take him so far from Algiers unattended. It was asking for trouble in a land of horsemen who stole where they could not buy and who would consider the theft of a noted stallion, that a foreigner purposed to remove from the country, as an act of merit rather than otherwise. All her young life she had ridden alone. But it would be useless to try and explain to Clyde the overpowering desire for solitude that had driven her out yesterday morning without the groom whose constant presence put a period to her enjoyment and took from her all the pleasure of her rides.

The clock on the mantelpiece struck seven. She hardly glanced at it. If Clyde did come, the train would probably be late. It usually was. And for nearly an hour more she lay still, striving to concentrate her tired mind on trivialities, becoming momentarily drowsier as the room grew darker. She was nearly asleep when the sound of a loud blustering voice echoing from the hall sent her bolt upright on the sofa, her heart beating violently, her wide eyes fixed apprehensively on the door.

She stumbled to her feet as he flung into the room, a tall heavily-built man whose big frame seemed to almost fill the aperture as he stood for a moment in the entrance peering for her in the dim light.

"What the devil are you sittin' in the dark for?" The truculent tone gave her the key to the mood in which he had returned and her heart beat faster as she heard him fumbling at the electric switchboard by the door. Then the room flashed into brilliance as he swept his hand downward with an impatient jerk, and she blinked at the sudden glare of light with a nervous little laugh.

Without waiting for an answer he strode towards her and caught her in his arms with the rough masterfulness that was habitual with him. "Been asleep—tired of waiting for me? You look like a baby with your hair all ruffled and your cheeks the colour of a two-year-old," he said, with a short laugh of satisfaction, drawing her closer and bending to kiss her. The hot breath fanning her face was rank with spirits and it took all her resolution to suppress the repugnance his nearness caused her, and meet the heavy eyes that glowed with sudden passion as he crushed his mouth on hers. She was trembling when at last he released her but he did not seem to notice her agitation. He laughed again, looking her slowly up and down with the frank appraisement of a proprietor. "I wanted that," he remarked complacently, "a fortnight's a bit too much without your charmin' society, my dear. You'll come along too the next time. And the trip wasn't worth it. No decent heads worth speaking about, not a sight nor smell of a panther, and that ass Malec mucked up the arrangements as I knew he would—a rotten show from start to finish. And the train was nearly an hour late getting into Algiers, waited an infernal time at a potty little wayside station for some dam' chief or other to get aboard with most of his tribe. Thought we were going to be there all night. Can't think why they let the beggars travel by train. I'm as hot as hell and my throat's on fire. I want a drink and I want a bath. Tell 'em to have dinner ready in half-an-hour." And with a parting curse at the inefficiency of the Algerian railway service he flung out of the room as he had flung into it.

With her hand pressed tightly against the lips that were still quivering from his kisses Marny stood struggling to regain her composure and starting nervously as she listened to the angry bellowing that came from her husband's dressing room. But she drew a swift little breath of relief at the thought that he obviously knew nothing as yet of The Caid's disappearance, that it was not any fault of hers but only the non-success of the shooting trip that had annoyed him. If she could only keep the disastrous knowledge from him until tomorrow—the horse might be back by then. She smothered a sigh and, ringing the bell, gave the order for dinner. His rough handling had further disarranged her ruffled hair and while she smoothed it into order she stared at herself in the mirror with hostile eyes.

He had made her a coward—would he end by making her a liar as well? But at least she need not lie to herself. It was cowardice that made her defer telling him the story of her mishap. It was cowardice that had made her choose the hateful dress she was wearing tonight. She turned away with a gesture of disgust and self scorn, and fell to pacing the room until he joined her again.

During dinner her own silence passed unheeded while he launched into a detailed and grumbling account of the expedition that had fallen far short of his expectations. He cursed the country and its people and the sporting facilities with equal impartiality and with a wealth of highly coloured language that was peculiarly his own, breaking off frequently to swear at the servants who were, notwithstanding, doing their work quickly and well. She knew that he must have been drinking heavily during the day, but his thirst seemed unquenchable and as she watched him gulp down whisky after whisky, she wondered with a feeling of dread what form the inevitable reaction would take. His rages were easier to bear than the moods of maudlin sentimentality that sickened her.

Contrary to his usual custom he followed her into the drawing room when dinner was finished, and lighting a cigar took up a commanding position before the flower-filled fireplace with his hands thrust deep in the pockets of his dinner jacket, watching her through half-veiled eyes until coffee was brought.

"You're dam' pretty tonight, Marny," he remarked condescendingly as he took the fragile cup she held out to him. "I flatter myself that dress was a stroke of genius," he added, looking with no great favour at the coffee he raised to his lips. A moment later cup and contents went crashing into the flower pots behind him.

"Filth!" he exclaimed disgustedly, "if that chap can't make decent coffee he'll have to go." And consigning the cook to perdition he lounged across the room to a chair and turning to the tray-laden table beside him splashed neat cognac wrathfully into a glass. Marny put down her own cup without answering. There was nothing wrong with the coffee, it was perfectly made as usual, but expostulation was useless with Clyde in his present humour. And he seemed to expect no comment. Swallowing the brandy with slow enjoyment, he refilled the glass and, stretching his long limbs lazily, turned to her with the question for which she had been waiting all evening.

"Tanner been behaving—beasts all right?" he rapped, with a glance at the clock on the mantelpiece. And fearful that, even at this late hour, he might be meditating a visit to the stables, for the first time in her life she lied, her fingers clutching at the soft cushions of the sofa till they grew stiff and numb.

"Tanner has been exemplary. The horses are splendid," she said with forced easiness. And her answer apparently satisfied him for he grunted approvingly and settled more comfortably into his chair. For some time he did not speak, and she lay still striving to subdue the rapid beating of her heart, acutely conscious of the searching eyes that rarely left her face. But when the coffee tray had been removed he stirred restlessly. "Any letters?"

Accustomed to doing for him what he was too lazy to do for himself, she rose and fetched the pile of correspondence that had accumulated during his absence, and, going back to the sofa, watched him tearing open and throwing aside letter after letter until she could keep silent no longer.

"Aren't you going to the Club?"

He laughed shortly. "Not me," he said, with a glance that made her flinch. "You seem to forget I've been away for a fortnight. My wife's society is good enough for me tonight."

With an involuntary tremor she turned her head that he might not see the loathing she knew was written on her face, and picked up a novel with shaking fingers. She had not expected that he would go to the Club, and only a passionate longing to shorten the hours she must spend alone with him made her propose it. Her lips trembled as she turned the pages of the book mechanically, not reading but listening to his angry comments on the letters that were evidently not pleasing to him. He flung the last one from him with a snarl.

"That charming brother of yours is asking for trouble! Overrun his allowance again and has the cheek to write and ask for a cheque by return. I'll see him in Hades first. I've warned him before the allowance is ample and that I wouldn't raise it by a single halfpenny. Seems to think I'm made of money," he added, kicking the letter petulantly.

The book slipped to the floor as Marny sat up with a jerk, staring at him uncomprehendingly.

"His allowance—Denis—I don't understand," she said slowly, with a puzzled frown.

He looked at her with a curious smile. "Don't you, my dear?" he said unpleasantly. "Neither does Denis, apparently. No Irishman seems to understand the value of money, and I suppose Denis is only conforming to type when he fails to understand that the yearly allowance I make him has got to last a year. He can whistle for what he wants now, I shan't give it to him."

"But, Clyde, I don't know what you're talking about," she gasped, "the allowance *you* make him—why do you make Denis an allowance? Why can't he live on his own money?"

Lord Geradine smiled again.

"What money?" he drawled.

She jerked her head impatiently.

"His own money, the estate money, the rents of Castle Fergus. What he—what we have always lived on. Why can't he manage on that?"

"Because the Castle Fergus rents are paid to me," replied her husband shortly. She looked at him blankly, putting her hand to her head with a gesture of bewilderment.

"To you," she faltered, "the Castle Fergus rents are paid to you? But why—what have you to do with Castle Fergus? Oh, Clyde, I don't know what you mean, truly I don't."

Lord Geradine heaved himself sideways in his chair and poured out a whisky with slow deliberation. "You knew your brother was in a hole when I married you," he said at last, with a certain irritation in his voice. She winced, and the blood rushed into her white face. "I knew that," she said shakily, "but I didn't know it had anything to do with money. I thought it was something—something horrible he had done," she added with a shiver, her voice breaking pitifully.

Geradine emptied the glass and pushed it from him with a hard laugh. "The one sometimes follows from the other," he said contemptuously, "it was so with Denis. He ran through a very tidy fortune in an uncommonly short space of time, and then he did what you are pleased to call 'something horrible'. I don't set up to be a model of virtue myself but there are some things I jib at, and I'm damned if I'd soil my hands with the dirty game he played. But he played it once too often when I came on the scenes. He landed himself in the devil of a mess and jolly nearly ended in jail. But for my own reasons that didn't suit me, and he was dam' glad to take the terms I offered him. He wanted his liberty and money enough to make it amusing—I wanted you. And there you have it," he concluded with brutal candour.

She sat quite still, looking at him fixedly her face colourless, trying to realize the meaning of what he had told her. At the moment she hardly knew which she hated most, the brother who had held his sister so cheaply or the man who had been content to drive so shameful a bargain to obtain what he wanted.

"He *sold* me to you," she said at last. And the scorn in her voice sent him out of his chair with an oath that made her shudder, "Oh, for God's sake don't make a tragedy out of it," he cried angrily. "In any case it's ancient history. You knew that Denis had a reason for pressing our marriage. I don't know what fancy tale he told you, and I don't care. We are married and there's an end of it. And there's no earthly need to cut up so rough about it. You didn't do so badly for yourself, you blessed little innocent—and I'm not complaining. Don't be a little fool, Marny. I mayn't be a saint but I'm dam' fond of you. I wanted you the first minute I laid eyes on you, and I generally get what I want," he added with a complacent laugh, dropping down on the sofa beside her. Then his voice changed as he slid his hand slowly up the soft cool arm under the loose sleeve of her teagown. "I've been wanting you pretty badly this last fortnight," he whispered thickly, and flung his arms around her with sudden violence. For a moment he held her, trembling and helpless in his fierce embrace, and she felt the heavy beating of his heart as he stared down at her with hot desire flaming in his red flecked eyes. Then he laughed again, a laugh that made her want to shriek, that made every nerve in her body quiver with passionate revolt, and pushed her from him.

"Run along," he said quickly, "and don't keep me waiting the infernal age you usually do. Tell that old woman to clear out in double quick time if she values her place."

Beyond the door, free from his watching eyes, she buried her face in her hands with a groan of agony. For how many more years, oh, merciful God, must she endure this life of horrible bondage? Would she never be free—never escape from his brutality till death released her. If she could only die—but she was too strong to die. Misery did not kill. She would live—live until the beauty that was all he cared for faded, live until he had drained from her the strength and vitality that had attracted him. And afterwards? For her there was no afterwards, no hope, no consolation. There was only the present with its difficulties and suffering. The present! She started nervously. How long had she stood there? With a convulsive shudder she went swiftly across the dim lit hall.

And as she passed her husband's dressing room the door opened suddenly and she came face to face with his Arab valet. She had not seen the man since his return and, forcing a smile to her trembling lips, she nodded to him with the kindly greeting she gave invariably to every member of the household. But as he turned to her the words died in an inarticulate gasp and she halted abruptly, staring with horror at the terrible mark that, stretching from forehead to chin, disfigured his face—a mark that could only have been caused by the slashing cut of a powerfully driven whip. "Malec—" she cried aghast. But with a quick salaam the man drew back and, slipping past her, vanished down the passage with the lithe noiselessness of his race. She stood as if turned to stone, breathing heavily, her clenched hands pressed against her throbbing temples, sickened by what she had seen. "How can he—oh, how can he?" she moaned. Then with a backward glance of fearful apprehension she fled panic-stricken to the door of her own room. But there, with a tremendous effort of will, she regained her self command and went in quietly, smiling with apparent naturalness as Ann turned from the open window to meet her. The old woman's face was radiant. She almost ran across the room.

"Miss Marny, dear, it's all right," she breathed eagerly. "Tanner's just been in. The horse was brought back half an hour ago and he's not a penny the worse."

For an instant Marny looked at her strangely. Then she sank into a chair with a gasp of relief, and stretched out her hands tremblingly.

"Ann—oh, *Ann*!" she whispered.

IV

At the close of a hot afternoon, about three weeks after his return to Algiers, Carew was sitting in the Governor General's private room at the Winter Palace.

Staring out of the window, a neglected cigarette drooping between his lips, he was listening without attending to the faint strains of the Zouave band echoing from the Place du Gouvernement, drumming absently with his fingers on the table before him which was littered with maps and plans and scattered typewritten sheets. For the best part of two hours he had been repeating the story of his last journey, and the hardly won concession for the benefit of an interested and detail-loving representative of the Ministry of the Interior who was returning the next day to Paris after an extensive and carefully shepherded tour through the northern provinces of Algeria.

Carew's mission successfully terminated and his report duly handed in to headquarters, he had had no wish to be further identified with the enterprise. He was glad to be of use to the Administration; anxious always, when opportunity offered, to assist in promoting a better understanding between the rulers of the country and its native part of his life's work. He was not inclined to magnify the importance of what he did and he was actuated by no desire for personal gain or advantage. He was content to give his help when it was required and let others take the kudos. He worked solely for love of the country and admiration of its administrators. The Governor General and the Commander-in-Chief, both hard-working conscientious men who governed a difficult country with tact and discretion, were his personal friends, and he considered himself amply rewarded if his own endeavors in any way eased the burden of their responsibilities.

But today, for the first time, he had yielded to the often expressed wish of General Sanois—who administered the particular part of the Sahara under discussion—that his really valuable aid should be more intimately known to the home authorities.

The interview had passed off successfully. The illustrious visitor had shown a wide knowledge of and a deep personal interest in the affairs of the country which had gone far to lessen the instinctive feeling of hostility with which the two men primarily responsible for its well-being, had viewed his advent. He had listened carefully to Carew's story, gripping the major points of importance sanely and intelligently, and had been loud in his approval of the work done. With Gallic courtesy and enthusiasm he had congratulated all concerned, expressing his own and his country's indebtedness to the three men he addressed in a felicitous little speech that hinted at much he did not say outright, and, with a final interchange of compliments, had at last betaken himself to his waiting carriage whither the Governor and General Sanois had accompanied him.

And Carew, left for a few moments alone in the cool pleasant room, had fallen into a profound reverie that was in no way connected with the events of the afternoon.

The sound of approaching voices roused him and he turned reluctantly from the window as the stout, smiling little Governor bustled in, followed by his tall, grave-faced army colleague, and a slim, delicate-looking youth who went silently to a desk in a far corner.

The Governor dropped into a chair with a little grunt, mopped his heated forehead vigorously and beamed with evident satisfaction on his companions.

"That's over," he remarked in a tone of relief. "I usually have a *crise de nerfs* after these visits. But this one was better than most, *Dieu merci!* Some of them—*oh, la! la!*" He broke off with a comical grimace, flourishing his handkerchief expressively. Then with a shrug and a gay laugh he tapped Carew's knee confidentially with a podgy forefinger.

"Everything goes *à merveille*, my dear Carew. Our friend is charmed with all he has seen, has been pleased to compliment me on the state of the country, and has swallowed all the extravagant demands of our good Sanois here without turning a hair. Providing he remembers all he has promised, providing his interest is as great as he represents, there should be speedily allowed to us some alterations in administration we have long asked for in vain. Our hands have been tied too tightly, *voyez-vous*. He sees the necessity for loosening them somewhat. I am not expecting the millennium—I have lived too long to expect anything very much, particularly of politicians—but I am hopeful, decidedly hopeful. If it were not so exhausting I might even allow myself to become enthusiastic. But I gave up enthusiasms when I came to Algeria—so very detrimental to the nerves." Again he demonstrated languidly with his handkerchief, and then patted his chest significantly. "And some little decorations will probably follow, *hein*? We need not attach too much importance to them, perhaps, but they are pleasant to receive, oh, yes, decidedly very pleasant to receive."

"For me, I would rather receive the extra battery I asked for," growled the General.

The little Governor looked up at him with an expression of pained protest. "Ah, you soldiers—you and your guns! Brute force, brute force—that's all you think of," he murmured reprovingly. Then he smiled again, waving his hands as though dismissing the unpleasant idea his colleague's words suggested.

"You will dine with me tonight," he said genially, "both of you? We must celebrate the occasion. And afterwards, perhaps, for an hour or two, the opera? Not very amusing but—" he shrugged whimsically and offered Carew his cigarette case.

For a few minutes longer they talked of the possibilities of the new régime in prospect, and then the General rose to go with a vague reference to a mass of correspondence awaiting his attention.

"Are you coming my way?" he asked, turning to the Englishman. But Carew shook his head.

"I've an appointment in the Casbar this evening," he said, shuffling some papers together and slipping them into his breast pocket.

Sanois laughed grimly and looked up from the sword-belt he was buckling with a suspicion of eagerness in his keen eyes. "It would be indiscreet to ask with whom, I presume? You know more about the Casbar than I do," he said, almost grudgingly. "You've friends everywhere, Carew. Some of them I'd like to lay my hands on," he added meaningly.

Carew smiled faintly. "Possibly," he said coolly, "but my 'friends' are useful. And until they let me down I can't very well help you to any information you may want concerning them. That was agreed," he added, his voice hardening slightly.

"Word of an Englishman, eh?" said the General with another grim laugh, and stalked off.

The Governor looked at the closing door with his smiling features puckered up disapprovingly. "An excellent fellow, but blood thirsty— very blood thirsty," he murmured, with the least little touch of regret in his voice as if he deprecated an attitude with which in reality he thoroughly concurred.

But Carew's thoughts were not concerned with the man who had just left the room.

Crossing to the open window he stood for some time without speaking, his hands plunged deep in his jacket pockets, scowling at the palms in the garden beneath. And accustomed to his frequent and protracted silences his host, pleasantly somnolent with the beat and tired with the excitement of the day, made no attempt to force conversation. Stretched comfortably in a capacious armchair he toyed idly with a cigarette and sipped the vermouth his guest had declined, thoroughly content with himself and the world at large, until Carew's voice broke in suddenly on thoughts that were lightly alternating between the happy results of the afternoon's interview and the gastronomic delights of the coming dinner.

"There is a compatriot of mine, a certain Viscount Geradine, who has de Granier's villa this winter—can you tell me anything about him?"

The cherubic little Governor looked vaguely embarrassed. "Nothing of very much good, I am afraid," he said slowly, "he is not, unfortunately, an ornament to your usually so distinguished aristocracy. I personally know very little of him. But one hears things—one hears things," he repeated uncomfortably.

For a moment Carew hesitated, then:

"As—what?" he asked bluntly. Surprised at the question, the Frenchman shot him a look of undisguised astonishment. It was unlike Carew to be curious about anybody, and in all the years he had known him he had never heard him even refer to a member of the English community.

"Patrice knows more about these things than I do," he fenced, lighting a fresh cigarette with delicate precision. And turning to the pale youth in the corner who seemed absorbed in his secretarial duties, he raised his voice slightly.

"My good Patrice, can you tell us anything about the Englishman, Lord Geradine, who is living at the Villa des Ombres?"

The young man looked up quickly with a laugh which showed that his attention was not so wholly centered on his work as it appeared to be.

"I can tell you what happened *chez Fatima* last night, *mon oncle*," he replied promptly, with a boyish grin that was faintly malicious. But the Governor raised a plump white hand in horrified protest. "I beg of you—no," he said hurriedly. "Spare us the disgusting details, *mon cher*. Generalities will be amply sufficient, amply sufficient."

His nephew shrugged acquiescence. "As you will," he said complacently, "but it was amusing—oh, yes, distinctly amusing," he mimicked, with the assurance of a highly privileged individual. And for five minutes he sketched with racy frankness the character and failings of the man who had won for himself an unenviable reputation even in a not too straight-laced society. It was an unsavoury revelation that provoked little exclamations of disgust from the visibly distressed Governor, but Carew listened with apparent indifference to the delinquencies of his fellow-countryman. "—a drunkard and a bully," concluded the attaché, ticking off the final accusations on his fingers as if he were tabulating them for a formal process. "And married," he added with a burst of indignation, "married, *imaginez-vous*, to a beautiful young girl with the face of an angel—"

"Yes, yes, quite so," interrupted his uncle dryly, "they usually are married, *ces gens là*, to a beautiful young girl with the face of an angel! But we are not discussing Lady Geradine, my good Patrice. Not a pleasant character, I fear," he added, turning deprecatingly to Carew as if apologising for his nephew's outspoken comments, "but rich, immensely rich, I understand. If it is the question of a horse, perhaps—" he suggested tentatively, as a probable reason for Carew's inquiry suddenly occurred to him. But Carew shook his head with a curt gesture of disdain.

"I value my horses too highly to sell them to a man of that type," he said shortly, and took leave without vouchsafing any explanation of his curiosity.

Outside in the Place du Gouvernement he glanced at his watch as he turned his steps toward the native quarter. It was later than he had imagined. He would have to hurry to keep his appointment and get back to his own villa in time to dress for the dinner the Governor had planned so gleefully. Heedless of the traffic, too familiar with the varied types to even glance at the jostling crowd of cosmopolitan humanity about him, he strode through the busy streets with a heavy scowl on his face, immersed in his own thoughts. What on earth had made him ask the Governor that idiotic question? What on earth did the fellow matter to him! If the voluble young attaché's story was true—and Patrice Lemaire was a social butterfly who knew everybody and everything in Algiers—he must be a pretty average blackguard. And if he were—what business was it of his? It mattered not one particle to him if the tenant of de Granier's villa was a devil from hell or a saint from heaven. If the girl had married a scoundrel it was her own look-out. It was of no moment to him. He had no interest in either her or her husband. He had been forced to help her in her exigency, but the affair was over and done with—thank heaven.

Finished as far as he was concerned when he had been fortunate enough to get her horse back, which he had done far sooner than he had expected. It had been a stroke of luck, that second chance meeting with Abdul el Dhib. Carew smiled despite himself as he remembered the wily horse stealer's discomforted curses when he reluctantly surrendered the stolen stallion which he had already mentally disposed of at considerable profit to a Sheik in the south who paid well and asked no questions. But it had been touch and go, half-an-hour later and he would have missed him. With what result? Quite suddenly he seemed to be looking into a pair of wide, blue eyes, strained and dark with agonised terror, and he flung his shoulders back angrily, cursing the trick of memory that had brought the girl's white face before him with vivid distinctness. For years he had never consciously looked at a woman. Why did this woman's face haunt him so persistently? He had no wish to remember her, he hoped never to see her again, but for the last three weeks the remembrance of her had been a nightmare. The tranquillity of mind he had won after years of mental struggle had been torn from him, first by the coming of Micky Meredith and then by the circumstance that had flung this unfortunate girl across his path. The quiet villa that for so long had been his haven of rest seemed now neither restful nor solitary. It was peopled by shadowy figures that crowded day and night upon his thoughts, breaking habits that had become second nature and stirring him painfully to the recollection of emotions he had long since deliberately cut out of his life. He was in the grip of a tremendous revolt that acted equally on mind and body. He seemed, for the second time in his forty years, to be facing a crisis that was overwhelming. He tried to analyse dispassionately the agitation of mind that had taken so strong a hold on him, to probe honestly for the reason of the strange unrest that filled him. But self-analysis brought him no nearer to an understanding of his feelings, brought him no kind of alleviation.

And yet, in reality, there was only one solution, he argued doggedly as he made his way through the narrow streets, a solution that was simple enough, ample enough in all conscience—if he had only sense enough to leave it at that. It was, it could only be, reaction from the sudden awakening of the old pain, the old memories he had thought done with forever. There was no other possible construction to put upon his state of mind—he would allow no other construction. And yet, the humiliation of it! That the chance meeting with an old friend should move him so strongly; that he should be fool enough, weak enough to permit himself to brood over the past he had buried so many years before. Had he not even yet conquered the moral cowardice that in the early days of his sorrow had driven him from England and made him avoid association with his fellow countrymen rather than face the scandal that would always be connected with his name. It had been rank cowardice. And he was a coward still, it appeared, too cowardly even to be honest with himself.

His face hardened as a wave of self-disgust passed over him. And wrenching his thoughts resolutely from the morbid introspection to which he had given way he forced his attention to the immediate matter in hand.

And as he plunged deeper into the heart of the Casbar he thought with a slight feeling of amusement of General Sanois' parting words for the astute old Arab who awaited his coming was distinctly one of those "friends" the General yearned to lay his hands on.

Turning from the steep street he was ascending, he entered a gloomy alley of squalid, sinister-looking houses and walked slowly along the narrow footway, counting the closed doors carefully as he went.

The house before which he eventually halted was, if possible, more sinister, more wretched-looking than the rest, the cracked walls bulging ominously in places and stained with leperous-like patches where the plaster had fallen off, the twisted iron balcony that projected a few feet above his head clinging by what seemed a miracle to the crumbling fabric from which it threatened momentarily to detach itself. There was no knocker on the nail-studded door, and the tiny grille was closed, but Carew had not expected an open welcome and he was too well versed in the ways of the Casbar to advertise his presence by any noisy demonstration. Though apparently deserted, he knew that life was teeming behind the seemingly empty walls. The whole street bore the same abandoned tenantless appearance, but he was well aware that unseen peeping eyes had followed his leisurely progress from the moment he had set foot on the filthy cobble stones that were damp and reeking with undrained refuse. He knew that he was expected, but it was not his custom to make visits of ceremony to the Casbar in European dress, and, an unfamiliar figure, in all likelihood, some minutes would elapse before the door opened to receive him. It was probable that his coming was watched for from behind the close lattice-work of the forlornly drooping little balcony and he moved further out into the street that he might be more plainly seen, lighting a cigarette as he set himself to wait until the hidden watcher should satisfy himself of the visitor's identity. And the cigarette was smoked through before he heard the dull clank of heavy bars being removed. Still with no show of haste he sauntered to the door that opened narrowly to admit him and passed into gloom that became absolute blackness as the faint light, filtering in from without, was shut off by the closing of the entrance. Again he heard the rattle of formidable bolts, then a hand touched his sleeve and he was led along an interminable passage that curved and twisted tortuously. It was impossible in the darkness to form any idea of the way he was being conducted and with the frequent turnings he speedily lost all sense of bearing. He only knew that the house he had entered was certainly not the one in which he would eventually find himself. That the passage occasionally widened into rooms was apparent for he could feel the difference in the atmosphere, and his hand outstretched to the dank wall beside him met from time to time with only space. But his silent guide moved forward unhesitatingly with a sure step that made Carew wonder suddenly if he was blind.

Dumb also, it would appear, for he made no answer to the one remark addressed to him.

A doorkeeper who was a deaf mute and blind, a mysterious building which was approached by devious ways and secret passages—Carew's lips twitched with amusement. To him the situation was sufficiently ludicrous, though to one less sure of his welcome, less acquainted with the way of the people, there might have been more than a suggestion of unpleasantness in this curious reception. It was all so typically eastern, so fraught with childish intrigue and suspicion. The wily old Arab who, after years of absence, had ventured into Algiers again for cogent reasons of his own was evidently taking no chances of a surprise visit from the authorities who were presumably unaware of his return. That he had come himself directly from the Palace and from the company of General Sanois was a humorous coincidence that made Carew smile again.

His eyes were just beginning to become accustomed to the darkness when the guide's fingers pressing on his arm brought him to a sudden stop and he waited without moving while more bolts were removed and a tiny door swung inward revealing a narrow winding staircase which was lit by a solitary earthenware lamp placed in a niche in the wall. Seen by the dim light his conductor proved to be a powerful negro of gigantic height, blind as he had thought. And feeling more than ever that he had stepped into an episode from the Arabian Nights, Carew followed him up the staircase to a door that was covered with a curtain of matchless embroidery. He was ushered into a room which, for sumptuousness of furnishing and barbaric splendour, he had never seen equalled. The rugs and hangings were priceless, the divans and mats gorgeous with vivid colourings, and the many lamps of beaten silver, lit already, for the daylight was excluded by thick curtains, were finer even than those which hung in the mauresque hall of his own villa. The atmosphere was stifling and heavy with the sweet pungent scent of incense.

Blinking at the sudden light he hesitated on the threshold for an instant and then went forward to meet the superbly-dressed Arab who rose quickly from a heap of cushions to greet him with unusually demonstrative expressions of pleasure.

Their last meeting had been under very different circumstances, circumstances attendant on the intertribal warfare that waged perpetually between the belligerent Arabs of the far south. Travelling in a district that was new to him, Carew had become involved in a bid for supremacy between two powerful chiefs which had ended in victory for the one who was now greeting him with such wealth of flowery hyperbole—a victory that at the time it had seemed impossible he could live to enjoy. In the course of his wanderings, Carew had seen many appalling sights and had attended to wounds that appeared well-nigh incurable, but never in the whole of his experience had he attempted to restore a body so horribly mangled and broken. For weeks he had wrestled to save the chief's life and it had been mainly owing to his care, though helped by a magnificent constitution and a passionate desire to live, that the Sheik had eventually recovered to swear eternal friendship with the man who had literally snatched him from the jaws of death.

The mutual interchange of formal compliments and good-will was followed by the customary coffee and sweet-meats, and cigarettes that were the Sheik's one lapse from strict orthodoxy and which he proffered with a grave smile and a jest at his own expense. The conversation ranged over many topics, and used though he was to the circumambient methods of the oriental when any particular point is in view, Carew began to wonder when the special subject which he understood was the main reason of his visit would be approached. But when the Sheik at length abandoned generalities and came with unexpected directness to the heart of the matter he had dallied with so long, Carew listened to information that coming from such a quarter, filled him with amazement. The man was no friend to France, and out of favour with the Government, but he was calmly imparting intelligence that would be very useful to the Administration and for the moment Carew was nonplussed. Was the surprising confidence for his ears alone or was he being used as an intermediary to bring about a rapprochement between a refractory chief and the rulers of the country? He put the question with his usual bluntness.

"Is it thy wish that the Government should learn of this?"

The Sheik's gem-laden fingers touched lightly first his forehead then his breast.

"It is my wish that through *thee* the Government should learn that which they are too blind to see. Thus do I, in part, pay my debt," he answered, with a sudden gleam in his fierce old eyes. Carew nodded and studied the glowing end of his cigarette thoughtfully for a few moments.

"And thou, O Sheik," he said at last, "do I speak for thee to the Government? The day is fortunate. Tonight I dine with His Excellency and General Sanois—"

"May Allah burn them!" interposed the Sheik fervently, and spat frankly and conclusively on to the priceless carpet. Carew laughed.

"And thy news?" he asked, rising to his feet after a glance at the watch on his wrist and pulling his waistcoat down with a jerk.

"Use it—or withhold it, but speak no word of me. Am I their dog?" replied the Sheik, with a flash of anger, as he prepared to take leave of his guest.

But there was a constraint in his manner, a hint of something left unsaid, that made him appear preoccupied as he accompanied Carew to the head of the little winding staircase where the negro was still waiting. And it was not until the elaborate farewells had been spoken and Carew had started to descend that the old Arab gave utterance to what was in his mind. Leaning forward he spoke in a swift undertone. "There was a dweller in the wilderness who had a garden filled with rare flowers— culled from the gardens of better men than he—a garden overflowing with sweetness and delight. Yet was he not satisfied, for his questioning eyes had glimpsed the beauty of a stranger blossom brought from a far-off land, and he burned with desire to gather it for his own. Chance gave him the prize he longed for—and chance wrested it from him again. And now the fire of desire is quenched in the greater fire of hatred and revenge. Take heed for that same gardener, my friend," he added meaningly, and turned away with a parting salaam.

Carew went on down the stairs with a faint smile at the oriental ambiguity with which the veiled warning had been conveyed to him. Though no name had been mentioned it was perfectly obvious who threatened him. He had thwarted the desire of no other Arab. But as he followed the negro again through the blackness of the winding passage he turned from the thought of that particular Arab with a shrug of annoyance. Abdul el Dhib was too intimately connected with what he wished to forget to allow him to dwell on the possible results of the horse-thief's threats. Threatened men live long, and Abdul was in some ways wise in his generation. There seemed no need to take the warning too seriously and, besides, he was too deeply imbued with the fatalism he had learned in the desert to dread death that was always more or less imminent in the hazardous life he led. He had always held his life cheaply, there was no reason now to go out of his way to take precautions that would probably be unnecessary. He lived or he died as Allah willed—a comfortable creed he found amply sufficient.

Dismissing Abdul from his mind his thoughts reverted to the other as plausible but more clean-handed Arab he had just quitted. The intelligence the Sheik had imparted ought, without question, to be passed on to headquarters, and that as speedily as possible. Perhaps tonight he would find opportunity to approach the General on the subject—and Sanois; certain demands for the source of his information were going to be the very devil to parry.

The return journey through the dismal cellars seemed shorter than the first and Carew was not surprised when he was ushered into the outer world again to find himself, as he had expected, in a totally different street from that in which he had waited to gain admittance to the sinister-looking house. But the locality was known to him and very soon he was back in the rue Annibal, swinging quickly down the unusually empty street. Preoccupied he rounded a sharp corner without noticing the noisy clamour that ordinarily would have warned him of some special excitement in progress and came suddenly upon a yelling crowd of ragged youths and boys who fought and screamed and tore at each other as they surged round some central object that was hidden from him. The noise was deafening, the narrow roadway completely blocked, and Carew glanced at his watch with a gathering frown. He was late enough already, he had no mind to be further delayed by a band of young savages employed probably in their usual amusement of torturing some unfortunate dumb animal that had fallen into their clutches.

He was familiar with the callous cruelty of the Arabs, but familiarity had not lessened the abhorrence with which he viewed this particular pastime of the native youth. And the scowl on his face deepened as he sought to find some way of passing the squalid rabble who had taken possession of the footway. Argument was impossible, his voice would be drowned in the shrill cries that filled the air. Action, prompt and decisive, was the only expedient. Selecting a spot where the throng seemed less dense he gripped two of the taller lads, who were engaged in a private sparring match on the fringe of the crowd, and dashing their heads together drove them before him a living wedge into the heart of the press.

The unexpectedness of his attack made his task an easy one, and in the sudden silence that ensued he cursed them fluently and with picturesque attention to detail that left nothing to the imagination.

There were some who knew him by sight—he heard his Arab title uttered warningly—for the rest he was a representative of law and order whose coming put a period to their amusement. Before he had finished speaking they had begun to slink away and in a few moments he was alone in the again deserted street, looking down with a variety of feelings on the slim girlish figure crouched on the filthy cobblestones at his feet. Hatless, her white dress stained and crumpled, she seemed oblivious of everything but the pitiful little cur whose mangled bloodstained head lay on her knee. She was crooning to it softly, brushing the matted hair from its fast glazing eyes and stroking the broken palpitating limbs with tender caressing fingers. And when the tortured creature's agony was over and she had laid the little dead body gently aside she still sat on motionless, shivering from time to time as she tried to wipe the crimson stickiness from her fingers with a scrap of lawn that was already a soaked red rag.

With a gesture of impatience Carew dropped his own larger and more adequate handkerchief into her lap.

"It is unwise to meddle with these Arab *gamins*, Lady Geradine." He spoke curtly, his tone patiently disapproving, and at the sound of his voice she started violently. For a moment she scarcely seemed to breathe, then she stumbled to her feet looking up at him quickly and he saw the sudden bewilderment that leaped into her eyes as they travelled slowly over the length of his tall figure and then sought his face again to linger on the tell-tale scar across his cheek that gave her the clue to his identity.

"You are English," she stammered, the colour rushing into her white cheeks. "I thought—that night—you were an Arab." Then she flung her hands out to him with a little choking cry. "Oh, why didn't you come sooner," she wailed, "it was horrible! That poor wee beastie—those *devils*! You don't know what they did—it nearly drove me mad—I can't bear to see an animal suffer—" she broke off with a shudder and for a moment he thought she was going to faint and caught at her arm instinctively. But she pulled herself together, moving away from him slightly with a fleeting smile of acknowledgment.

"I'm all right, thanks, only it makes one—just a little bit—sick," she said jerkily, her hands busy with her loosened hair, and looking about for her hat which had been torn from her in the scuffle. She spied it at last wedged in the grating of a window and rescued it with a rueful laugh that ended shakily. Brushing the dust marks from her tumbled dress she turned again to Carew. He was waiting with the detached air of aloofness she remembered so well and which sent a little chill through her, making her feel that again he had been constrained to render a service that was totally against his inclination.

"I seem to be fated to give you trouble," she murmured shyly. But he did not choose to notice her tentative reference to their first meeting.

"Are you alone?" he asked bluntly. "It is too late in the evening for you to be in the Casbar without an escort."

She flushed deeply at the undisguised reproof in his tone, and found herself eagerly defending her imprudence as if she admitted his right to censure and could not bear that he should put a wrong construction on her actions.

"I know—but I didn't realize how late it was. I was shopping, and after I had sent my man home with the parcels I remembered a piece of embroidery I wanted. I thought I could find it easily but I had to hunt for it a long time. Then I forgot all about the time in watching the people, and I wandered on until, finally, I lost myself. I was trying to make my way back when—when I saw the dog. I suppose it was stupid of me to attempt to do anything—but I just had to," she concluded, with sudden vehemence. A curious look she was unable to read flashed across his face as he glanced from her to the wretched little body stiffening on the cobbles, but he made no comment as he moved forward with an almost imperceptible shrug. "I can find you a *fiacre* in the rue Randon," he said coldly, as if his sole desire was to be rid of her society at the earliest moment possible.

And chilled again by his brusque manner she walked beside him silently. She was more shaken by the incident than she had realised, and for the first time she began to wonder what would have happened if he had not come. But he had come, and once again she was his debtor for a service he rendered unwillingly. By no stretch of imagination could she deceive herself into believing that, he was even interested, much less glad, at seeing her again. Why did he so grudge the help he voluntarily offered? And why had he let her think that he was an Arab? She looked at him covertly, but after the first shy glance she had no hesitation in continuing her scrutiny for he seemed as unaware of her regard as he was negligent of her company. She realised it with a curiously bitter little feeling of pain. Yet why should he be other than he was? She was only a stranger, forced upon his notice by what he must consider as deliberate acts of folly on her part. And yet it was not so. She had been thoughtless, but on neither occasion had she willfully gone out of her way to court either excitement or danger. The morning when she had ridden alone it was an imperative desire for solitude that had made her leave Tanner behind. And today the sight of the tortured dog had driven all thoughts of herself out of her head. She had not stopped to think of the possible consequences that might ensue when, carried away by horror and pity, she had endeavoured to restrain the most fiendish cruelty she had ever witnessed.

She stifled a sigh as she looked at him again, sure of his preoccupation.

The change of dress seemed to alter him completely. In the well-fitting blue serge suit that clung closely to his muscular figure he appeared taller, slenderer than she had supposed; but he looked older, too, and the gravity of face and demeanour that had seemed natural in an Arab struck her even more forcibly now that she knew his true nationality. The soft felt hat, pulled far forward over his eyes, shaded features that to her looked sterner and more rigidly set than when she had first seen them. It was a strong face, she decided, too strong, too hard perhaps for absolute beauty but, clean cut, and bronzed as a native's, lean and healthy looking, it was a face that arrested and compelled attention. Strength seemed the key note of his composition. His spare frame appeared to be made up of only bone and muscle, his long slow stride was springy and elastic, and he carried himself magnificently. Again she found herself wondering who he was, wishing she might ask him, but fearing the same rebuff she had met with before. And yet, if she only knew his name! It would be something to remember, something to cling to. And as the thought came she turned her head away hastily with a feeling of acute and miserable shame, realising how completely he had filled her mind during what had seemed to her the longest and most unhappy weeks she had ever experienced. She had wrestled with herself, striving to forget him, hoping that time would obliterate the image that seemed to possess her every conscious moment. But this second meeting had shattered the resolutions she had formed so bravely. She would always remember, always care. The memory of him would go with her through life—the memory of a man who was indifferent to her, whom honour demanded that she should root out of her heart. Did love always come like that, so suddenly, so irresistible, so unsought? Could she have conquered it if she had really tried to do so from the first moment of realization? She had tried. She had fought against it, shuddering from what seemed to her a sin, praying desperately for strength to put it from her. But her prayers had been unavailing and daily, hourly, the love she could not deny had grown stronger and more insistent. Only in the last three weeks had she come to know how starved her heart had been. Love had entered very little into her life. Her father had loved her but she was a child when he died, and since his death she had had no outlet for the affection lying dormant in her. She had lived in the open, a boy's life rather than a girl's, finding abundant happiness and contentment in sport and outdoor pursuits. She had had no girlish dreams of the possible lover who might some day come to win her heart, no opportunity of filling her imagination with tales of sentiment and romance. During the long winter evenings in the lonely house in Ireland she had read much but the books that formed her father's library were books of travel and the histories of many countries. She had been singularly innocent, singularly young. Then she had married, and marriage had brought her not the joy and wonder of a man's devotion but the loathing of a man's possession. All that was brutal, all that was sordid and degrading in such a union she had learned with horror and amazement. Forced to hide the revulsion that filled her, forced into a mode of life that shocked her every sense of decency, she had steeled herself to endure until she had come to look upon herself as a thing of stone, a heartless, lifeless automaton. The hope of a child, that might have been another woman's salvation, had never touched her. She shrank with abhorrence from the thought of possible motherhood. It would have been the last drop in her cup of bitterness. In spite of the disappointment and anger of her husband, who never ceased to reproach her for failing to give him the heir he desired, she prayed God passionately to spare her the shame of bringing into the world the offspring of such a man. That through her his vices might be perpetuated was a fear that never left her, a fear that year by year as she learned more thoroughly her husband's character and innate viciousness had grown into an obsession. And now the dread that filled her continually had become a thousand times more poignant, a thousand times more horrible for the strange overwhelming emotion that had leaped into being that awful night three weeks ago. Love she had never thought to know had come to her—and come too late. Free, she could have loved him though he had never turned to her; bound, to even think of him was disloyalty to the man who had the right to claim her affection. The right to claim—but when had he ever claimed it! When had he ever shown by look or word that he even desired it? Her feelings were nothing to him, obedience was all he demanded—slavish submission to his domination, absolute surrender to his will, his caprices, and his inordinate passion. The pride he displayed in her beauty was the same he exhibited for any animal his wealth enabled him to acquire. The pride merely of arrogant ownership. And as he treated his animals so did he treat her. And as they flinched from him so did her whole soul recoil from his proximity. The last three weeks had been purgatory. He had been more intolerant, more hard to please, more insistent in his selfish demands than he had ever been. He had also been drinking more heavily than usual with disastrous results to his temper which had been felt by all the household. Malec, the Arab valet, the scarcely healed cut across his face a burning, throbbing reminder of his master's heavy hand, went sullenly about his duties with hatred in his half-veiled eyes, and Tanner was in open rebellion.

This evening for the first time since his return he had allowed her out of his sight, and had given reluctant permission for the shopping expedition to the Casbar. For two hours she had been free, free of the suspicious eyes that watched her every movement, free of the hated caresses that in his maudlin humour he showered on her. She shivered at the thought of going back to him. With an unconscious movement she drew nearer to the man who walked beside her, marvelling anew at the strange feeling of security his presence brought her, marvelling that she should feel so little astonishment at seeing him again.

It seemed perfectly natural that he should once more come to her aid. If it had been Clyde instead—a spasm of pain crossed her face. Clyde would only have been amused! She clenched her hands as she strove to stem the tide of bitterness that rushed over her. Why must she torture herself with making comparisons. The contrast between them was sufficiently hideous without allowing herself to dwell on it. And she had no right to dwell on it, no right to make comparisons. She was Clyde's wife—Clyde's wife. The clenched hands tightened until the nails bit deeper into the soft palms. Silence became impossible. She must speak, if only to turn the current of her thoughts.

"I haven't thanked you for sending back The Caid," she said nervously, forcing her voice to steadiness. They were passing down a narrow street where grave-faced Arabs, lost apparently in contemplation, sat smoking in the open doorways of their shops regarding the passers-by with unconcerned aloofness, ostensibly disdainful of possible sales, yet quick to notice all who came and went, for, watching them, Marny saw with growing astonishment the frequent and profound salaams which greeted her companion. As she spoke he had stopped to acknowledge the salute of a venerable greybeard who lounged indolently amongst the fine carpets and heterogeneous collection of brasswork and antique firearms that formed his stock in trade. For a moment Carew paused to handle the keen-edged Moorish dagger proffered to him with an accompanying murmur that was barely audible, then shook his head smilingly as he returned the weapon with a shrug of careless indifference and an equally low-voiced rejoinder.

With complete unconcern the Arab tossed the knife aside and resumed his pipe, and Carew turned again to Marny with a slight gesture of apology.

"I can recommend old Ibraheim, if you are interested in embroideries, Lady Geradine. Most of his things are genuine, and he has seen you with me—he won't rob you too unmercifully," he said, with the first smile he had yet given her. "I was fortunate in finding your horse," he continued, raising his hand to fend from her the swaying head of a heavily laden camel that lurched past with a snarling grunt of ill-humour, "but, if you will permit me to say so, I strongly advise you not to ride him again unattended. His worth and pedigree are well known, and there are a number of Arabs in and about Algiers who are very averse to valuable stallions being sold out of the country. It is only natural when you come to think of it! I should hold the same view myself—were I an Arab."

"You are very like one." The words escaped her involuntarily and she glanced at him quickly, fearful that he would think her impertinent. But he did not appear to resent the comparison and taking courage she yielded to the longing that came over her to learn more of the man who had come so strangely into her life.

"You have lived much amongst them?" she suggested diffidently. His curt assent was not conducive to further questioning but her wistful interest overcame her shyness.

"In the desert—the *real* desert?" she asked eagerly.

"Yes, in the real desert," he answered shortly, a slight frown gathering on his face. And as if regretting the slight lapse from his former rigidity of manner he seemed to draw once more into himself, cold and unapproachable as he had been at first. And, flushing sensitively, Marny relapsed into silence that lasted until they reached the rue Randon. A passing victoria plying for hire rattled up in response to Carew's signal, and he had placed her in it almost before she realized that they were clear of the Casbar.

For a moment she leant forward without speaking, looking at him as he stood bareheaded on the pavement beside her. Then she thrust her hand out to him with a brusque boyish gesture.

"Thank you—for all you've done," she said shakily, her lips trembling despite her efforts to keep them steady.

For the fraction of a second he hesitated, staring gloomily at the little outstretched hand, then his tall figure stiffened suddenly and, drawing back with a deep un-English bow, he signed to the Arab coachman to drive on.

V

Without bestowing a second glance on either the carriage or its occupant Carew jammed his hat down savagely over his eyes and leaped into another cab that had drawn up expectantly beside him.

He leant back against the dusty cushions, his arms folded tightly across his chest, scowling wrathfully at the busy streets. He had not seen the look of hurt disappointment that flashed into the girl's eyes when he ignored her outstretched hand, nor heard the sharp sob that burst from her trembling lips. He had been conscious only of the raging tumult of his own feelings, of the intolerant anger that this second wholly undesired meeting had provoked. It had been an effort to be even civil—if indeed he had been civil at all, which he very much doubted. How like a woman to forget one peril so readily and court further danger without a moment's consideration. Had the lesson of three weeks ago made so little impression on her? The little fool—did she imagine that Algiers was teeming with knights-errant seeking beauty in distress! His fine lips curved contemptuously as he lit a cigarette and looked at his watch with a deeper scowl. Though indifferent to his own meals he disliked causing annoyance to others and the cheery little Governor was a gourmet to whom a retarded dinner was a catastrophe. By now he should have been starting for the Palace instead of toiling up the road to Mustapha behind two extremely tired half-starved Arab hacks. It was useless to urge the driver, the hill was steep and the miserable little beasts were doing their best.

Stretching his long legs out more comfortably and pulling his hat further over his eyes he settled himself to wait, his mind wandering back to the desert he had so recently left but towards which his thoughts were already turning eagerly. Time to complete his arrangements for another protracted trip, to restock his depleted medical equipment, and he could leave this confounded town again for the life he loved best. A life of hardship and danger, but to him a life eminently worth living. And in the end—far out amongst the sandy wastes, he hoped, where the fierce sun would beat down scorchingly on the whispering particles that would hold him in their shifting embrace, where the jackals would wail their nightly chorus under the marvel of the eastern stars—the requiem of the desert.

The desert! He drew a deep breath of heart-felt anticipation. It was calling him more compellingly than it had ever done, bringing memories of long hot rides beneath the burning sun, of the silver radiance of the

E.M. HULL

peaceful moonlit nights and the never failing glory of the dawn. He smiled a little at his own enthusiasm. It was not all peace and beauty and marvellous silence. There was battle and murder and sudden death, cruelty that was inconceivable and suffering that made him set his teeth as he thought of the needless agony he had witnessed more times than he cared to remember. But despite its savagery he loved it. It was his life. It was there he had found his chosen work, it was there he hoped to die. Even the thought of it was soothing to him in his present mood, and dreaming of it, he forgot the annoyance of the afternoon, forgot everything but the irresistible charm it had for him.

The villa was reached at length, the sweating horses expending their remaining reserve of strength in a final spurt of activity rushing the last fifty yards of level ground under a storm of abuse from the Arab driver who drew up at the nail-studded door, set in the enclosing wall, with a self-satisfied grin that widened broadly as he caught the liberal fee tossed to him. At the sound of the approaching wheels the door had opened silently and Carew passed through and went swiftly along the flower bordered pathway to the house. The single storied building was the most beautiful in Mustapha Superieur. Built forty years before for Carew's delicate mother it was a miniature palace and stood in a garden that rivalled even that of the Villa des Ombres. But, preoccupied, Carew had tonight no eye for the beauty of either house or garden and he did not linger as was his wont before entering the spacious mauresque hall where Hosein was waiting for him in a state of visible agitation that was foreign to his usual impassive demeanour.

"Praise be to Allah, my lord has returned," he murmured, his gloomy eyes lightening with evident relief. Carew stared at him for a moment in puzzled astonishment, then he smiled a trifle grimly. Hosein too! This was becoming monotonous. He was fully conversant with the rapidity with which reports spread in a land of rumour and intrigue, but Abdul, who had unorthodox proclivities, must have been drunk indeed to boast so openly of his intentions.

"To Allah the praise," he returned conventionally. Then he laughed and shrugged indifferently. "'The jackal howls where he dare not slay,'" he quoted, adding over his shoulder as he moved away, "Telephone to the Palace that I have been detained, that I beg His Excellency will not wait for me. I will join him as quickly as possible."

He crossed the open courtyard round which the house was built and entered his bedroom, passing through to the dressing room beyond.

There he found the blind boy sitting on the floor, his hands folded in his lap, his face turned towards the door with a look of strained attention. As it opened he sprang to his feet and bounded forward impetuously. With a word of warning Carew caught him and swung him high in his arms. "What mischief to confess, O son of wickedness?" he teased, as he felt the slender limbs trembling against him. But the time-honoured jest did not provoke the peal of laughter he expected. Instead the little face was grave and strangely set and Carew put him down with a quick caress.

"Who has troubled thee, Saba?" he asked quietly, moving across the room to empty his pockets before changing. The boy followed him with outstretched fumbling hands. "No man has troubled me," he answered slowly, "but, lord, my heart is sick within me. I dreamt a dream—an evil dream. And, waking, the dream is with me still. There is danger, lord, that threatens thee. In my dreams I saw clearly, but now I cannot see—I cannot see—" he broke off with a sharp little wail of anguish. A queer look crossed Carew's face as his hands closed firmly over the tiny fluttering fingers. It was not the first time that Saba had shown himself to be possessed of an almost uncanny sensitiveness where the safety of the man he worshipped was concerned. Ordinarily a happy, healthy-minded child there was in him an odd streak of mysticism that cropped up at rare intervals with curious results. On two previous occasions he had had a presage of danger menacing his protector that subsequent events had fully justified. Too familiar with the occultism of the east to be sceptical Carew was not disposed to minimise the importance of a warning that was identical with the plainer, more substantial hints he had received that afternoon, but he was in no mind to treat it with undue seriousness or show too great a credulity to the nervous boy whose upturned sightless eyes were wet with tears. He soothed him with the tenderness that marked his every dealing with him. "Thou hast dreamt before," he said gently, "and the danger has passed. So will this danger pass—"

"If Allah wills." The childish treble broke on a quivering sob and Carew accepted the qualification of his assurance with a little smile. "All things are with Allah," he answered, "and it is written 'seek not to discover that which is hidden, for behold, when the day cometh all things shall be revealed.' And again, 'no accident happeneth in the earth, nor in your persons, but the same was entered in the book of our decrees.'"

E.M. HULL

A deep sigh escaped the boy and he pressed his lips on the strong brown hands clasped on his.

"So it is written—yet if thou die, I die," he exclaimed passionately.

With wonderful gentleness Carew disengaged himself.

"Time to think of that when I die," he said lightly. "Meanwhile I live—and the French lord's dinner grows cold while I chatter with a dreamer of dreams," he added, turning away to the dressing table.

He changed quickly, and flinging a black cloak over his evening clothes paused irresolutely with his hand over a revolver that lay on the table. He was not in the habit of carrying firearms in the town of Algiers but tonight there seemed justification for so doing. He might have doubts as to the truth of the warnings he had received but he would be a fool to utterly ignore them.

Slipping the weapon into his hip pocket he left the room with a cheery word to Saba, who was sitting mournfully amidst the discarded clothing that littered the floor, and went out to his waiting carriage.

And as the spirited black horses drew him swiftly through the night his thoughts were busy with the pathetic little figure left disconsolate in the dressing room. If anything happened to him what would be the fate of the blind boy whose whole life was bound up in his? It was a problem that had often troubled him. He had made full provision for his protege's future and Hosein, while he lived, would serve him faithfully. But Saba in his blindness and with his highly-strung mystical temperament needed more than bodily comfort and faithful service. He needed what apparently only Carew could give him. Without Carew he would pine and droop like a delicate plant torn from the parent root from which it draws its strength. For Saba's sake, then it behooved him to take precautions he would otherwise have neglected.

The town was quieter than it had been earlier in the evening and Carew's coachman, who was a noted whip, took full advantage of the empty streets, driving with customary Arab recklessness but handling the excited horses magnificently until, with a fine flourish, he drew them foam-flecked to a standstill before the Palace.

The Governor, as Carew hoped, had taken him at his word. Dinner was in full swing when he entered with apologies for his lateness and slipped into the place reserved for him.

It was, in compliment to his known peculiarity, a strictly bachelor entertainment, enlivened by the presence of Patrice Lemaire and another equally light-hearted attache.

The Governor, hospitable to his finger tips and still pleasantly excited with the success of the day's work, was overflowing with good humour. Even General Sanois had relaxed somewhat of his usual gravity and condescended to occasional bursts of heavy pleasantry. But he was obviously distrait and his spasmodic attempts at conversation were punctuated by lengthy silences during which his eyes wandered frequently to Carew who was sitting opposite to him. And towards the close of dinner, when the Arab servants had left the room, he leaned forward with a sudden remark that was fraught with more meaning than the actual words implied.

"Your friends in the Casbar were exigent, it seems."

But Carew, who knew him, was not to be drawn. General Sanois was usually possessed of more knowledge than he was willing to admit, and his seemingly inocuous questions were often actuated by a deliberate policy and were rarely as guileless as they appeared. And tonight his thinly veiled curiosity met with scant success. Carew had no intention of being trapped into saying more than he wished to say, or of imparting what he preferred to withhold. He met the General's intent gaze with a tolerant smile.

"Don't jibe at my friends, *mon général*," he replied. "As I said this afternoon, they are useful. They serve you through me and they know it—most of them. But I picked up one piece of information this evening that will interest you—"

"Tomorrow," interrupted the Governor hastily, "tomorrow, my dear Carew. Business tonight is taboo. If our good Sanois once starts talking of his eternal affairs he will talk all through the opera, and I shall behave badly. Yes, badly, I warn you. I—" The remainder of his protest was lost in the shout of laughter that burst from his irrepressible nephew.

"Latest news from Algeria," chanted Lemaire in the shrill nasal tones of the street newsvendor. "Regrettable scene witnessed last night at the opera. Fracas in the Governor General's box. His Excellency and the Commander-in-Chief engaged in mortal combat in the presence of an excited audience. The Governor not expected to recover. General Sanois has fled to the desert and proclaimed himself 'Emperor of the Sahara'—My dear General, I offer my service as Aide-de-Camp. I'm bored to extinction with writing Uncle Henri's despatches," he added with an ironical bow, dodging the dinner napkin the Governor flung at his head. And in the general laugh that followed they rose from the table.

E. M. HULL

They were late in reaching the opera house and the first act was in progress when the Governor, a music lover at heart, tiptoed silently into his box and settled himself attentively to listen to a work he had already heard a score of times.

Carew, sitting on his left, drew his chair into the shadow of the heavy side curtain and leant back to pursue his own thoughts which the mediocre company on the stage failed to distract. The house was full, one box only—that directly facing the Governor's—being empty. Carew's gaze turned to the crowded seats with indifferent interest. It was more than two years since he had last visited the garish little theatre; it would probably be another two years before he was in it again, he reflected, as his mind ranged back to the all absorbing topic of the new expedition he was scheming. And now it seemed possible that his schemes might meet with an unexpected check. The information he had promised General Sanois at dinner, which he had gleaned that afternoon during his interview with the old chief in the Casbar, had in a measure upset his original calculations. It might mean a total change of plan. The needs of the Government had not been included in his forthcoming trip. He had purposed a tour that should be wholly devoted to his own work, and he viewed with some dismay the possibility of further political activity. He was a free lance, of course. He could take or reject any work offered him, but the mere fact of his freedom seemed to make the sense of his moral obligation more binding. He would have to go if it became really necessary—devoutly he hoped that the necessity would not arise. He was tired of intrigue and the endless palavers of political negotiations. He was anxious to pursue his own vocation unhindered, and to travel where inclination took him rather than follow a definite route in furtherance of Government schemes. There was a district, far away in the southwest, he had long wanted to visit. A district inhabited by a tribe he had heard of but with whom he had never yet come in contact. His plans of the last three weeks had centered more and more round this unknown locality that seemed to promise everything he demanded in the way of work and adventure. A strange and hostile people who guarded the secret of their desert fastness with jealous activity, fiercely resenting not only the advent of foreigners but also the encroachment of contiguous tribes. The tales he had heard of the impregnable walled-in city—a medieval survival if all the extraordinary stories anent it were true—had fired him with a desire to penetrate its hidden mysteries, to gain a footing amongst its prejudiced population. His calling had proved a passport to other inhospitable tribes, he counted on it confidently to win his admission to the secret City of Stones—the name by which it was known to the nomads who avoided its vicinity. The thought of it moved him deeply. Surely there was work for him within that rocky fortress could he but once pass its closely guarded gateway. The call seemed imperative, the call of suffering ignorant humanity whose misery he longed to alleviate. The need must be great, and alone he could do so little. Still even the little was worth his utmost endeavour, was worth the hazardous experiment. He could but try, and trying, succeed or fail.

And as he meditated on the chances of the success he earnestly hoped for, the little theatre with its crowded seats seemed to fade before his eyes. He saw instead an endless stretch of undulating waste, sun scorched and shimmering in the burning heat, and a caravan that wound its tortuous length across the wavy ripples of the wind-whipped sand labouring towards the mirage-like battlements of the secret city towering grimly against the radiance of the western sky. The imagery was strangely clear, singularly real. The gloomy pile stood out against his mental vision with almost photographic distinctness, and as he gazed at it wonderingly he seemed to feel between his knees the easy movements of the big bay stallion, to hear the voices of the men who rode behind him, the grunting protests of the lurching camels, the creak of sweat-drenched saddles and the whispering murmur of the shifting sand.

The desert smell was pungent in his nostrils, his eyeballs ached with the blinding glare. . .

The burst of applause that greeted the fall of the curtain woke him abruptly from his abstraction and he turned with a momentary feeling of confusion to join in the general conversation that ensued. Would he ever in reality come so near to the mysterious city as he had seemed to be in imagination five minutes ago, he wondered, as he declined the Governor's invitation to smoke a cigarette in the corridor. He was still pondering it when, left alone, he rose to stretch his legs, cramped with the confined space. He made a noticeable figure standing in the front of the box, a figure that attracted universal attention. But with the complete unselfconsciousness that was so markedly a trait in his character he was unaware of the interest he aroused. Incurious himself with regard to others, and reserved even with his intimate friends, he had no knowledge of the extravagant reports that for years had circulated about him, or of the excitement caused tonight by his appearance at the opera. That he was the subject of endless speculation, that he was the most discussed personage in Algiers, had never entered his head. And now, absorbed in his own thoughts, he was totally oblivious of the opera glasses and lorgnettes turned in his direction.

But his wandering attention was caught at last by the arrival of late comers in the opposite box—a man who stopped in the doorway to argue noisily with the theatre attendant, and a slim white-robed girl who moved slowly to the front of the box without heeding the stormy altercation behind her. She stood looking down on the crowded seats with a curious little air of detachment as if her thoughts were far away, toying nervously with the long curling feathers of a huge ostrich fan, her heavy sable cloak slipping from her shoulders. And with the same strange irritation, the same wholly unreasonable anger he had felt before Carew found himself staring at the pale sensitive face of the woman from whom he had parted only a few hours ago. Was he never to be free of her, never to be free of the haunting eyes he had striven for three weeks to banish from his thoughts? Was the remainder of his peace of mind to be wrecked by the continual remembrance of a woman he had no desire to remember? Surely her very womanhood was sufficient reason for forgetting her. He hated women. And in the intolerant antagonism that filled him he felt that above all others he hated this particular woman whose need had forced him to lay aside his prejudice and break the oath he had sworn so many years ago. Young and beautiful, she was the incarnation of all he distrusted and despised. His face darkened and he made a movement to return to his seat. But something that was stronger than his hatred stayed him. Despite himself his gaze lingered on the slight girlish figure. And presently, as if drawn by some subtle telepathic influence, she seemed to become aware of the compelling stare fixed on her and slowly raised her head. For a second, across the width of the theatre, her eyes met his. But though the quick blood flamed into her face she gave no sign of recognition and turned, as from the unwarrantable scrutiny of a total stranger, to the man who was with her—the husband, Carew presumed, to whom she had alluded so briefly and with such evident constraint on that first night of meeting. The husband who doubtless knew nothing of the hours she had spent in his camp; who, probably, also knew nothing of this evening's incident in the rue Annibal. His lips curled in a sneering smile and he turned with cynical amusement to look at the heavy figure lounging beside her. But the smile faded swiftly and his amusement gave place to a rush of feeling he did not at the moment understand as his eyes ranged over Geradine's massive almost ape-like limbs and coarse sullen features. An odd look swept across his face and he drew his breath in sharply. For the first time in twelve years he felt pity for a woman. But he had no time to ponder it. All thought of the girl was swamped in the wave of strange and terrible emotion that was pouring over him, shaking him with a force he had never before experienced—a sudden overwhelming sense of hostility that had sprung into violent life within him at the sight of the man in the opposite box, a fierce instinctive hatred such as he had never conceived. The realisation of it staggered him. There was no reason for it, he told himself angrily. It was preposterous, absurd. He had heard of hatred at first sight, and laughed at it. But he did not laugh now as he dragged his eyes from the face of the man he felt he hated from the bottom of his soul. He was very far from laughter. He was conscious instead of a feeling of fear—fear of himself, fear of the consequences of the appalling forces which seemed suddenly let loose within him. He had thought himself to be possessed of a perfect self-understanding. He wondered now did he know anything about himself at all. Nothing, it seemed. Nothing that had ever led him to imagine that some day, for no apparent cause or reason, he would contemplate the destruction of an utter stranger. For that was what it amounted to—the violent impulse that was actuating him was a passionate desire to kill. God in heaven, what had happened to him! Had his whole nature undergone some sudden and horrible metamorphosis—had the wild life he had led in the desert been influencing him unconsciously until at last he had himself succumbed to the savagery and lawlessness of the people amongst whom he lived? What devil was prompting him? His mission was to save life, not to destroy it. True that during the course of his wanderings there had been occasions when he had been forced to take life, but that was different. He had killed in self-defence or in the defence of others, as he would unhesitatingly kill again if need be, as he would without compunction have killed Abdul el Dhib if it had proved necessary in the deserted village three weeks ago. But there was a wide gulf between justifiable homicide and murder. Murder! Perspiration gathered in icy drops on his forehead as his rigid lips framed the word. Was he going mad! He knew that he had never felt saner in his life. It was not madness that possessed him but an inexplicable feeling of deadly enmity that was almost overmastering in its intensity.

The atmosphere of the theatre seemed suddenly stifling. The blood beat in his ears and with a sense of suffocation he brushed his hand

E.M. HULL

before his eyes trying to clear the bewildering mist that had risen before them, blurring the crowded seats and the rapidly refilling orchestra. To sit out the remainder of the opera seemed an impossibility, but to surrender weakly to the impulse of the moment and leave the building was equally impossible. Gripping himself he turned to go back to his seat. But as he moved a hand was thrust through his arm and Patrice Lemaire's eager voice sounded close beside him, murmuring in his ear.

"Look, *monsieur*, in the opposite box. The compatriot of whom you spoke—Lord Geradine, and his wife. Beauty and the beast, *hein*? *La! la! quelle brute!*"

For a moment Carew stood motionless, then, with a tremendous effort he forced himself to glance naturally in the direction indicated by the interested attache. A glance of the briefest possible duration. Freeing himself from the nervous clasp of the impressionable young Frenchman who he knew would have had a great deal more to say had his auditor been other than himself, Carew drew back with a shrug of assumed indifference.

"As you say—a brute," he said coldly, "for the rest, you are more competent to judge than I."

Lemaire accepted the retort with a little laugh of perfect good temper.

"Each to his taste, *monsieur*. For you—horses, and for me—the ladies," he replied gaily, and continued to stare with undisguised admiration at the fair occupant of the opposite box until the entrance of his uncle and General Sanois drove him to his own seat there to evolve schemes, with his more sympathetic fellow attache, for obtaining an introduction to the beautiful Englishwoman who reigned, for the moment, supreme in his susceptible and fickle heart.

To Carew the time dragged out with maddening slowness. He envied Sanois who, screened by the curtains as he was himself, was frankly nodding. His whole body was still throbbing from the rush of extraordinary rage that had swept him, his head was aching with the effort to understand his own feelings, to find some sane and logical reason for the mental disturbance that had seized upon him with such cataclysmic suddenness. The whole thing was inexplicable, as inexplicable as the agitation of mind that had possessed him for the last three weeks. Was there any connection between them—was the one a corollary of the other? The startling thought almost forced an exclamation from his lips and he clenched his teeth as his eyes leaped involuntarily to the opposite box. What possible connection could there be—what had he to do with either of the strangely assorted couple who had each in their turn stirred him so powerfully? Towards what was fate pushing him! He was conscious all at once of a feeling of helplessness. Since the day that Micky Meredith had come so unexpectedly, reviving memories of the bitter past, everything seemed to be changed. He appeared to be no longer master of himself. He seemed to have been plunged into a vortex of circumstances over which he had no control, the end of which he could not see. The sense of impotence was galling, and he repudiated it angrily. He was damned if he was going to submit to any force of circumstance that ran counter to his own inclination. And he was damned if he would take the easy way out of the difficulty. Once before in his life he had played the coward's part and run away from a situation he was not morally strong enough to meet. He could never, if he hoped to retain the least shred of self-respect, do it again. And what, after all, was it he was trying to evade? The problematical results of an extraordinary hatred suddenly conceived for a total stranger, and the haunting recollection of a woman's face with which he had become obsessed—he, who hated woman. Good Lord, what a fool! And reduced to the level of dispassionate reasoning how futile it all seemed! It was time he got back to the desert if this was the effect that civilization had on him. With a shrug of self-contempt he turned for distraction to the stage he had hitherto ignored. And until the close of the act he forced his attention to a representation that appeared to him to be hardly more fantastic and unreal than his own extravagant thoughts.

He welcomed the Governor's decision to leave during the following interval and followed him out of the box with a sigh of relief.

In the foyer, where His Excellency lingered for a few moments chatting with his habitual courtesy to the director of the opera house, General Sanois, whose policy was to strike while the iron was hot, seized on the opportunity to draw Carew aside and ask point blank for the information that had been promised during dinner. They were still talking when they went out to the waiting carriages. The Governor paused with his foot on the step of his victoria and beamed affectionately at the two tall men towering beside him.

"You are going on to the Club—for a little game of bridge, perhaps?" he enquired genially.

"The Club—yes. Bridge—no," replied the General bluntly. "Carew and I have some business to discuss."

The Governor cast his eyes heavenwards. "Business at this time of night—*grand Dieu*!" he exclaimed. "Cards I could understand, but business—" he shook his head despairingly. "You are incorrigible—and this good Carew who encourages you! Go and talk your business, my friends. For me, I have had an exhausting day, a very exhausting day. I shall go home to bed—at a reasonable hour for once in my life. It has been a charming evening, a charming evening. My thanks to you both." And smiling and bowing he fluttered into the victoria and drove away.

As Carew's carriage moved into place General Sanois, who had accepted his offer of a lift, shot a glance of faint surprise at the two mounted Arabs who were drawn up close behind it.

"You ride *en prince*, tonight, my friend," he said, frankly curious. And Carew who had himself only at that moment noticed the men, shrugged with mingled amusement and annoyance. The idea of an escort would never have occurred to him, but Hosein was evidently determined his master should run no risk that forethought could prevent.

"It would seem so," he replied curtly, "but you must blame Hosein, not me, for this piece of theatrical nonsense."

The General settled his angular frame into a corner of the carriage and hitched his sword between his knees. "He probably has his reasons," he said, with a shrewd smile that left Carew wondering how much he knew and how far his own steps were dogged by the secret police whose activities extended over a wider district than was generally known. But he let the comment pass unanswered. The General was his very good friend, but with Sanois, friendship went by the board where the needs of the country were concerned and even his most trusted agents were subjected to an espionage that was all part of an elaborate and well-organized system. He stuck at nothing to obtain information he wanted and maintained that any means justified a desired end. That he was intrigued by Carew's visit to the Casbar today was obvious but he was restricted from openly voicing his curiosity by a compact that had been agreed between them years ago. Though he knew, and had good cause to know that Carew was whole-heartedly attached to the land of his adoption, he knew also that the Englishman was governed by scruples that debarred him from certain lines of action. Tonight Carew felt convinced that the General was on the track of something other than the information he had been promised and, for his part, he was equally determined to disclose nothing but the matter in hand. Though his host of the afternoon might have been guilty of certain indiscretions that had put him out of favour with the Government his own visit to the Casbar had been a purely personal one—and it could rest at that.

The Military Club was full when they arrived and it was some time before the two men could find a quiet corner in which to continue the conversation they had begun in the foyer of the opera house.

Ordering coffee the General produced the map that seemed to live permanently in the inside pocket of his tunic and spread it out on the table between them. For an hour or more they talked uninterruptedly, and when at last General Sanois pushed back his chair with a little grunt of satisfaction, the club had emptied of all but a small number of inveterate card players whose voices echoed fitfully from an adjoining room.

"It is understood, then, that you will act for us," he said, refolding the map carefully into its creases, "if it becomes necessary."

"If it becomes necessary—yes," said Carew, reaching for his cloak, "but I would prefer that you arranged this affair without my assistance. I have a scheme of my own on hand, and I am anxious to get back to my work."

"You can do your work and ours at the same time."

But Carew shook his head. "Not conscientiously," he said as he rose to go, "and besides, you want me to go south. I want to go west."

The General glanced up with sudden interest from the notes he was hastily scrawling in a bulky pocket-book. "The City of Stones?" he suggested, with the suspicion of a chuckle in his voice.

"Yes, the City of Stones," the other admitted slowly, "but how did you know?"

The General laughed. "I didn't know. I guessed. It is a sufficiently impossible undertaking that would naturally appeal to you. I have been wondering when you would attempt it."

Carew made a gesture of dissent. "I don't think it impossible."

"No, you wouldn't," returned Sanois dryly, "but it is impossible for all that. Many people have attempted to penetrate into that very intriguing and mysterious city—it has been told me that the charming inhabitants use their bones to form a unique and picturesque embellishment to their battlements."

Carew swung his heavy cloak over his shoulders. "They are welcome to my bones," he laughed, "the probable alternative being jackals."

"And your men—and the little Saba?" drawled Sanois, drawing patterns with his pencil on the marble-topped table.

Carew eyed him with a faint smile. Sanois' solicitude was touching but not convincing.

"How much for my men and Saba—and how much for your own schemes, General?" he retorted. The General grinned frankly, as he hoisted himself on to his feet. "*Touché!*" he said with a little bow, "but my schemes are less mad than yours, my friend. In the meantime we can count on you?"

"Only if it becomes absolutely necessary," Carew replied again quickly. And unwilling to risk a total refusal by premature argument Sanois reserved his inducements for a future time. "We can talk of it again," he said pleasantly, and shook hands with even more than his usual cordiality. To Carew the cool night air was a welcome relief after the heated atmosphere of the club. The fresh wind blowing against his face seemed to clear his brain and enabled him to think more calmly of the disturbing incidents of the evening. But calm reflection did not elucidate the extraordinary and violent hatred that had come to him. It was as much beyond his power of comprehension as it was beyond his power to ignore it. It seemed burnt into him. And the girl—he swore at himself angrily. He had thought enough about the girl. What had he to do with her or any other woman—he, who had cursed all women. Had he no strength of mind, no strength of purpose left? He sneered in bitter self mockery as the carriage stopped before the villa gateway.

Utterly weary of himself and the turmoil of his thoughts he walked up to the house wondering how he was going to get through the remaining hours of the night. Sleep in his present state of mind seemed out of the question. It was not rest he wanted but hard physical exercise that in bodily fatigue he might forget the mental upheaval that had assailed him during these last three weeks of comparative inactivity. He paused at the foot of the verandah steps, looking up at the star-lit sky, and the drifting scent of orange blossom made him think with sudden regret of the camp he had left amongst the hills near Blidah. What a night for a ride! If he started now he could be there by dawn. For a few minutes he played with the idea and then reluctantly put it from him. Despite his whole inclination something seemed to be dragging him back, something that made it impossible for him to leave Algiers.

With a heavy sigh he went slowly into the house.

VI

During the days that followed it became more and more borne in upon Carew that his cherished dream of visiting the mysterious City of Stones was doomed if not to failure certainly to indefinite postponement. General Sanois, who had thrown himself heart and soul into the new scheme for which Carew's information had paved the way, was plying him hard, pressing for his acceptance of the mission offered him. Carew's success in the past had made the General very sanguine of the outcome of the present proposed embassage and very tolerant of the Englishman's lack of enthusiasm in a venture that presented far fewer difficulties than others which had been negotiated and which, moreover, promised to further the prestige of the military governor of the Sahara. By turns he argued and expostulated, throwing forward every possible inducement to secure his voluntary agent's co-operation and losing no opportunity of urging his insistent demands. To each and every objection Carew raised he responded with an unusual flow of rhetoric that was wasted on his silent and equally determined listener whose desire to return to his own work he brushed aside as secondary to the needs of the country. Mounted orderlies arrived at the villa at all hours of the day, and it seemed to Carew that the telephone bell never ceased ringing. In despair at last of obtaining the peace and quiet for which he longed, he had taken Hosein and slipped away for a couple of days to the camp near Blidah. Within a mile of his own camp he found the tents of a desert sheik who was making a leisurely way to Algiers for the annual gathering of chiefs.

The Arab was an old acquaintance whose hospitality Carew had enjoyed on several occasions and an interchange of visits was both necessary and advantageous. But it was not to listen to the querulous outpourings of a chief with a perpetual grievance that he had fled from General Sanois' importunity, and foiled in his purpose, he had set out alone this morning an hour or so before the dawn to return to Algiers, leaving Hosein to follow later in the day when he had completed some arrangements in the camp.

But in spite of the tedious interruptions which the old sheik's demands on his time had made the two days had proved beneficial to him. Away from Algiers he had in a measure conquered the agitation of mind that had possessed him since the night he had rescued Lady Geradine from Abdul el Dhib.

And it was of the frustrated horse-thief and his unfulfilled threat that he was thinking as he drew Suliman to a standstill on the crest of a hill, a few miles outside the town, to watch the glory of the sunrise that was to him a never-failing pleasure.

Abdul had so far made no attempt to put his murderous intention into practise and, still sceptical himself as to the real truth of the warnings he had received, Carew would never have given him a second thought but for the behaviour of his attendants whose continual and obvious watchfulness was a constant reminder of the menace hanging over him. Hosein was still anxious—there had been difficulty in persuading him to remain behind at the camp this morning so loath was he to let his master ride alone—and Saba was still unhappy, a pathetic little figure of misery who clung to his protector refusing to be comforted. And daily the revolver that Carew wore naturally thrust in the waistcloth of his Arab dress sagged uncomfortably in the pocket of his serge jacket until he laughed at himself for carrying it. Clad in the native robes he preferred for the last two days he had forgotten it, but as he glanced now around the little hillock on which he stood he pushed it further into the silken folds of his embroidered shawl with a slight smile of amusement. The locality was reminiscent. It was here, after leaving Lady Geradine on the outskirts of Algiers, that he had chanced across Abdul and forced him to reveal the whereabouts of the stolen horse. But the smile passed quickly and his face clouded as his thoughts swung from the recovered stallion to the girl who had ridden him. Since the night of the opera he had not seen her but the memory of her was present with him always. The intolerant anger she had once roused in him was gone and he was at a loss to actually define the feeling he now felt towards her. It was not interest, he told himself almost angrily, he had no interest in her, no wish to think of her, and he fought against the perpetual remembrance that never left him. Unable to combat what seemed to him a veritable obsession he resented the deep impression she had made, resented the humiliating breakdown of the will he had trained to obey him. More than ever was he determined to get out of Algiers at the first possible opportunity. He had come to hate the town and the disturbing associations that would always be connected with it. The call of the desert, the lure of the legendary City of Stones was urging him powerfully as he sat with slackened reins looking dreamily at the golden sunrise, cursing the half promise he had made to General Sanois. But he had promised, or as good as promised, and facing his decision squarely for the first time he knew that the City of Stones must wait. With a little sigh of regret he searched for a cigarette in the folds of his waistcloth as he watched the glowing disc of the sun rise higher in the crimson flecked sky until the full light came with a sudden rush and the distinct city stood out before him clear and distinct in every detail. He scowled at it with sudden irritation and tightening his grip on the bridle, turned Suliman in the direction of the little village of Birmandreis. It was still very early. But for an occasional goatherd stalking gravely at the head of his flock, he had seen no sign of human life since he left the cross-country track he had taken from the camp and joined the plane-bordered highway that led to the village. Too early to return to the villa, he decided as he rode slowly along the well laid road listening to the sharp clip clop of his horse's hoofs and breathing in the fragrance of the fresh morning air that was blowing against his face. There was no need to hurry. Time enough this afternoon to see Sanois and give him his long delayed answer. Until then he could forget it.

Birmandreis was awake and stirring as he cantered through its miniature square and headed in the direction of El Biar. A short distance beyond the village he left the main road and turned down a narrow pathway in search of a tiny Arab café that was known to him. The picturesque little building, almost hidden by a wide spreading fig tree, was at this early hour of the morning silent and apparently deserted, but the clatter of hoofs and Carew's shout produced a sleepy and yawning proprietor who awoke into sudden and obsequious activity at the sight of this visitor. Slipping Suliman's bridle through a ring in the wall Carew sat on a bench in the shadow of the fig tree while he waited for the Arab coffee for which the place was famous. It was brought at length by the half-caste *aubergist* who hovered about his early guest with eager loquaciousness. He had heard that his excellency had returned from the desert, he had hoped before this to have seen him at the Café Meduse. He trusted that the protracted journey had been propitious. Monsieur was pleased to return to civilization? Monsieur was *not* pleased! *Hélas!* and yet Algiers was gay this season—fuller than it had been for many years. Trade was good. For himself he had nothing to complain of, the café prospered and the visitors, the English visitors in particular, paid well—to Allah the praise!

Undeterred by Carew's monosyllabic replies he rambled on half in French half in Arabic discussing the district and the crops and the government taxes with fine impartiality, but with due regard to his listener's well-known intimacy with the administrators of the country. But under his seemingly careless manner there was a suggestion of uneasiness that was very apparent. He moved restlessly as he talked, from time to time glancing almost furtively about him, and once or twice it seemed as if he were on the point of imparting some confidence that nearly reached utterance but which died away in mumbled ambiguity before it was spoken.

But when Carew had paid his modest score and was once more in the saddle the man appeared to come to a sudden decision. Pressing close up to the restless horse he stooped down under pretence of tightening a loosened girth, his fingers fumbling nervously at the scarlet leather straps. "There is venom in the jackal's bite, O Sidi," he muttered in the vernacular, pure Arab in his agitation, and drew back hastily as if already repenting the words he had nerved himself to say. And Carew, glancing down at his twitching face, knew that to question him would be useless, so he made no sign of understanding but with a careless nod and a perfunctory, "Go with God," reined his horse back into the little lane and held him, sidling and catching at his bit, to a walk until a bend in the road hid them from the prying eyes that were doubtless watching from behind the dense foliage of the fig tree. Then he gave Suliman his head wondering, as the spirited creature broke into a headlong gallop, how near to attempted assassination he had been during the last half hour. That Abdul el Dhib, biding his time with oriental pertinacity, was somewhere in the vicinity, seemed beyond all question. But why he risked his rascally neck so near to Algiers or what were his relations with the half-caste owner of the café Carew was at a loss to conjecture. Sufficient that once again he had been warned and that the warning had been given reluctantly and under stress of great personal fear. It spoke volumes that the fellow had found courage to say what he had said.

With a muttered word of impatience Carew bent forward and ran his fingers soothingly over Suliman's glossy neck. Abdul was becoming a nuisance, and he found himself almost wishing that the difference between them could have been settled definitely once and for all at the Café Meduse that morning. Half tempted to retrace his steps and force the affair to an immediate conclusion he pulled up suddenly, turning in the saddle to scan the road behind him. But what was the good! Abdul had had his chance and for reasons of his own had neglected it. There was nothing to be gained and probably a good deal to be risked by putting temptation in his way a second time. After all, the quarrel was Abdul's, not his. Let Abdul then make the first move—if, indeed, he intended to move at all. To Carew it seemed almost that his enemy had talked too much to be really dangerous. Babblers were seldom doers, he reflected, and dismissing the outlaw from his mind he rode on, leaving the road for a rough mule track by which he could skirt El Biar and reach Bouzaréa from where he meant to return to Mustapha.

Already the fresh morning wind had dropped and the day began to give promise of great heat unusual for the time of year. But to Carew, accustomed to the fierce sun of the desert, the warmth was welcome and, more at peace within himself than he had been for weeks, he turned his whole attention to the district through which he was riding, a district known to him from boyhood but which he had not lately visited. The intervening years seemed to drop away as he noted and recognised each succeeding landmark. There was little change to be seen in the fruit groves and vineyards he was passing and gradually he fell into a reverie, leaving Suliman to choose his own way along the stony track.

Influenced by his surroundings he let himself dwell on early memories; memories of the handsome brilliantly clever father who had given up a public career of great promise to devote himself to the delicate wife who was his idol; and memories of the beautiful fragile mother whose influence, had she lived, might have made so great a difference in his own life. With all the strength of his boyish heart he had adored her and the memory of her had made him very tender with the wife who had repaid his devotion with coldness and deceit. But with the tragic ending of his own short married life he had closed his heart to the softening influences of memory and in the drawing room of the villa, a room he never entered, the portrait of his mother was veiled by heavy curtains that for the last twelve years had never been drawn. Twelve years! Twelve years of self-banishment and loneliness. At first it had been little short of hell, there had been times when the temptation to end it all had been almost overpowering, when only his strong will had kept him from self-destruction. But now he could think of it calmly—except for the one aching memory that never left him. Despite himself his thoughts turned to the child he had lost, the little son in whom so many hopes had been centered, and a passion of longing and regret filled him. If only the boy had been left to him! A look of intense pain swept across his face and his firm lips quivered as he tried to visualise the boy as he might have been now, a lad of fourteen, on the threshold of manhood. His son! God, how he wanted him still! And from the child of his body who was lost to him his thoughts veered with sudden compassion to the child of his adoption, the little Arab waif he had saved from death to assuage his own loneliness, who was in his blindness and helplessness so utterly dependent on him. Poor little dreamer of dreams, besieging Allah hourly with prayers for the safety of the beloved protector who was all his world, he too was longing for the desert, for the freer, wilder life to which he had been born.

Carew's mind leaped forward to the coming interview with General Sanois. His promise given today, he would move heaven and earth to expedite matters and get away from Algiers as soon as possible. A speedy departure should be a *sine qua non* of his acceptance.

With a little laugh he bent forward to ease his weight off Suliman as the horse started to climb a steep ascent that led to the woods behind Bouzaréa. The mule track was little used, rough and boulder strewn and in places almost overgrown with cactus among which the stallion picked his steps with careful precision born of experience. Carew let him take his own way and sat with slackened rein as the big bay, straining and heaving, breasted the last hundred yards of sharp incline, his powerful muscles rippling against his rider's knees. With a final effort, the loose stones flying from under his heels, he reached the summit and stood breathing deeply and whinnying in response to the caressing hand laid on his sweat drenched neck. Then he moved slowly forward with pricked ears and nervous gait along the track that had dwindled to a narrow hardly perceptible path. Desert bred, to Suliman the dense silent wood was a place of lurking unknown terror to which he had never become accustomed and, snorting and starting, he evidenced now his disapproval of a route that was highly distasteful to him. But wrapped in his own thoughts and used to his horse's moods Carew did not heed his uneasiness. Like the district through which he had just passed the wood was alive with memories, a favourite haunt of childhood where he had roamed for hours at a time with Hosein as companion and playmate. Then the wood had been a region of mystery and enchantment, peopled with the malevolent djinns and horrible afreets that loomed so large in the Arab's creed and of whom he discoursed with all the fluency and imagination of his race—tales to which the English boy, already deeply imbued with the spirit of the country, listened half credulous, half unbelieving but always interested, wriggling for sheer joy even when his hair crisped on his head and he peered involuntarily into the depths of the thick undergrowth for the monstrous shapes and fiery eyes that Hosein's eloquence made so real. Carew looked about him with an eagerness that brought a smile to his lips. Near here there had been a tiny clearing, always connected in his mind with a tale of especial weirdness that had been Hosein's masterpiece—a tale of necromancers and demons, of beauty in distress, and the extravagant adventures of a sultan's son whose heroic exploits had transcended all human possibility. How he had revelled in it, listening wide eyed and absorbed to Hosein's sing-song intonations. Here, so went the story, the sorrowful princess, escaping from the enchanter who held her captive, had met the wandering knight whom fate had sent to rescue her; here, more beautiful than all the houris of paradise, sitting patiently upon the ground and veiled in her night black hair she had waited for her lover.

The old tale was running through his head as a sharp curve in the path brought him to the entrance of the little clearing. Smaller it seemed than when his boyish eyes had looked upon it, and robbed somehow of the mystery that had been associated with it. To the man's eyes now just an ordinary glade in an ordinary wood.

But it was not the well remembered spot that held his attention. His gaze was rivetted on a figure sitting, like the princess of the story, motionless upon the ground at the foot of a gnarled cork oak. Not swathed in shimmering eastern silks nor veiled in a cloud of dusky hair, but clad in the close fitting boyish riding suit in which he had first seen her she leant back comfortably against the tree, her bare head resting on the crinkly bark, her arms wrapped round her updrawn knees, whistling softly to a small green lizard palpitating on the moss beside her. The tiny creature with swelling throat and languorous swaying head was listening fascinated to the clear sweet trills charming it into immobility. Suliman's neat feet made no sound on the soft earth and the girl was obviously unaware of the increase to her audience. To back his horse silently and slip away before she noticed his presence was Carew's first impulse, but despite his every inclination something stayed him in undecided hesitation. And the opportunity neglected he was given no second chance. Resenting the tight grip on his mouth and the sudden convulsive pressure of his rider's knees Suliman, with a display of temper that was unusual, bounded high on his hind legs snorting his indignation. Submitting to the inevitable with the best grace he could muster Carew dragged him down and swung to the ground, raising his hand to his forehead in the graceful salute that was in accordance with his Arab dress.

"Good morning, Lady Geradine."

The lizard had fled but Marny had neither moved nor altered her position. She responded to his greeting with a faint smile, her eyes sweeping him frankly from head to foot as he stood, a picturesque commanding-looking figure, leaning against his horse whose muzzle was thrust contritely into his hand.

"Good morning—desert man."

There was the least possible pause before the last two words and Carew's tanned face flushed dully. "My name's Carew," he said gruffly. She nodded, looking at him with wide grave eyes and hunching her knees up closer to her chin.

"I know," she said, "Mrs. Chalmers told me before she left Algiers. You are Sir Gervas Carew—and you hate women. Why did you do it?"

"Do what—" he asked, failing to grasp the context of her question.

"Why did you trouble to interfere that night near Blidah?" she said quietly, but the quick blood sprang to her face as she spoke.

He was silent for a few moments then, with a slow shrug: "Because you were English," he answered tersely. She shook her head with a little smile of amusement.

"But I'm not. Sure it's Irish I am—glory be to God." The brogue was unmistakable and despite himself Carew's grave face relaxed.

"It's the same thing," he said with indifference. But she negatived his assertion with a scornful wave of the hand.

"Not to us," she said laughingly. Then she grew grave again, looking at him with undisguised interest. "Do you mean it, really?" she said with deliberation. "Do you mean that if I had been an Arab or a Frenchwoman you would have done—nothing?"

He nodded in silent assent.

"And because I was English, or you thought I was English, you set your prejudice on one side and did what you did—just to satisfy your *esprit-de-race*?"

"Yes."

She looked away with an odd little laugh. "You are very refreshing."

Carew scowled at the hint of mockery in her voice.

"How so?" he asked stiffly. But she laughed again and shook her head, refusing to enlighten him. Then with a sudden change of manner she turned to him again, eyeing him almost wistfully.

"You refused to shake hands with me—twice, Sir Gervas," she said slowly, flushing slightly, "and I cut you dead at the opera. Shall we call quits—just for this morning—your prejudice against my rudeness? Can't you forget, just for once, that you are talking to one of the sex you despise—I can't help being a woman, I would much rather have been a man—and tell me the things you know so well, the things that nobody I meet with in Algiers seems to care about—the Arabs, the desert, and all this wonderful country. Not the desert the tourists go to but the real desert, far away in the south there," she added eagerly, kneeling up suddenly to point with unexpected precision towards the region of which she spoke. Mechanically his eyes followed her outstretched hand. He was trying to understand his own strange hesitation. It would have been easy to excuse himself, alleging any plausible excuse that offered, and go as he had come leaving her to the solitude he had interrupted. But he did not want to go. The astounding truth came to him suddenly and his lips curved in cynical self-scorn. What sort of a fool was he, what strength of purpose had he that, professing to hate all women, he should surrender to the charm of this one woman? And wherein lay the charms he reluctantly admitted? Her beauty? He smiled more bitterly than before—he had learnt the worthlessness of outward loveliness. Was it then the diversity of mood she displayed? He glanced at her covertly as she sat leaning against the cork tree, apparently indifferent to his silence, her eyes fixed not on him but on the tips of her neat riding boots, whistling as she had whistled to the lizard. A boyish graceful figure, pulsing with life and health, bearing this morning no kind of resemblance to the white-faced fainting girl he had carried in his arms or the proud weary-looking woman he had seen at the opera. Which was the real woman? And what was her present motive? Was it really a disinterested and genuine desire to learn something of the real life of the country that led her to endeavour to detain him at her side—or was she merely amusing herself at his expense, flattered at having claimed the attention of a man known as a determined misogynist? His face darkened and meditated refusal sprang to his lips. But the words died away unspoken. Flight was tantamount to a confession of weakness against which his pride rebelled. If she was playing with him—so much the worse for her. If, on the other hand, she was sincere in the request she had made—with a shrug he turned and led his horse to the further side of the little clearing, tethering him with no show of haste to the branch of a tree.

And as he went Marny Geradine's eyes followed him with a look of yearning sadness, and a deep sigh that was almost a sob escaped her. What had she done! What right had she to intrude herself upon him? Why add to her own unhappiness by prolonging an interview that would only bring her further sorrow. The joy of seeing him, of speaking with him, could lead to nothing but greater misery and regret. But the temptation had been stronger than she could withstand. She loved him so. And what harm could there be when his own indifference was so great! Why did he hate women? Mrs. Chalmers' information had not gone beyond the bare fact and, herself reserved almost to fastidiousness, she had not sought to probe the reason of his hatred. What, after all, did it matter? The secrets of his past, if there were any secrets, were not her affair. Enough for her that he was a man who had devoted his life to relieving the suffering of the desert people amongst whom he lived. From the doctor's warm-hearted wife she had learned the significance of the title by which he had called himself that night of terrible memory. So would she have him—the ideal she would treasure in her heart, a man magnificent in his singleness of purpose.

He came back to her slowly, his face inscrutable as the people whose dress he wore, and sat down leisurely, Arab fashion, on the ground near her. Taking her literally at her word and prompted by her eager questions he found that speech was easier than he had anticipated. It was a subject on which he was well qualified to speak, a subject that lay very close to his heart, and gradually his attitude of barely concealed hostility wore away and he talked as, weeks ago, he had talked in his tent to Micky Meredith. But not of himself and his own work. Of these he said nothing, speaking only of the desert and its nomad inhabitants, of the charm and cruelty of the vast sandy wastes, of the petty wars and feuds that raged perpetually amongst the savage and belligerent tribes. His low even voice ran smoothly on, drawing no fanciful picture but relating faithfully the things that were the things he had himself seen, the life he had shared. While he dwelt on the glamour and fascination of the desert wilds he spared her nothing of the squalor and misery, the ghastly needless suffering that was bound up inextricably with the scenes he depicted.

Eagerly she listened to him, happy with just the fact of his nearness, enthralled by the story he told so graphically and which held her spellbound. Her eyes fixed on the sunburnt face that was turned persistently away from her, she was no longer in the little clearing or even near to the Algiers that had proved so great a disappointment to her. She was far away in the burning south, riding beside him over the undulating sweeps of the restless sand, camping under the argent stars and living the life of which she had dreamed—a life that with all its savagery and primitive violence was yet cleaner than the one to which she was condemned. To be with him there, far from the artificial existence that sickened her, to live out her life beside him aiding him in the work of which he would not speak and serving him with all the strength of the love that was consuming her! She clenched her hands with the pain of her own imagining. A dream that could never be realised. There was no room for a woman's love in the life he led. Alone, and always alone, he would follow the course he had set himself, a solitary dweller in the wilderness pitting his individual strength against the pain and suffering he sought to minimise. And, bound, what would be her loneliness when he rode for the last time out of her life leaving her to a misery that would be greater even than she had known before?

A gasping sob escaped her and horrified at her lack of control she hid her burning face in her hands. But to Carew her agitation seemed only the natural consequence of the grim tale of ruthless Arab ferocity he had just concluded.

"It is cruel, of course," he said with a slow shrug, "but it is the way of life the whole world over—the strong preying on the weak, the eternal battle for existence, and a callousness that is born of necessity. And Arabs are only children, as all men at heart are children, fighting for what they want and often, from mere perversity, for what they do not want."

She nodded assent, not trusting her voice to answer him and furtively brushing away the tears of which she was ashamed. And he too fell silent, playing absently with a length of creeper he twined and retwined between his long strong fingers, wondering at the interest she had evinced, wondering at the ease with which he had spoken to her.

At last, through the silence that neither seemed able to break, came the trampling of horses' hoofs. He looked up with a start and leapt to his feet, his hand reaching instinctively for the revolver in his waistcloth. For himself he did not care, but if Abdul had tracked him here what of the girl beside him? Alone he would have been content to give his enemy the benefit of the doubt—but because of her he could take no chances. He would have to shoot at sight, or be shot himself. He moved quickly, screening her where she sat, and slid the heavy weapon from its resting place. But the next moment he jerked it back with a smothered exclamation of relief. It was not Abdul el Dhib who rounded the bend in the narrow path but a neat typically English little man straddling with a jockey's gait between the two horses he led. Only when he turned to find Marny close at his elbows did Carew realise that his face was wet with perspiration. With a gesture of impatience he brushed his hand across his forehead but he did not vouchsafe any explanation. She must have seen the revolver in his hand—explanations could wait. And standing quietly beside him, she did not seem in any hurry to ask but remained silent until the arrival of the groom. The little man brought the horses to a stand with no sign of surprise at the sight of the tall Arab-clad figure towering behind his mistress.

"Nine o'clock, m'lady," he announced stolidly, and backed her horse into position.

Marny laughed as she placed her foot in the stirrup Carew moved forward to hold.

"Tanner is my timekeeper," she explained, swinging easily into the saddle, "he always has a watch, and I lose mine as fast as I buy them," she added, gathering up the reins and settling herself comfortably.

Carew patted the neck of her horse for a moment without answering, then he looked up slowly and at sight of his face the laughter died out of her eyes.

"Keep your man in sight when you come to the woods again, Lady Geradine," he said gravely. She looked at him questioningly.

"Do you mean it—seriously? I thought that so close to Algiers—"

"You were close to Algiers before, and I would not warn you if I did not mean it seriously," he interrupted with a touch of irritation in his voice, and stepped back with a salaam that she felt to be almost a dismissal. And it was without waiting to watch her ride away that he strode across the clearing to his own horse. He had no intention of accompanying her back to Algiers, he had outraged his principles sufficiently for one morning he assured himself with a smile that was not mirthful.

Nor did he feel inclined to return immediately to the villa.

During these last few weeks he had grown almost to hate it. He would go on to Bouzaréa, telephone to Sanois and spend the rest of the day at the little suburb with a French doctor of his acquaintance. Perhaps in Morel's laboratory he would be able to forget the unrest that this morning's meeting had revived so poignantly.

It was late in the afternoon when he rode into Algiers to keep the appointment made over the telephone that morning.

At the moment General Sanois was living in barracks and Carew found him in his private room sitting alone before a huge desk that was heaped with a mass of papers. At his entrance the general rose and held out a welcoming hand.

"Well," he said eagerly, "you have decided?" and sank back into his chair with a little exclamation of satisfaction as Carew nodded affirmatively.

"You relieve me of a difficulty, *mon cher*," he went on, pushing papers and telephone on one side to make room for the map he spread out with almost affectionate care. "I was at my wits' end to find a substitute. My own men are no use, an officer would never get past the frontier. And the same applies to the accredited agents—those, that is to say, whom I have at my disposal. Remains you. And I think I shall not be wrong in saying that you will not fail," he added confidently.

Carew smiled faintly at the implied compliment which he knew to be no idle one but a genuine expression of opinion.

"I'll do my best," he said briefly, with a slight shrug of embarrassment, "but I am not infallible," he added, "and if I fail—"

"You will at least have had a charming excursion," cut in Sanois laughingly. "You will have broken new ground. You will probably have found a new disease and we shall have to send an expensively equipped medical mission to follow up your discovery, and you will end by costing us the deuce and all of a lot of money. But that's not my affair," he added, tapping the gold lace on his sleeve significantly, and turned once more to the large scale map he had laid out.

Carew hitched the folds of his heavy burnous closer round him and drew his chair nearer to the table.

"I am ready to start almost at once. My own preparations can be concluded in a week. I am anxious to get out of Algiers, and if you keep me waiting indefinitely—well, then, I can't promise that when you want me you will find me." He smiled at Sanois' whistle of dismay for there had been an undertone of peremptoriness in his voice that the general recognised.

"A week?" he said rather doubtfully. "You don't give us much time, my friend. It will take longer than a week to settle this affair. But I'll do what I can. And now to business."

When the details of the expedition had been discussed in every particular and Carew rose at last to go night had fallen. He refused the general's invitation to dine with the mess and found himself obliged to repeat his refusal more than once before he reached the barrack yard. Usually he was glad to accept the hospitality of the officers with whom he was a frequent and popular guest but tonight he wanted to be alone.

Riding through the crowded streets Suliman occupied his exclusive attention, but when the town had been left behind and the ascent to Mustapha begun he let his thoughts range forward to the coming journey. Regretfully he put away from him the temptation of the City of Stones. It would have to be for another time. He was pledged to Sanois now and, the general himself bound down to a promise, he had at last something definite to go on. Not that there was much for him, personally, to arrange. The change of route called for little alteration in the preparations he had already made for an extended tour in the desert. And the boy would go in either case. He had spent most of his young life in the saddle and his apparently frail little body was capable of astonishing endurance. To leave him behind would be to break his heart—and Carew could not do without him. Tonight the air was strangely soft, heavy with the scent of flowers, and a brooding silence that was reminiscent of the solemn hush of the desert seemed to have closed down over all nature. Not a tree moved, not a dog barked, and Carew had the curious feeling that he was riding through a place of the dead. Amongst the Arabs it was an omen of death, a sure and certain sign that for some human soul the wings of Azrael were beating downward from the realms of the blessed. For his? With a philosophical shrug he turned in the saddle to look back at the newly risen moon, a crescent slip of silver in the sky, and then sent Suliman flying in the direction of the villa.

The door of the wall was open, and Hosein, ghostlike in his white draperies, emerged from the deep shadows of the entrance as Carew dismounted. He took the horse in silence, still evidently nursing his grievance of the morning, and half amused, half annoyed by his servant's tacit expression of disapproval Carew omitted his own customary greeting and swinging on his heel walked up to the house.

In the Moorish hall, brilliantly lit by three large hanging lamps of beaten silver, Saba was waiting. And as his sensitive ears caught the almost imperceptible sound of soft leather against the marble pavement he darted forward with a wild cry of joy and fell, laughing and sobbing together, into the arms stretched out to catch him. Tossing him up on his shoulder, Carew carried him, chattering with excitement, through the jasmine scented courtyard to the big bedroom at the back of the house, there to cope with a flow of endless questions which ceased not but penetrated shrilly even to the distant bathroom. And standing beside the dressing table, his slim fingers straying caressingly among the orderly arranged toilet appointments, he was still talking when Carew came back from his tub. Then the questions gave place to a detailed description of his own small doings during the last three days and he rambled on discoursively, while Carew changed into the fresh robes laid out for him, carrying his listener through endless imaginary adventures and concluding with the grave announcement that Derar, the fat butler, had assuredly incurred the wrath of Allah for his wife had presented him that morning with yet another unwelcome daughter "—which, as your lordship knows, is the *fifth*," he added with fine scorn.

And glad that for the moment the boy appeared to have forgotten his fears, Carew let him talk and finally took him with him to the dining room where, perched cross-legged on a cushion beside the table and made happy with a plate of fruit and sweetmeats, he continued to chatter throughout the formal dinner served by a dejected, tearful-looking Derar and Hosein, who had recovered his accustomed serenity.

Though preferring the simplicity of camp life, Carew, in his town house, followed early traditions and maintained a certain state and ceremony. Many of the servants were old retainers, and Derar had been butler to the late Sir Mark Carew. And the elderly survivor, conservative to the backbone and highly endowed with a sense of his own importance, was largely responsible for the continuance of the old régime that still prevailed at the villa. And so it was that, even when he was alone, Carew dined nightly in the huge room where the table seemed a tiny island set in the midst of a vast marble sea. But this evening he had glanced about him once or twice during the protracted meal with a faintly puzzled look in his sombre eyes. What made the room tonight appear so empty—so chill and lifeless? It was not the lack of guests that troubled him, he was used to being alone, but a strange yearning for something he was at a loss to define. Was it the preliminary warnings of middle age that, urging a remembrance of his forty years, had induced the unaccustomed feeling of lassitude and melancholy that seemed to have taken hold of him? He almost laughed at the thought. For some it might be the beginning of a gradual decline of force and ability, but for himself, he had never felt fitter or stronger. It was just Algiers, he told himself as he lingered over the cup of thick, sweet coffee that had become as indispensable to him as to any native of the country, Algiers—and a consciousness of intense and profound boredom. Thank heaven it wouldn't last much longer. Life on the march was too strenuous to admit of ennui.

Calling to Saba he went to the study adjoining his bedroom and from there out on to the wide verandah that overlooked the garden.

For a while he smoked in silence that was punctuated at intervals by the blind boy's fitful remarks to which he replied briefly with an inattention that was not lost upon his small companion, for gradually he, too, fell silent.

The night was very still. Directly before the verandah a broad streak of moonlight stretching like a path of silver to the distant boundary wall made blacker the darkness that enveloped the rest of the garden where trees and flowering shrubs loomed large and fantastic in the murky gloom. The heavy scent of flowers was almost overpowering, languorous and sleep-inducing as the smell of incense. And the brooding hush that Carew had noticed earlier in the evening seemed now even more penetrating and intense. There was in the air a feeling of unnatural suspense, a breathless sensation of expectancy like the deep hush that precedes a storm. In the desert Carew would have known what it portended, but here in Algiers he could not account for it. Was it perhaps only his own imagination magnifying the quiet of an ordinary evening into something that approached the abnormal? He was not given to imagination, but he could not rid himself of the impression of a coming calamity that momentarily made him more wide awake and alert. And with the sense of waiting there came again the feeling of depression and melancholy he had experienced during dinner. How empty and lonely the house had seemed! He had never noticed it before. Why did he notice it now? And as he pondered it there seemed to rise before him the semblance of a figure standing in the brilliant strip of moonlight, a slender, graceful figure whose boyish riding dress no longer moved him to intolerant disgust. For an instant he stared with almost fear at the delicate oval face that appeared so strangely close to his, looking straight into the pain-filled haunting eyes that seemed to be tearing the very heart out of him. Then a terrible oath broke from his rigid lips and in the revulsion of feeling that swept over him he wrenched his gaze away, cursing with bitter rage the day he had ever seen her. Not her nor any other woman—so help him God!

A stifled whimper and a tiny hand slid tremblingly into his, made him realise the passionate utterance that had been forced from him. He caught the boy in his arms and soothed him with remorseful tenderness. "Angry with thee—when am I ever angry with thee, thou little foolish one?" he murmured gently in response to the sobbing question that came muffled from the folds of his robes in which Saba's head was buried. Content with his answer the child lay still. And the clinging touch of his fingers, the soft warm weight of his slim little body brought a measure of consolation to the lonely man who held him.

For a long time Carew sat without moving, staring into the shadowy garden. Save for the shrilling of a cicada in the grass near by the deep silence was unbroken. And soon even the insect ceased its monotonous chirp, abruptly as it had begun.

Carew had been up since before daybreak, and lulled by the intense quiet and the heaviness of the night, he began to be aware that drowsiness was stealing over him. He was almost asleep when the vague impression of a distant sound, a curious slithering sound that ended in a faint thud, penetrated to his only half conscious mind and roused him to sudden and complete wakefulness. The noise seemed to have come from the further end of the garden. Who was abroad in the garden at this time of night? As he stared keen-eyed into the darkness his brain was working rapidly. He had thought the child to be asleep, but from a slight movement in his arms he knew that Saba too was awake and listening intently, as he himself was listening. To get the boy away before the happening he believed inevitable was his first care. Without altering his own position he slid him silently behind his chair with a low breathed injunction to go. But with a passionate gesture of refusal Saba clung to him and Carew was obliged to use unwilling force to unclasp the slender fingers twined desperately in his thick burnous.

"Go!" he whispered again peremptorily. And as the boy crept slowly away he leant forward in his chair once more, waiting with braced muscles and straining ears for any further sound that should betray his nocturnal visitor's whereabouts. But the few moments' attention given to Saba had been moments used by another to advantage. The attack came with unexpected and noiseless suddenness, from a quarter he least expected, and it was only his acute sense of smell that saved him. With the rank, animal-like odour of the desert man reeking in his nostrils he leaped to his feet, swerving as he turned. And his quick, instinctive movement saved his life, for the driving knife thrust aimed at his heart failed in its objective and glanced off his arm gashing it deeply. With a snarl of rage el Dhib thrust again. And, his right hand temporarily numbed and unable to draw the revolver at which his blood drenched fingers fumbled nervelessly, Carew caught the swinging arm with his left hand and flung his whole weight forward against his opponent. They fell with a crash, the Arab undermost, and grappled in the darkness twisting and heaving with straining limbs and labouring breath.

Crippled, Carew at first could do little more than retain his hold, but as the numbness passed from his wounded arm he managed with a desperate effort to jerk himself upward until his knees were pressing with crushing force on Abdul's chest and rigid forearm and, rolling sideways, he tore the knife from the fingers that clung to it tenaciously. But the manœuvre cost him the advantage he had gained. With a lithe panther-like movement of his sinewy body the Arab slipped uppermost, his hands at the other's throat. And conscious that he was fighting for his life, Carew put forward his utmost power to meet the strength he knew to be equal to his own. Locked in a mortal embrace that seemed to admit of only one ending they struggled with deadly purpose, writhing to and fro on the floor of the verandah until a sidelong jerk from one of them sent them over the edge and they rolled, still gripping fiercely, into the garden beneath. The drop was a short one, but in falling Carew's head struck against the abutment of the marble stairway and for a moment he lay stunned. And Abdul who had fallen on top of him was not able to complete the work he had begun. Warned by the lights that flashed up in the villa, unable to recover the knife he had lost, with a parting curse he turned and ran for the shelter of the shadowy trees, doubling like a hare as he sped across the strip of brilliant moonlight. And still dazed from the blow on his head Carew staggered to his feet and stood staring stupidly after him, swaying dizzily as he strove to think collectedly. But as the flying figure almost reached the friendly darkness that would cover his flight the momentary cloud lifted from Carew's brain and he wrenched the revolver from his waistband. Yet with his finger pressing on the trigger he paused irresolute. Not at an unarmed man—not in the back! That was *murder*—no matter how great the provocation. With a smothered exclamation he dropped his arm to his side. But the screaming whine of a bullet tearing past his head and a sharp crack behind him told him that Hosein was troubled by no such scruples. And with mingled feelings he watched Abdul el Dhib, caught at the moment he thought himself safe, plunge forward on his face and lie twisting in the agony of death.

When Carew reached him and lifting him with practised hands supported him against his knee, the dying man's eyes rolled upward to the grave face bending over him and his contorted features relaxed in a grin of ghastly amusement.

"This was ordained, lord," he gasped painfully, a pinkish foam gathering on his lips, "thou or I—and Allah has chosen. To Him the praise," he added mockingly, and choked his life away on the crimson tide that poured from his mouth.

VII

S ilence had settled again over the little oasis which an hour before had been the scene of noisiest activity.

Scattered amongst the palms and thorn trees the debris of a camp evidenced the passing of a caravan, and three or four miles away the train of lurching camels with its escort of mounted Arabs was still visible moving steadily over the rolling waste, heading for the south. Seated cross-legged on the warm ground, idly dribbling sand through his long, brown fingers, Carew watched it with a feeling of envy, longing for the time when he could once more lead his own caravan towards the heart of the great desert whither his thoughts turned perpetually.

But for the promise made to General Sanois he would already have left Algiers. The small attraction the town had once had for him had vanished completely in the mental disturbance that had dominated him during the last few weeks. And Sanois' preparations dragged interminably. Daily Carew was tempted to put his half-laughing threat into execution and abandon the whole enterprise. But the constant delays were no fault of the General who was straining every nerve to complete his arrangements—and Carew had given his word. There was nothing for it but to wait with what patience he could muster.

Out of tune with himself and his surroundings he had gone for distraction to Biskra to attend the annual race meeting, and for three crowded days he had been able, partially, to forget the strange unrest that beset him. But only partially. The little desert town, filled to overflowing for the great event of the year, was too small for chance meetings to be avoided and several times he had glimpsed Geradine, blustering and insufferable there as in Algiers. But keeping closely to his own circle of acquaintances Carew had escaped coming into contact with the man for whom he had conceived a hatred that was inexplicable. And in Biskra he had other interests besides the racing to engage his attention. Amongst the Arab chiefs who poured into the town from far and wide he had encountered many old friends. And it was in response to the earnest request from one of them, the strangest Arab he had ever known, that Carew had left Biskra early the previous day to ride with him the first couple of stages of a journey that would take the sheik weeks to accomplish.

It was long since they had met and the intervening years had brought startling and unforeseen changes into the life of the man

Carew remembered as a light-hearted captain of Spahis who had been more Frenchman than Arab in his tastes and inclinations.

Carew's gaze turned musingly to the chief who lay stretched on the ground beside him. Wrapped in his burnous, his face hidden in his arms, he had slept, or seemed to sleep throughout the hour of the siesta and not even the clamour and bustle of the departing caravan had roused him. Carew had watched the breaking up of the camp with more than ordinary interest. A headman had superintended the arrangements with precision and despatch that savoured more of military methods than the usual haphazard procedure prevalent among journeying Arabs; and the escort, of whom a dozen or so remained at the further side of the oasis chatting with Hosein, were all obviously fighting men, extraordinarily disciplined and orderly.

Still in disgrace with the Administration for the wiping out of a contiguous tribe ten years before, for what purpose had Said Ibn Zarrarah, ex-captain of Spahis and paramount chief of a large district, not only fostered the warlike instincts of a people with fighting traditions behind them but endeavoured, apparently with success, to engraft on them the European tactics he had himself learnt from the rulers of the country? It was an intriguing question Carew had pondered while his companion slept. In the old days France had had no more devoted adherent than the dashing young Spahi. Was there now any ulterior motive in the militarism he encouraged in his people, or was it merely a means by which he sought to distract his mind from a life that Carew knew to be uncongenial?

A younger son with no immediate prospect of succeeding to the leadership of the tribe, with aspirations that had never found fulfillment in his desert home, he had, on joining his regiment, become thoroughly Gallicised, spending long periods of leave in Paris and unlike the average semi-educated native assimilating only what was best in western thought and culture. Unspoilt by the flattery and attention heaped on him, notorious for his cold disregard of women, he had lived for his regiment and the racing stable he maintained in France. The death of his elder brother, killed in the raid that had put him out of favour with the Government, had called him from the life he loved to assume the cares and duties of a chieftainship he had never desired. Hotly resenting the heavy censure of the authorities on an action that had been misrepresented to them, and too proud to explain the necessity that had forced his hand, he had severed all connections with the past and had retired to his desert fastness to combat the suspicions of the elders of his tribe who had distrusted him for his want of religious zeal and for his adherence to the very people with whom he was in disgrace.

The irony of the situation had not been lost on him and it had been a certain satisfaction to prove conclusively his loyalty to his father's house. The Governor who had condemned his action had been superseded shortly afterwards, but the chief of the Ibn Zarrarah had ignored the change and made no effort towards reconciliation. His heart turned often in secret to the France he had known and loved, he held aloof from his old associates, keeping strictly to his own territory and immersing himself in the affairs of his tribe. He had lived down the mistrust of even the most conservative of his people, conforming outwardly to an orthodoxy that gave him no inward consolation.

This year, for the first time in ten years, he had yielded to the long suppressed desire to revisit the scene of former pleasures. In the old days he had been a conspicuous and well-known figure at the annual race meeting at Biskra, popular with Arab and Frenchman alike and famous for his stud of magnificent horses. The visit just concluded had been made under very different circumstances. Unrecognised and almost unremembered he had kept entirely to the company of his own countrymen, a spectator only where once he had been a moving spirit.

The experience had been fraught with more pain than pleasure. He was human enough to feel the difference keenly, philosophical enough to be contemptuous of his own bitterness. But all his philosophy could not heal the ache in his heart or still the longings quickened by the sound of the soft musical language he had spoken for years in preference to his own.

And now when Carew bent forward and touched him with a half-laughing "Ho, dreamer!" in the vernacular, he sat up with a jerk revealing dark melancholy eyes that were not dulled with sleep but hard and bright with concentrated thought. "For the love of God speak French," he exclaimed. "Oh, I know I'm a fool," he went on with a half-defiant ring in his voice, "a bigger fool than most—I always was. I was a fool to forget that I was an Arab, to try and imagine myself a Frenchman. I was a fool, when my brother Omair remained childless, not to realise that I might at any time be called upon to give up all that made life pleasant for me. And when he was killed I was a fool to do what I did. You know what happened. I went to Algiers to make my *amende honorable* for having broken the peace of the border, and the Governor—that fat old

Faidherbe who was always trembling for his own skin—waited for no explanation but lost his temper and cursed me. I was 'an ingrate to be viewed with the deepest suspicion,' I was 'a turbulent chief who was a menace to the country.' I was everything that was vile and contemptible and dishonourable. I lost my own temper in the end and cursed him back until I didn't know how I got out of the Palace without being arrested. I left Algiers within the hour and Faidherbe misrepresented the whole case to the Ministry of the Interior, and I have been under suspicion ever since. But what else could I do? I had to fight. I loved Omair. When it came to the pinch I found that my love for him was greater than my love for France. I fought to defend his honour, and what I did later I did to avenge his death—do you blame me?"

His restless eyes swept upward in frowning enquiry and a momentary gleam lit them as Carew shook his head.

"No! but France blames me, and it hurts—damnably. France—" his voice softened suddenly—"what she meant to me once! I loved her, I love her still—the more fool I! She is like a woman—fickle, undependable—courting you today, spurning you tomorrow. But I cannot hate her as I hate women though she has hurt me as women have hurt me. Women! God's curses on them!" he exclaimed violently. "I always detested them, always avoided them, but they made me suffer despite myself. For love of a woman Omair died. The love of a woman took from me my best friend, an Englishman as you are, just when I needed him most. *Bon Dieu*, how I loathe them!" He flung himself back on the sand with a harsh laugh.

The confidence Carew had been expecting ever since they left Biskra had come with a rush. Much of the story was known to him already. A garbled account of the chief's delinquencies had been given to him years ago in Algiers, more he had learned from his numerous Arab friends. That there were faults on both sides was evident, but it was clearly a case where leniency might very well have been extended to a chief who had been one of France's warmest admirers. It had been the last blunder of a weak and unscrupulous Governor whose term of office had been a series of unfortunate happenings. To curry favour with the home authorities he had screened his own hastiness and magnified the chief's offence, forgetting that his scapegoat had it in his power to retaliate in a way that would have cost France much. The Ibn Zarrarah were a large and powerful tribe whose sphere of influence was far reaching and, flushed at the moment with victory, a revolt of more than ordinary magnitude might easily have occurred. Their chief, seething under a sense of injustice, a very little might have turned the scale in favour of rebellion—and wars of suppression were expensive. And often Carew had wondered not at what Said Ibn Zarrarah had done but at what he had left undone. But now as he sat still raking the loose warm sand with his fingers he was thinking more of the chief's concluding words than of his grievance against the French Government.

He looked again at the distant caravan, a mere smudge now on the horizon. He had spent a day and a night with the Arab and his train of followers and he had reason to know that one of those slow moving camels carried the closely screened travelling box of the wife of the man who had cursed all women as heartily and as passionately as ever he had done himself.

"You loathe women—and yet you are married," he said slowly, without turning his head or altering the direction of his gaze.

The chief rolled over with a growl of angry impatience.

"For the sake of the tribe," he flashed. "Do you think by any chance that I did it to please myself! Do I do anything to please myself in these days? I put it off as long as possible, but my people were insistent—the house of Zarrarah had need of an heir."

"And your wife—?" The involuntary question surprised Carew even more than his listener. To an ordinary Arab the remark would have been beyond the bounds of all etiquette and convention; to Said Ibn Zarrarah, western in his ideas even with regard to the sex he despised, it was curious only as coming from the man it did.

"She is happy with her child," he said with a shrug of indifference, and searched for a cigarette in the folds of his burnous. But despite his outward show of unconcern it seemed as if his answer had scarcely contented himself for his black brows were knitted gloomily and his face almost sullen as he sat smoking in silence with his melancholy eyes fixed on the boundless space before him. "Why should she not be happy?" he burst out at length. "She has everything she asks for—the only wonder is she asks so little. She has more liberty allowed her than the average Arab woman—and is too rigid an Arab to make use of it. She is alone in my harem, she has no rival to make her life miserable—and she has borne a son to the house of Zarrarah."

She had borne a son—the supreme desire of the eastern woman.

A shadow crossed Carew's face as he turned and looked at his companion curiously. "And is that no compensation to you? There are those who would envy you your son, Sheik," he said, with a touch of bitterness in his voice. But his question went unanswered and he changed the conversation abruptly.

"You were a fool to leave it to Faidherbe," he said with friendly candour. "You knew what he was, and the attitude he was likely to adopt. You had your chance with the change of administration. His successor is a very different type. He would at least have listened to your explanations with an open mind. He would listen to them now if you chose to make them. But the first move must come from you. You cannot expect the Government to make overtures to one who is *suspect*. I heard the story at the time, of course—Faidherbe's version of it, that is to say. But I could do nothing then. I was practically new to the country and I was not—"

"You were not El Hakim—the eye of France," cut in the chief with a swift smile. Carew laughed.

"Is that what they call me? A blind eye, Sheik, where my friends are concerned." The chief nodded. "That I have also heard. And that is why you are trusted—trusted as few men are in Algeria," he added gravely.

And for a time he relapsed into silence and Carew waited for the suggestion he preferred the other to make. He had a certain influence now with the Government, he could pave the way for a reconciliation—if Said Ibn Zarrarah really desired it. But did he desire it? It was clear from what he had said that in spite of his very natural feeling of resentment the chief nourished no schemes of revenge and had no thought of turning the large forces at his command against the country he still admired. But wounded in his deepest susceptibilities, embittered by years of solitary brooding, would his pride allow him to make overtures that must of necessity be humiliating and would require a certain moral courage to perform? And his present position was a strong one, apart from the injury to his feelings he had little to lose or gain either way.

It was a problem the chief would have to decide for himself. In the years that Carew had worked in the country he had learned to keep his own counsel. He never interfered or gave gratuitous advice, and was chary even of advising when asked. He had come to have a deep insight into the workings of the native mind and he had long since realised the value of neutrality. His rôle of intermediary was possible only so long as his sympathies remained equally divided between the people of the land and their foreign rulers.

And now he waited long for Said Ibn Zarrarah to speak, so long that more than once he glanced covertly at the watch on his wrist. It was time, and past the time, that the chief should start to overtake the caravan that was now no longer distinguishable, and time that he himself set out on the fifty mile ride back to Biskra. Travelling with no camping impedimenta to hinder him he had reckoned on spending the night at a tiny village that was known to him and which made a convenient halting place. He would have to ride hard if the squalid little collection of mud huts was to be reached before the light gave out. Not that either he or Hosein minded a night spent supperless under the stars, but there were the horses to be considered. There was, too, an odd feeling in the air that he had only just realised. The heat that all day had been intense was now suffocating. And as he raised his hand to brush away the moisture lying thick on his forehead, it dawned on him that he had been doing so frequently during the last hour. Instinctively his eyes swept the horizon. There was nothing to break the uninterrupted view, and seen through the shimmering haze that eddied from its surface, the wide expanse of sand looked like the rolling waves of a vast leaden sea. A sullen angry sea that seemed to heave and writhe as though straining to let loose the tremendous forces lying dormant within its mighty bosom. And far off to the southeast, where sky and sand met, a faint dark line like an inky smudge caught Carew's attention and sent him to his feet with a sharp exclamation.

"You were better with your people, Sheik."

At the sound of his voice the chief looked up with a start and sudden anxiety flashed into his eyes as they followed the direction of the other's pointing finger. Then his gaze turned southward and for a moment he stood peering intently as if striving to visualise the caravan that had long since passed out of sight. Without moving he shouted to his men and almost before the words died on his lips his horse was beside him and he swung into the saddle.

Bending down he caught Carew's outstretched hand in a grip that conveyed much he did not utter.

"Some day I may ask you to speak for me," he muttered hurriedly, and was gone in a swirl of dust and sand.

For a minute or two Carew lingered, looking after him, then turned to Hosein who was bringing up the horses. The man jerked his head towards the east. "My lord has seen?" he murmured. Carew nodded. "It may pass," he said, running his fingers caressingly over Suliman's neck before gathering up the reins. But Hosein shook his head. "It will come," he asserted positively, "they know," he added, pointing to the horses whose nervous fidgeting and sweat-drenched coats evidenced uneasiness.

"Then in God's name let it come," replied Carew with a short laugh, "are we children to fear a sandstorm?" And Hosein's grim features relaxed in an answering grin as he held his master's stirrup for him to mount.

Riding, the air seemed less stagnant but the heat increased momentarily and the deep silence of the desert was more strangely silent than usual.

The horses were racing, urged by instinct, and splashes of white foam thrown back from Suliman's champing jaws powdered Carew's dark burnous like flakes of snow.

But it was Said Ibn Zarrarah rather than the approaching sandstorm that engaged his mind as he leant forward in the saddle to ease his weight from the galloping horse. Said's case was only one of thousands of others, he reflected. East or west the problems of life were very similar. The point of view might differ but the problems remained the same. The eternal struggle between duty and inclination was not confined only to the so-called civilized races but raged as fiercely here under the burning African sun as in many more temperate climes. And Said Ibn Zarrarah, trained from boyhood to despotism and self-indulgence, had shown more moral courage than he himself had done. Surrendering to a sense of obligation the Arab had gone back to the life he loathed and assumed duties that were distasteful to him, while he, for a private sorrow, had shirked the responsibilities that were his by inheritance. It was a humiliating truth that was indisputable.

And from Said Ibn Zarrarah, Carew's thoughts wandered to the young wife who was waiting for the coming of the husband who had married her only to satisfy the wishes of his people. It was a strange marriage even for an Arab woman. Though treated evidently with unusual consideration, her life must be a difficult one. Rigidly orthodox, as there was every reason to suppose she was, her lord's western tendencies and liberality of thought would alone be sufficient cause for perplexity and bewilderment. And solitary in a harem that was probably a marvel of oriental sumptuousness, surrounded by everything that a woman could desire, with no spoken wish ungratified, might she not still be longing for more than the cold and empty symbols of a lavish generosity that was prompted only by a sense of what was properly her due as the wife of a powerful sheik? "She has everything she asks for—the only wonder is she asks so little." Unloved and perhaps yearning for the love denied her, were her wants so few by reason of the one want that made all others valueless to her? Said, with his magnificent physique and fine features, was an arresting figure of a man who would appeal to any woman, more particularly to one who could have had little or no opportunity of seeing other men with whom to contrast him. Small wonder if the girl-bride had fallen in love with her stalwart, handsome husband. And he? Was love for her dawning in spite of his professed hatred of women—was the mother of his son already more to him than he realised? He was not as indifferent to her welfare as his words had seemed to imply. He had gone unnecessarily out of his way to endeavour to represent her as contented with her lot. That in itself was significant. And the look that had leaped to his eyes when Carew drew his attention to the threatening storm was certainly not anxiety on his own behalf.

What did the coming years hold for him and the woman he had married? The woman—Carew checked his wandering thoughts with a bitter smile. What had he to do with women and the love of women?

Jerking his head angrily he waved Hosein to his side, and as he turned in the saddle a sudden gust of wind, scorching as the heat from an oven door, struck against his face and a heavy peal of thunder crashed through the intense stillness, reverberating sharply like the prolonged rattling of artillery. For an instant the horses faltered, quivering and snorting, then leaped forward racing neck and neck and, together, the two men looked behind them. The inky smudge on the skyline was blacker and more apparent than it had been, rolling swiftly up like a dense impenetrable wall, and for the first time Carew realised the gloom that, preoccupied, he had not noticed before. There seemed no possibility now of escaping the storm that earlier he had thought would pass too far to the south to touch them, and the prospects for the night should they over-ride the tiny village in the darkness, were not cheering. But it was all in the day's work and he was accustomed to the vagaries of the desert. And there was something in the thought of the approaching struggle with the elements that stirred his blood and made him almost welcome the physical discomfort that would inevitably ensue. It was something tangible he could contend with, something he could do, and doing, forget perhaps for a few hours the strange unrest that had laid so strong a hold on him.

A vivid flash of lightning followed by another deafening roar of thunder stemmed the current of his thoughts and concentrated all his attention on his nervous mount. The pick of his stud, Suliman was the fastest horse Carew had ever ridden, and today, fleeter than usual by reason of his fear, it was difficult to restrain the headlong gallop that threatened to carry him far beyond his companion.

Tightening his grip Carew leant forward soothing the terrified animal with voice and hand. The gloom was increasing, the gusts of hot wind more frequent and of longer duration, bringing with them now the stinging whip of driving sand. There was a distant muttering like the far off surge of waves beating against a rocky coast and suddenly the sun went out, hidden by the racing clouds that swept across the heavens, and with a tearing, whining scream the storm broke.

Reeling under the terrific impact of the wind that staggered even the galloping horses, blinded with the swirling sand, the two men crouched low in their saddles, wrestling with the flapping cloaks they strove to draw closer about them, struggling to keep near to each other, their voices lost in the roar of the tempest. The surrounding country was obliterated and a thick darkness enveloped them. Between his knees Carew could feel the great bay trembling and starting but the strain was eased somewhat from his arms for the need of companionship had driven Suliman close beside the horse Hosein was riding. It was pure chance now where they would find themselves when the storm abated for the darkness and the whirling clouds of sand obscured every landmark. But it was not a matter with which Carew concerned himself. He had been through many sandstorms, fiercer and more prolonged than this one was likely to be. And here they were only catching the fringe of it. Further to the south Said, with his slow moving camels and the burden of women on his hands, was probably in a far worse case and would spend a more uncomfortable night than they would. With a shrug he spat out a mouthful of sand and dragged the heavy burnous higher about his face. The flying particles stung like showers of spraying glass and the reins were rough and gritty between his wet fingers. From time to time he shook off the clinging accumulation but it gathered fast again filtering up his wide sleeves and penetrating through his thick clothing till his whole body was tingling and pricking. But in spite of the discomfort he was happier than he had been for weeks. The fighting instinct in him leaped to meet the fury of the storm. There was no time to think. He lived for the moment, every nerve strained to the utmost, his sombre eyes glowing with a curious look of pleasure, his knees thrust tight against his horse's ribs, his powerful limbs braced to resist the violent gusts that threatened to tear him from the saddle. The fierce howling of the wind, the savage pitilessness of the scene filled him with a strange excitement, making him exult in his own physical strength, the strength that had enabled him to pursue the wild and strenuous life he had made his own. It was nature, capricious and changeful as he had learned to know her—the nature he had turned to in his time of need, the nature he would go back to with undiminished pleasure and confidence. A hard mistress, cruel often, but alluring and compelling for her very waywardness.

The storm had been raging for some time before the rain came, a heavy tropical downpour that, unexpected as it was short lived, drenched the men's thick cloaks and caked the sand on the horse's bodies. It passed quickly and with its going the gloom lessened slightly and the wind abated somewhat of its violence. But Carew placed no faith in the temporary lull. It would blow again later, or he was very much mistaken, and probably harder than before. Meanwhile it was an opportunity to push on, to increase the pace of the horses, whose mad gallop had gradually slackened while the storm was at its height. It was only nerves and the strong wind that had slowed them down. They were capable of a good deal yet in spite of the strain they had gone through. It was not such blind going now but it was still impossible to distinguish any of the outstanding features of the district and the village they were making for could be easily passed within a stone's throw and yet missed. And night was falling rapidly. There was nothing for it but to carry on and trust to luck.

For an hour they rode steadily, huddled in their dripping cloaks, silent as they usually were when together. And the moment, to men even more communicatively inclined than Carew and his taciturn servant, was not conducive to conversation. The air was still impregnated with drifting sand that sifted through to mouth and nostrils in spite of the close drawn cloaks, and the wind made speech difficult. And furthermore, Carew was succumbing to an intense and growing feeling of drowsiness. He had not slept during the hour of the siesta at the oasis and he had been up the greater part of the previous night attending to one of Said's followers who had taken an ugly toss from a stumbling camel. Suliman, his panic subsided, had resumed his usual smooth gallop and his easy movements were sleep inducing. More than once

Carew found his sand-rimmed eyes closing. It was Hosein who noticed the first indication that luck had favoured them and that they were on the right track for the village they had scarcely thought to find. A clump of withered palms clustered beside a broken well that had been dry for years. Carew recognised the mournful little spot with a half-somnolent feeling of detachment and nodded sleepily in response to his servant's exclamation. And it was again Hosein who made the further discovery that drew from him a second exclamation that effectually banished his master's drowsiness.

Almost hidden by the palm trees and the crumbling masonry of the well, two riderless horses stood with dejected, down-drooping heads, ridden to a standstill apparently for even Suliman's angry squeal failed to attract their attention. Motionless like creatures of bronze, their backs to the driving sand, their dangling bridles flapping in the wind, there was something singularly forlorn in their attitude. At sight of them Carew scowled in momentary indecision. He had no wish to be hampered with the care of two spent horses, but it was not a night to pass even an animal in distress. With a word to Hosein, he swung Suliman towards the little dead oasis. The weary beasts took no notice of their approach and did not move as Carew drew rein beside them. A quick glance about him and he slid suddenly out of the saddle. Near by lay an Arab, face downwards on the ground, and a few steps away a powerfully built European sat with his back propped against the broken wall of the well nursing a heavy riding whip across his knees. His head was sunk between his shoulders, his face hidden by the wide brim of the helmet pulled low on his forehead. Rain-drenched and spattered with mud and sand that caked his once immaculate boots and clung closely to the rough surface of his tweed coat, he presented a sorry spectacle, but his plight had evidently not impaired his power of speech for there came from his lips a steady flow of uninterrupted blasphemy that sounded oddly in such a place and at such a time.

Carew was no purist himself, but the unnecessary foulness of the words that assailed his ears roused in him a feeling of disgust and he turned abruptly to the prostrate Arab who seemed in more immediate need of attention. But as he touched him the man rolled from under his hands and stumbling to his feet, shrank away with upraised arm as though to ward off a blow. His eyes were dazed but mingling with the pain in them there was a look of deep hatred, and his bruised and bleeding mouth told their own tale. The individual by the well was evidently a hard hitter as well as a hard swearer. To Carew, the sullen, twitching features were vaguely familiar and it was obvious, when after a few moments the Arab collected himself sufficiently to speak, that he himself was recognised. But he could not place him and the name that was reluctantly vouchsafed conveyed nothing—he knew dozens of Arabs with the same designation. More he could not ask. Whatever were his feelings on the subject he could not interfere between master and servant. But his expression was not pleasant and he was conscious of a rising anger as he swung on his heel to go back to the well. He did not reach it. With slow clenching hands he stood where he had turned staring at the man who was leisurely coming towards him—the man he had been trying to avoid since the night, weeks ago, of the opera. The sodden helmet was pushed back revealing clearly, even in the dim light, the blotched, dissipated looking face that had stirred him to so strange and deadly a hatred. And now, in their close proximity, that strange hatred seemed to increase a thousandfold and it was all Carew could do to preserve semblance of passivity and conceal the boiling rage that filled him. It was like nothing he had ever experienced in his life before. As on that night in Algiers it was sweeping him with a force that was beyond all reason, all explanation. He could not explain it. He could not conquer it. He could only hope to retain the self-command that seemed perilously near to breaking point, for again the same appalling desire to kill was pouring over him. Aghast at the horrible impulse that was almost more than he could resist he thrust his hands behind him to keep them from the weapon that lay hidden in the folds of his waistcloth. And completely oblivious of the storm of passion his presence had evoked, Geradine strode up to him with the swaggering gait and overbearing demeanour that characterised him always, but which was especially notable in his dealings with any native, irrespective of rank. A native to him was a native, an inferior creature little better than the beasts of the field, to be dominated by fear and kept in his place. He stood now, his legs planted widely apart, slapping his boot with his riding whip, surveying Carew through insolent half-closed eyes.

"Look here—" he began, his tone a mixture of truculence and arrogant condescension. "I'm in the devil of a mess. Came out from Biskra for a day or two's camping—missed my people in this infernal sandstorm—all the fault of that fool there. What'll you take to get me out of this bally graveyard? My beasts are knocked up—yours look pretty fresh. Name your price, and for heaven's sake get a move on, I—oh, *damn*!" he broke off with a petulant shrug of annoyance as Carew continued to stare at him with a purposely blank face that was neither helpful nor encouraging. For a few moments, imagining himself to be not understood, he glared wrathfully at the supposed Arab, favouring him with a string of personal epithets that were neither complimentary nor parliamentary. And with contemptuous indifference Carew let him curse. If Geradine had accepted him as an Arab, an Arab he would remain—but not an Arab to be either browbeaten or bribed. He was not in a mood to make things easier for the blustering bully who was working himself up into a state of childish rage. He could alter his tone if he wanted assistance. Nor at the moment was Carew very certain that his assistance would be forthcoming. Why should he go out of his way to help a man he hated! To be left in the predicament in which he was would be a salutary experience that might have a chastening effect on one who was obviously unused to opposition or discomfort in any shape or form. A few privations would do him no harm. And if he died in the desert, which was not in the least likely, his death would probably be a source of relief rather than grief to his friends and relations. Quite suddenly Carew thought of the wife of the man who was facing him. She certainly, if all reports were true, would have no cause to lament a husband she evidently went in dread of. But what was that to him! A surge of anger went through him as his down-bent eyes swept upward to meet the insolent stare fixed on him. The foul-mouthed brute! God, how he hated him! Almost unconsciously he moved a step forward, and there was something menacing in his expression that checked Geradine's flow of language.

With a shade more civility in his tongue he began to repeat his demand in halting French that was scarcely comprehensible. And with typical Arab aloofness Carew waited for him to come to the end of his stumbling explanations. But it was not on his account that he listened to him. It was the need of the wretched servant and the two exhausted horses that swayed him and moved him finally to a reluctant decision.

With a cold word of assent, and a curt gesture that sent the quick blood rushing to the other's face, he turned haughtily as though from an inferior and walked back to the horses, leaving Geradine to stare after him spluttering with rage, twisting and bending the pliable whip between his coarse hands, in two minds whether to follow him or not. Curse the dam' nigger and his infernal cheek, looking at him as if he were dirt! A bit above himself, that chap. That's what came of treating natives as the French did—equality, fraternity and the rest of it, by Gad! A rotten country! Who did the supercilious beggar think he was talking to, anyhow? A silly tourist to be impressed by his dam' airs of superiority? He was hanged if he would stick impudence from any Arab. Coming the free son of the desert over *him*, was he? The blighter could go to blazes, and his horses too for that matter. *He'd* not truckle to any eternally condemned son of a—But a freshening gust of wind that, sand laden, whipped against his cheek with unpleasant suggestiveness cut short his muttered imprecations and quashed his half-formed intention of revoking his demand for assistance and relying on himself to get out of an uncomfortable situation he was convinced was due entirely to the muddle-headedness of his servant. Curse the fool—there hadn't been a job yet that he hadn't mucked up! Recommended for his capabilities, by jove! A well-trained valet and an efficient dragoman, was he? He'd be a bit more trained and efficient when his present employer was done with him. There was only one way of dealing with cattle of that kind, and Malec wouldn't be the first nigger he'd licked into shape, not by a long way. But Malec could wait—he could deal with him later.

With a snarl that boded little good for the unfortunate valet Geradine went with no show of haste to join the group of men and horses by the well-head. Carew was already mounted, wrestling with Suliman who was backing and rearing impatiently. He swung him round as the Viscount approached.

"You can ride my servant's horse," he said in French, "yours can hardly carry themselves. The men will have to walk."

With a grunt which was certainly not an expression of courtesy Geradine took the bridle Hosein offered him and climbed stiffly into the saddle. His drenched condition and his resentment at the authoritative tone addressed to him did not tend to improve either his manners or his temper, and with characteristic pettiness he vented his ill-humour on the object nearest at hand. The horse that had been lent to him was plunging in furious protest at the raking spurs that were being used with unnecessary violence and, losing command of himself, he slashed savagely at the little shapely head with his whip. Twice the heavy thong rose and fell, then a hand like steel closed on his wrist and it was wrenched from him. And, turning with an oath, he found himself confronted by a pair of blazing eyes in which he read not only rage but a totally unexpected hatred that sent an odd sensation of cold rippling down his spine. He flinched involuntarily, dragging his horse aside, conscious for the first time in his life of a feeling of fear. But the strange look that had startled him was gone in a flash and Carew's face was impassive as he reined his own horse back. "Your pardon, *monsieur*, he is unused to a whip," he said icily, and sent the offending weapon spinning into the mouth of the empty well where it fell beyond recovery. Speechless with fury Geradine glared at him, and then, his French too limited to adequately express his feelings, let out a string of curses in his own language which would have given him more pleasure had he known them to be understood. But his hands were fully occupied with the enraged mount and Carew had already ridden on. It was blowing again steadily. Carew, sure now of his bearings, was heading more to the east and the swirling sand was driving straight at them. Muffled in his burnous, his face shielded somewhat by the close drawn haick, he felt it less than Geradine did. But he had no sympathy to waste on the huddled figure behind them with the exhausted horses. For them he was glad that the village lay only a bare three miles away. And even three miles, over rough uneven ground and against a strong wind, was a sufficiently tedious tramp for men unused to walking and hampered by two jaded beasts who required constant encouragement to induce them to move at all. Progress was necessarily slow and more than once Geradine, impatient of the snail's pace at which they were proceeding, let out his fretting horse and dashed on ahead. But ignorant of the way and not relishing the prospect of losing sight of his companions in the growing darkness he was forced each time to curb his impetuosity and wait for the others to come up with him.

For a time he kept silence, but at last his annoyance found utterance. "See here," he exploded angrily, as Carew for the fifth time ranged alongside without seeming to notice the temporary separation, "this isn't a bally funeral! For heaven's sake push on a bit." And as Carew turned to him with an indifferent "*Plâit-il?*" he lost his temper completely. "*Plus vite*, you silly ass," he bellowed. "*Pas un cortège, n'est-ce-pas*—confound you!"

For a moment Carew hesitated, his own temper rising dangerously. Then he shrugged and raising his hand pointed behind him. "The men are walking," he said shortly, and wondered how long it would be before he was goaded into retaliation. To profess ignorance of his mother tongue was easy, to sit quietly under a storm of abuse and personal epithets was rather more difficult. But he had brought it on himself, he

E.M. HULL

had allowed Geradine to think him an Arab and an Arab he would have to remain. To tardily admit his nationality was impossible, it would only make Geradine feel that he had been made a fool of and might probably lead to a quarrel that could easily end disastrously. As it was, his mere presence was almost more than Carew could endure. He had kept a firm hold over himself so far but he knew that a very little more would shatter his self-control. He had voluntarily decided on a certain line of action and he would have to go on with it, if only for the sake of the wretched Arab. Left in the lurch, Geradine would undoubtedly wreck his wrath on the servant who had been already sufficiently manhandled. And again Carew racked his brains to recollect where he had seen the man before. He rarely forgot faces and now, for want of something better to engage his attention, he set himself to discover why the dimly remembered features were familiar. It flashed across him at length. De Granier's man—taken on with the villa, probably, poor devil. A fairly recent addition to the Frenchman's household, Malec had made no very definite impression on the guest he had served but once. But having identified him Carew, casting back in his mind, remembered that de Granier had spoken of him as a curious character, responding to kindness, but sullen when corrected and quick to take offence.

The change from the easy-going Frenchman to service with a brute like Geradine must have been great, and Carew wondered suddenly what induced him to remain with a master he obviously hated. High wages— or a more sinister purpose?—He checked himself abruptly. He would be doing murder by proxy, and rather enjoying it, if he let his thoughts race in this fashion. His own incomprehensible hatred was deep enough without allowing himself to dwell on another's grievances. And for him there was not even the excuse of a grievance. For no reason or cause whatsoever he had hated Geradine at sight. With a shrug of perplexity he drew his cloak closer round him and shook the stinging sand from his bridle hand.

The wind was gathering in force every minute and the light fading rapidly. If it failed entirely and they missed the little village in the darkness there was no other shelter available and Carew did not welcome the thought of a night spent in the open with his present company. At this slow pace the way seemed more like thirty miles than three. But he could not increase it. Even kept to a walk, the horses had outpaced the men and they were some distance behind. Deaf to Geradine's snarl of protest, Carew pulled up and waited until Hosein was alongside of him. And as the man's hand touched his stirrup the storm broke again with redoubled fury and a tearing gust enveloped them in a cloud of blinding sand. For a few moments the horses became almost unmanageable, wheeling backs to the storm and crowding together in a plunging, kicking bunch. They were pulled apart at last and the little party struggled on in the teeth of the wind, choked with the driving particles and straining their eyes through the gloom.

And complete darkness had fallen before they stumbled upon the squalid little collection of mud huts that formed the village. Tenantless, it seemed at first, for no lights shone from the tiny barred windows that were blocked with rags to keep out the drifting sand. But Hosein, despatched in quest of the headman, returned shortly with an elderly Arab who, shrouded in a multitude of filthy coverings, salaamed obsequiously in answer to Carew's shouted enquiry and led them to a hut a little distance away.

Only a hovel it was, but sheltering an amazingly large family—vague, shadowy figures, sexless in their close drawn draperies, who shrank from the vicinity of the strangers and slipped away stealthily into the night with heads bent low and shoulders hunched against the sweeping wind as the headman routed them out unceremoniously to give place to the unexpected visitors. One room, the further portion screened for the use of the women of the family, and indescribably dirty and comfortless. It was nothing new to Carew, use had accustomed him to even greater squalor than this, but Geradine's disgust was evident as he stared about him with curling lip, spitting the sand from his mouth and shaking it from his clothing. Wet and angry, and in no mood to be further inconvenienced, the sight of the horses vigorously propelled into the hut through the narrow entrance moved him to noisy expostulation. With frequent and profanatory lapses into English he managed to convey his total disapproval of the shelter provided for him, which he described as unfit even for pigs, and wrathfully announced his disinclination to share the limited accommodation with "those dam' brutes"—horses and men-servants grouped impartially. His own tired beasts stood shivering and listless but Suliman and Hosein's horses were nervous of their surroundings and for a short space pandemonium reigned in the hut and his remonstrances passed unheeded. When he could hear himself speak again he reiterated his demands loudly. But Carew, who was stooping to unloosen Suliman's girths, waved an indifferent hand towards the door and intimated sharply that if he preferred the sandstorm he was at liberty to remove himself, but that as far as he—Carew—was concerned men and horses remained where they were until the weather conditions improved.

Unused to opposition, and too selfish to think of anything but his own comfort, the flat refusal was all that was needed to stir Geradine's smouldering rage to a white heat of fury. An ugly look swept across his lowering face and he started forward with a threatening gesture. And for a few seconds it seemed as if the open quarrel Carew had feared was now inevitable. Tired and on edge, goaded by the other's insolence and overbearing manner, driven by his own hatred, nothing would have given him greater pleasure than to respond to the provocation offered him. Every instinct urged him to retaliate. He had done already all that could be humanly expected of him, and for two hours he had borne patiently with insults and abuse. He had done enough, and now his patience had reached its limit. And it was Geradine, not he, who was forcing the quarrel. Then why not give him what he asked for? By every means in his power he had tried to avoid him—and fate had thrust them together. Carew's heart beat with a fierce exultant throb, and the atmosphere of the little room seemed suddenly to become electric—alive with naked passions—as the two men stared into each other's eyes. Behind them the Arabs, sensitive of the tension, were watching intently, and Hosein was edging nearer to his master, his hand stealing to the knife in his belt. Then with a tremendous effort Carew thrust from him the temptation to which he had almost succumbed and swinging on his heel without a word turned back to his horse. And checked, despite himself, by a silence he did not understand, Geradine made no further protest, but fell back with an inarticulate growl and crossing the room, dropped down heavily on the cleanest spot he could find, as far removed from the others as possible.

Lighting a cigar with difficulty, for his matches were wet, he smoked sulkily until the horses were unsaddled. Then fumbling in the pocket of his sodden coat he produced a good-sized flask and, gulping down the remaining contents, shouted to the sullen-faced Arab—who was leaning moodily against the wall beside the steaming horses—to bring him more brandy. Apathetically, the man unstrapped the leathern holster from his master's saddle. And, following him, Carew saw the savage kick aimed at him as Geradine snatched the second flask from his outstretched hand. To the multifarious odours that filled the little room was added the reek of raw spirit for the Viscount, whose hand was shaking, spilled as much as he drank of the undiluted cognac with which he sought to quench an unquenchable thirst. Even so, added to what he had previously taken, the allowance was a generous one. But, beyond deepening the colour in his already congested face and further dissatisfying him with his environment, it seemed to make no difference to him for he cursed as fluently and as intelligibly as before as he shivered closer into the corner where he was sitting in a vain attempt to avoid the sweeping draughts that whistled through innumerable cracks in the broken, mud walls of the hut.

With growing hatred and disgust Carew listened to the uninterrupted flow of filthy language, wishing passionately that Geradine's hand had been steadier. Dead drunk he would at least have been silent. Half tipsy and vituperative he was intolerable. Was this what the girl listened to day after day and night after night—Carew flung his wet cloak back with an angry jerk, scowling at the sudden thought. It was no business of his, no business of his, he whispered doggedly as he searched for a cigarette. No business of his—but remembrance, stimulated, was easier than forgetfulness and for long he stared sombrely at the wreathing clouds of faint blue smoke that, curling upward in fantastic spirals, seemed to frame the exquisite oval of a pale, pure face. When at last, by sheer strength of will, he forced his mind back to the immediate present, Geradine's grumbling had ceased and he seemed to be asleep. The men, too, were dozing, though Hosein's hand moved mechanically each time the restless Suliman stamped. The room was perceptibly darker, and looking for the cause, Carew saw that one of the two little earthenware lamps left by the routed family had burnt out and the other was flickering feebly. He wondered if he also had been asleep. And listening for the gusts of wind that before had shaken the crumbling building he realised that the storm had passed. The atmosphere was stifling, and going to the door he wrenched it open and went out into the night. There the change was almost magical. Swept clean, the heavens were blazing with stars and the desert lay calm and still in the soft, clear light of a rising moon whose slanting beams shone silver on the sand. A peace and silence that was gripping. To Carew, still seething with the hatred that a little while since had almost mastered him, the marvellous beauty of the night was like the touch of a healing hand and, watching it, for a time he forgot even Geradine.

E.M. HULL

Behind him the tiny collection of huts straggled dark and mysterious in the deep shadow of a great bare rock that, stark and solitary, rose out of the level plain at some distance from the chain of mountains to which it properly belonged. But he did not look at the sleeping village. It was the desert that held him—the desert that with its silent voice was whispering, enticing, as so often it had whispered and enticed before, drawing him with the glamour of its hidden secrets. Caressingly his eyes swept the moonlit plain. He was one with it now, a nomad for all time. More than the stately house in England, more than the miniature palace in Algiers, it was his home. For ten years he had lived in it. For ten years, seeking to cure his own hurt, he had tried to bring relief to others, fighting misery and disease, appalled by the magnitude of his task and seeming to have accomplished so little. But even the little was worth while. By even the little he was repaid. His toil had not been altogether in vain. By God's grace he had been enabled to do something, and by God's grace he would do still more. In the deep stillness of the eastern night the sense of the Divine Presence was very near and, in all humbleness, Carew prayed from his heart for strength to continue the work that had become his life.

As he arose from his knees Hosein came to him, uneasy at his absence and the unwilling bearer of a message.

"The English lord is hungry," he announced briefly, with patent scorn in his voice that Carew affected not to hear. The situation was already sufficiently difficult without having to reprove his servant for a lapse that was due entirely to Geradine's own behaviour.

With a last glance at the shining stars he went reluctantly back to the hut.

Half hidden in a haze of cigar smoke and aggressively wide awake Geradine hailed his appearance with no more civility than before.

"Clear out those cursed beasts," he shouted truculently. "I can't sleep in a damned stable! And get me something to eat. Something—to— eat. *Quelque chose à manger, comprenez?*—you blasted fool!" he added, pantomiming vigorously. The blood rolled in a dark wave to Carew's face but determined to keep his temper he swallowed the retort that sprang to his lips and gave the required orders with apparent unconcern. But he smiled inwardly as he watched the men lead the horses away. It was very doubtful whether food of any kind would be procurable at this time of night, and even if Hosein's endeavours met with success it was not likely that Geradine would appreciate the rough fare of the necessitous little village. Nor, he was convinced, would the handful of crushed dates he carried in his waistcloth prove any more acceptable.

And when at length Hosein returned with a bowl of curdled camel's milk he was not surprised that the Viscount, after one glance of mingled dismay and repugnance, rejected both it and the unsavoury looking little mass of sand covered fruit with a disgusted "Lord, what beastly muck!" and retired into his corner with his hunger unsatisfied to curse himself to sleep. He was still sleeping heavily when Carew woke with the dawn and went out to find Hosein and the horses and make arrangements for Geradine's return to Biskra. It was not his intention that they should ride together. His sole desire was to get away as quickly as possible from the vicinity of the man he hated more vehemently than ever.

Last night he had controlled himself only by a super-human effort. This morning he felt he could no longer trust himself. To escape the leave taking that was otherwise unavoidable he did not go back to the hut when, an hour later, he was ready for the road and had concluded his interview with Malec and the headman of the village.

But as his foot was in the stirrup Geradine appeared, yawning sleepily, and swinging his arms to get the stiffness out of them. Having wakened for once without his customary morning headache he was in a better temper than usual. Apparently oblivious of his incivility of the previous evening he lounged forward with an air of condescending geniality, prepared evidently to make himself agreeable. His shouted greeting terminated in a loud laugh as he glanced at Carew, clean shaven and immaculate as Hosein always contrived he should be, and then at his own soiled clothing.

"You look smart enough, by Gad," he said, fingering his rough chin tenderly, "where the devil do you find water and a razor in this filthy little hole? You're off early—what's your hurry? Oh, damn it, I forgot you can't speak English. Well, never mind, you're a sportsman whatever you are. I'd have been in the soup last night if you hadn't come along. Many thanks—dash it, I mean *très obligé, mille remerciments*—and all the rest of it, don't you know." And with another laugh he thrust out his hand.

But incited by the gentle pressure of his rider's heel Suliman plunged wildly and shot away leaving Geradine with his arm still outstretched, half annoyed and half amused at Carew's abrupt departure.

　　　　　　　　　　　　　　　　　　　　E.M. HULL

Proud as Lucifer, like every other potty little chief he had ever met—but the beggar could ride, he reflected as he stood looking after the galloping horsemen, and the man he had with him was worth a dozen of the fool *he* was landed with. And yawning again he turned back to the hut and roared for the fool in question.

VIII

In her bedroom at the Villa des Ombres Marny Geradine was standing before the open window staring out into the darkness. She stood very still, her colourless face set like a mask of marble, her hands clasped tightly behind her. Only the tempestuous rise and fall of her delicately rounded bosom betrayed the inward tumult that was raging within her. Five minutes ago she had dismissed a white faced and pleading Ann and now, alone, she was facing a decision that took all her courage to sustain.

It was the night of the Governor's annual ball. By now she should have been dressed. But the wonderful Paris creation that Geradine had insisted on ordering specially for the occasion still lay in shimmering folds on the *chaise longue* and Marny had not changed from the simple teagown in which she had dined.

She was not going to the ball. She was not going to submit again to the open shame and humiliation that had been her portion throughout her married life but which during the last few weeks had reached a culminating point of horror. Her husband's gross intemperance, his notorious infidelities, his callous disregard for anything beyond his own pleasure, had driven her at last to rebellion. She had reached the end of her endurance. She knew that at home she must continue to suffer the brutal treatment he meted out to her but she had resolved never to appear in public with him again. How would he receive her decision? How would she brave his anger? Why did she think only of his strength, of the hectoring bullying voice she dreaded, of the merciless hands that made her shrink in physical fear that was an agony? Intolerant of the least opposition to his lightest wish what would he do to her! A shudder of pure terror ran through her. If he would only come—as she knew he would come to demand the reason of her lateness. Waiting was torture.

And yet when the door burst open and banged violently to again and she heard his heavy step behind her the dread she had felt before was as nothing to the paralysing fear that now rushed over her robbing her of all power of movement.

She could have shrieked when his hands closed with crushing force on her shoulders and he swung her round to face him. But she managed to control herself and meet his furious stare courageously. He was in the quarrelsome stage of semi-intoxication that of late had been his usual state, drunk enough to be cruel and vindictive, sober enough to be dangerous.

"Not dressed yet! What the hell have you been doing all this time? You're damnably late!"

She was used to being sworn at, she had come to feel that nothing he could say could hurt her any more, and tonight it did not seem to matter very much what he said.

She forced herself to answer him.

"I'm not going to the ball, Clyde."

He glared at her in speechless anger, his hands slipping from her shoulders, his dark red face flushing deeper, the veins on his forehead standing out like whipcord.

"The devil you're not! And why, might I ask?" he bellowed furiously. Panic driven, the temptation to evade the issue she had raised, the cowardly impulse to plead illness to allay his wrath was almost more than she could suppress. But she fought back the words that rushed to her lips and turned away with a little hopeless gesture.

"You know why," she said in a low voice.

"I'm damned if I do!"

She turned to him swiftly.

"You know, Clyde," she said steadily, "you know perfectly well why I dread going out with you. You've known ever since we were married."

"I know you're a little fool," he retorted angrily. "Look here, Marny, I've had enough of this nonsense. You'll go to this dam' ball whether you like it or not, just as you will go anywhere and everywhere I choose you shall go. I'll give you ten minutes to be ready—not a second more. And you can keep your infernal objections to yourself in future. I'm not going to be preached at by anybody, much less by you. Look sharp and don't keep me waiting any longer. Ten minutes—that's your limit," he shouted and moved as if to leave the room. She shivered, her pale face whiter than before, but her determination was stronger than her fear.

"It's no use, Clyde. I'm not going," she said slowly. And for the first time he heard a ring of obstinacy in her voice. He swung back towards her, staring at her for a moment incredulously, rocking slightly on his feet, his big hands clenching as he worked himself up to a pitch of passionate rage.

"You mean that?" he said thickly. Her dry lips almost refused their office.

"Yes," she whispered faintly.

"You deliberately disobey me?" She wrung her hands in sudden agony. "I've always obeyed you, always done what you wished—but this—oh, I can't. I *can't*!"

He towered over her, his bloodshot eyes menacing. "You can't?" he sneered. "I rather think you both can and will. There's only one person in this house who says 'can't'—and that's me. You'll do what you're told, now and always. Put on that dress—and God help you if you keep me waiting!"

She lifted a quivering face of desperate appeal.

"Clyde—I—*Clyde*!" Her voice broke in a cry of terrible anguish as he struck her, the whole weight of his powerful body behind the smashing blow that sent her reeling across the room to fall with a sickening crash on the parquet floor.

He looked down at her callously, his crimson face twitching, his big frame shaking with passion. Then he walked slowly across the room and sat down heavily on the bed, his smouldering eyes still fixed with a look of cruel satisfaction on the prostrate little figure that lay so still. He had no compunction for what he had done. She had come to the wrong shop if she thought she was going to roughride him with any of her silly notions. He would jolly well make it clear to her tonight that he would brook no disobedience, no questioning of his habits, no thwarting of his wishes. Damned little puritan—who shrank from his embraces as if she were a ravished nun instead of a normal athletic young woman with healthy red blood in her veins. He wanted a mate in his arms not a beautiful piece of statuary whose reserve and coldness infuriated him. She was his wife—and dam' lucky to be so. She might have been on the streets if it hadn't been for him. If she wasn't satisfied—well, he'd a grievance himself if it came to that. They'd been married five years, why the devil hadn't she given him the heir he wanted? And lashing himself to greater fury he waited, making no effort to aid her until she regained consciousness. She stirred at last, moaning with pain, her slender body convulsed with terrible shuddering. Dragging herself to her feet she stood swaying giddily, her hands pressed on her throbbing temple, her heavy eyes looking listlessly about her till they rested at length on Geradine's massive figure and into them there flashed suddenly the horror of dawning remembrance. With a little choking sound she turned and staggering a few steps fell into a chair before the dressing table, burying her head in her arms amongst the costly appointments that littered its shining surface, her shoulders shaking with hard tearless sobs.

And as Geradine had watched her insensible so did he watch her now, pitiless and unmoved. He had no use for half measures. If she had to be taught a lesson it should be at least a thorough one. He lurched to his feet and strode across the room, halting beside her with his arms folded across his broad chest, his foot beating with angry impatience against the floor. "How much longer are you going to keep me waiting?"

The harsh words jarred like a stab of actual pain and sick and faint she raised her eyes to his. One look convinced her of his determination. He meant it, oh, very well she knew he meant it! Too dazed, too broken to oppose him further she knew that she would have to obey; that, cost her what it might, she would have to dress and go with him. With a stifled gasp of pain she struggled to her feet, her head reeling, and caught at the table for support, pushing the heavy hair off her forehead and wincing as her fingers touched her injured temple.

"If you will please go I will ring for my maid," she muttered indistinctly, choking back the hysterical sobs that rose in her throat. "I'll go when it suits me, and you'll ring for no maid," he said sharply. "You'll dress a dam' sight quicker with me in the room. It won't be the first time I've valeted you, and it won't be the last I'm willing to bet. And I'm hanged if I'll have that grim faced old harridan you call your maid poking her nose in where she isn't wanted. I'm about fed up with her as it is. She's not the kind of woman I want about you, anyhow. She'll have to go, and the sooner the better. You can pay her her wages tomorrow and tell her to clear out by the first available boat."

"*Clyde!*" The sharp cry was wrung from her. And forgetting her pain, her fear, everything but the heartless ultimatum he had launched at her she sprang towards him, clutching at him with trembling hands, her face working convulsively, pleading as she would not have stooped to plead for herself.

"Clyde, Clyde, you don't mean it, you *can't* mean it! You can't send her away, you couldn't be so cruel. She's old, I'm all she's got, it would kill her to leave me. And you promised—you promised me faithfully I might keep her. It will break her heart. Oh, Clyde, be generous. Do what I ask, just this once. If you let me keep her I'll never oppose you again. I'll do anything you wish—I'll be anything you wish—"

A sneering look of triumph crossed his face as he flung her from him. "You'll do as I wish without any bargains, my lady," he said significantly. "You've had your orders and there's an end of the matter. The thing's finished. And might I remind you that the horses have already been waiting an hour?"

That was apparently all that mattered to him. Of less value at the moment than the pedigreed animals he prided, distress of mind, the pain and weariness of her bruised and aching body was beyond his consideration. A feeling of numbness came over her, a kind of frozen apathy that seemed to turn her into a mere automaton, and without a word she turned slowly to do his bidding. She had a curious impression that the white-faced weary-looking woman reflected in her mirror was some other than herself, that, divorced from her own body, she was watching the suffering of a total stranger. And as she dressed with mechanical haste only one thing was clear and instant with her—the consciousness of menacing eyes that followed her every movement until their burning stare became a veritable torment. But, throughout the process of her toilet he spoke only once, a characteristic remark: "Put a bit o' colour on your face. You're as white as a ghost."

"I haven't any," she faltered.

"Haven't—any? Good God!" he exclaimed and relapsed into silence. But when she was dressed he came to her, and as his critical gaze travelled slowly over her slim figure the heavy scowl smoothed from his face and the old look of proprietory admiration crept back into his eyes. With the quick change of mood that was so marked in him he caught her in his arms with sudden passion. "Damn it all, Marny, what the devil do you want to make me lose my temper for?" he grumbled petulantly. "Give me a kiss, and don't be such a little fool again."

Sick with loathing but helpless against his strength perforce she lifted her face to his. But unsatisfied he laughed with angry contempt. "Do you call that a kiss? Gad, you've a lot to learn!" he said scornfully, and crushed his mouth once more against her trembling lips. Then he let her go and, swelling with the sense of his own magnanimity, hurried her with heavy jocularity to the waiting carriage, there to soothe his ruffled feelings with a cigar which he smoked in silence during the short drive into Algiers.

And huddled in her own corner of the roomy victoria Marny leaned back and rested her aching head against the cushions, staring before her with fixed unseeing eyes.

During the five years that had been a physical as well as mental martyrdom she had suffered much at her husband's hands. In the furious rages to which he was liable he had often hurt her cruelly but until tonight he had never deliberately struck her. But it was not of his brutality towards herself that Geradine's wife was thinking now as the carriage rolled swiftly along the deserted road. Her mind was filled with only one thought. Ann! How to tell her. How to break to the faithful old woman the fact that her lifelong service must end so abruptly, so callously? Where would she go, what would she do? To face the world again at seventy! Marny's hands clenched in sudden anguish. Would she even be allowed to help her if necessity arose? Herself she was penniless, Castle Fergus had passed to Geradine and she was dependent on him even for the very *sous* she flung to the Arab beggars who clustered round her carriage. How, after tonight, could she ever appeal to him again. And yet, for Ann's sake, she knew that she would have to make that appeal and court not only his almost certain refusal but the consequent anger that would assuredly be directed against herself. Why was she such a craven, why did the thought of her own miserable suffering obtrude when it was Ann, and only Ann, who mattered!

Her husband's impatient voice roused her to the fact that the carriage was at a standstill. Tonight, the gala night of the year, the Governor's palace was filled to overflowing, a scene of vivid animation, gorgeous with oriental splendour, rioting with colour and echoing with a confusion of voices laughing and chattering in a score of different languages. The spacious rooms, flaming with lights and decorated with a wealth of scented flowers, were crowded—a motley gathering of nearly every race and creed moving in a never ceasing stream to the strains of the crashing military band.

The gaudy costumes of the desert sheiks, the crimson burnouses of the grave-faced Caids, the striking and picturesque uniforms of Spahis and Zouaves made distinctive notes in the brilliant assembly that eclipsed even the radiant hues of the marvellous toilettes of the French and English ladies.

To Marny, dazzled by the light and deafened by the uproar, it seemed as if she had stepped suddenly into pandemonium. For once she was even glad of the nearness of her husband whose burly figure was an effectual barrier against the press that thronged them as they moved slowly towards the low dais where the Governor, heated and weary with handshaking but beaming with happiness and hospitality, stood amongst a group of highly placed officials and European consuls. Near him General Sanois, less obviously enjoying himself, was deep in conversation with a tall and venerable-looking Caid. And at the foot of the dais was clustered a little group of sheiks from the far south, gazing about them with calm aloofness but keenly alive to every detail and circumstance of the evening's entertainment.

There were many curious glances that followed and many eager tongues that discussed the tardy appearance of the two important English guests as they made their slow passage across the room, and the Governor whose twinkling eyes were roving constantly in quest of new faces was quick to notice their arrival. Punctilious to a nicety he stepped forward to greet them with a deference that was due to Geradine's rank and to the beauty of his wife. But as she responded to his gallant and happy little speech of welcome Marny's voice faltered slightly and her pale face flushed with a wave of beautiful colour, for near her in the little group of desert men beside the dais she saw Carew standing clad like them in native robes but distinguished by the dark blue burnous he affected. And Geradine, whose French was as limited as was the Governor's English, while replying somewhat laboriously to his host's courtesies had also noticed the tall Arab-clad figure and grasped eagerly at the chance of cutting short a conversation that bored him infinitely.

"I'm hanged if that isn't my friend of the sandstorm," he exclaimed, and waved pointedly at Carew who, unwilling to add to the public attention already aroused, came forward reluctantly and submitted to a boisterous greeting. With a loud laugh Geradine turned again to the visibly astonished Governor. "Seems a decent sort of chap," he said condescendingly. "Pulled me out of no end of a hole in the desert a week or two ago. Introduce him to my wife, will you? She's interested in the natives. And, Marny," he added, his own slight interest already evaporating, "you speak the lingo better than I do, say something civil to the fellow—only for heaven's sake remember he's a Mohammedan and don't put your foot into it and enquire for his wife and family. And when you're tired of him His Excellency will find you partners if you want to dance. I'm off to get a drink." And with a careless nod he swung on his heel in search of the nearest buffet.

His graceless incivility was no more than much that Marny had been called upon frequently to endure but tonight his boorishness was almost more than she could bear. His mistake with regard to Carew though regrettable was a perfectly natural one, but his cavalier treatment of the courteous little Frenchman was unpardonable. Scarlet with shame and confusion she could find no words to break the awkward silence that ensued. But the Governor, whose saving sense of humour was fortunately greater than his feeling of mortification, plunged nobly into the breach and made the best of the embarrassing situation in which he found himself. "Madame," he stammered, with twitching lips, "I—I have the honour to present to you Monsieur Carew—a compatriot of your own," and fled to hide his secret enjoyment of a contretemps he found exquisitely amusing. Carew the woman hater—and he had just introduced him to the most beautiful woman in Algiers. *Bon Dieu, quelle comédie!* But to Marny it was no comedy. Miserable and tongue-tied, giddy with pain, she tried vainly to collect herself, to formulate some adequate excuse that should cover her husband's blunder and lessen the resentment she was sure the man beside her must feel at being publicly forced into an action that was totally against his universally known principles. Would he blame her for being the cause, though the unwitting cause, of his present predicament? Would he too leave her in this crowded room, the cynosure of curious eyes, to find her way alone to the group of English dowagers with whom she had the slightest acquaintance? Super-sensitive and innately shy the very thought of it made her shrink. The few seconds that had passed since the Governor's hurried departure seemed magnified into hours. Angry at her own gaucherie she had nerved herself to make some halting apology when the opening bars of a waltz rising above the din of conversation occasioned a general rush for partners and in the comparative quiet that followed she heard the deep soft voice that had become so dear to her speaking with the slow hesitancy she had noticed before.

"You are looking very tired, Lady Geradine. Shall I take you out of this babel?"

And almost before she realised it she found herself walking beside him down the length of the long room, piloted skilfully between the dancing couples who already filled the floor. Once or twice he paused to exchange a nod and a passing word with a uniformed officer or an isolated group of Arabs, but she hardly noticed these slight interruptions and at length they reached the rapidly emptying entrance hall. Crossing it he turned down a short corridor that opened into a little winter garden where chairs were placed amongst palms and banks of tropical plants. At the moment the place was deserted. And quiet and dimly lit to Marny it seemed a haven of refuge after the glare and noise of the crowded reception rooms. With a feeling of relief she followed him to a fern-screened couch at the further end of the conservatory and sank into the low seat, stripping the long gloves from her hands and closing her eyes wearily. And looking down at her Carew saw her face convulsed with a sudden spasm of pain.

He was still inwardly raging at the incident of a few minutes ago, still seething with the strange hatred that had laid so strong a hold upon him—hatred that, aggravated by Geradine's discourteous and overbearing manner, seemed tonight to have reached its culminant pitch. It was with difficulty that he had controlled himself just now in the ballroom. But something had restrained him, something—more impellent even than his desire to avoid a collision that could only have ended in a public fracas—that had risen up within him at the sight of the girl's strained face. And as he looked at her now with his black brows drawn together in a heavy scowl he was still wondering at the impulse that had come to him to shield her, still trying vainly to understand his own motive in bringing her here. What had prompted him?

Was it anger or pleasure or only pity he felt as he stared again at the little drooping figure? A curious expression crept into his sombre eyes. What a child she looked—what a weary white-faced child!

"You ought to be at home and in bed," he said, almost roughly. "Can I get you anything—champagne or a cup of coffee?"

She glanced up with a start.

"No, please, it's nothing. Only a headache," she stammered. "I don't know what's the matter with me tonight," she added with a shaky laugh. "I'm not given to headaches. I'm as strong as a horse, really." But as she uttered her valiant little boast her voice broke and she looked away, twisting her gloves nervously between her hands. He could see that she was struggling with herself but he made no attempt to forestall the explanation he guessed was coming and waited, still standing, for her to speak. She turned to him at last, her troubled gaze not reaching his face but lingering on the picturesque details of his Arab dress.

"Sir Gervas—I'm sorry—that stupid blunder—" she faltered. Then suddenly her eyes met his and words came tumbling out in breathless haste. "—but you were with him that night in the desert, you let him think you were an Arab. He couldn't possibly know you were English, that you could understand—"

"Do you think I mind being taken for an Arab?" he interrupted, pulling his heavy cloak closer round him and sitting down beside her. "It was a perfectly natural mistake and not worth a moment's consideration, certainly not worth the value of a pair of gloves," he added with a faint smile. And reaching out he drew them deliberately from between her twitching fingers. His voice was extraordinarily gentle but there was in it an underlying note of finality that made further apology impossible, and with a little sigh she relapsed into silence.

For a time she watched him smoothing the creases from the crumpled gloves, wondering at his unexpected presence.

"I didn't think you would be here tonight," she said at length. "You don't really like—this sort of thing, do you?" she added, with a vague movement of her hand towards the distant ballroom.

"Loathe it," he answered promptly, moving slightly to face her and settling his long limbs more comfortably into the corner of the sofa. "But I make a point of coming to this particular function if I happen to be in Algiers. I meet old friends."

"Desert friends?"

He nodded assent to the eager question.

"Is that why you wear Arab dress?"

"Partly," he shrugged, "they would hardly know me in European clothes. But principally because I prefer it."

"As you prefer to speak Arabic or French, rather than English?" she hazarded.

"How do you know?"

She flushed under his stare and looked away with an odd little smile.

"When you talk you stop sometimes as if you were searching for a word," she said, rather hesitatingly, "and the other day, in the Bouzaréa woods, half the time you were speaking in French."

"I have scarcely spoken English for twelve years," he said shortly. Then as if to cover the slight piece of personal information he had let slip he added:

"There is no longer any need for you to restrict your rides, Lady Geradine. The woods are safe enough now."

She turned to him swiftly. "What do you mean?" she said with sudden breathlessness. And as she listened to his bald unvarnished account of the end of Abdul el Dhib the colour that had risen to her face died out of it leaving her white to the lips. She was shivering when he finished, her hands clenching and unclenching in her lap. "And it was because of me—because of what you did for me that night," she burst out passionately. "Oh, I never thought, I never guessed the risk you were taking! And you knew all the time! It was he you meant when you warned me not to ride alone. It was he you thought was coming that morning in the woods when Tanner brought the horses, and that very night—oh, if he had killed you, it would have been *my* fault! And I—I—" She pulled herself up sharply, aghast at the sound of her own voice, at the confession that had been almost wrung from her. A wave of burning colour suffused her face and tingling with shame she averted it hastily, veiling her eyes with the thick dark lashes that swept downward to her cheek—but not before he had seen the look that flashed into them, a look that sent the blood racing madly through his veins and made his heart leap with sudden violence. For a moment he sat rigid, stunned with self-realisation, the hands that were clasped around his knee tightening slowly until the knuckles shone white through the tanned skin. Then with a tremendous effort he mastered himself.

"Nobody's fault but my own, I'm afraid," he said with forced lightness. "I knew the man I was dealing with. I have good friends in Algiers who gave me warnings in plenty and because I chose to ignore them what happened was due to my carelessness."

"It still doesn't lessen my obligation," she said in a stifled voice. But his quiet tone, his imperturbable manner was fast restoring her own self-possession. Indifferent himself, why should he guess the true cause of her agitation? Perhaps what had seemed so blatant to her had escaped him, and he had seen in her outburst only a natural womanly distress for the danger of a man who had risked his life on her behalf. And the formal courtesy of his next words further reassured her. "There was never any obligation," he said quietly. "I merely did what anybody else would have done under the circumstances." And abruptly he changed the conversation to the recent race meeting at Biskra. Convinced that he had not divined her secret, her feeling of self-consciousness and restraint wore gradually away and only the joy of his companionship remained. She would get from it what she could, she would live for the moment and its transient happiness and leave to the future the misery and loneliness that was going to be so much harder to bear than it had ever been. Enough that she was with him and that she loved him, loved him as she had never thought it possible to love. A love that should be her secret strength in the bitter years to come.

Silence fell between them again. And content to wait until he should choose to speak she sat very still beside him, watching him covertly as he leant back with his hands clasped behind his head, his half-shut eyes staring straight before him as if he saw more than the ferns and fairy lights at which he was looking. Tonight his face seemed graver, sterner than she had ever seen it. A tragic face it appeared to her, a face that bore the deep-cut marks of sorrow and disappointment. And she wondered, with a dull pain in her heart, what had been the tragedy that had driven him to the solitary wilds of the desert. She knew nothing of his history, his name and the nature of his work amongst the Arabs were all that Mrs. Chalmers had confided, and she had no means of ever knowing. A being apart, a type that had been a revelation, he would pass out of her life, abruptly as he had come into it, to forget her in the greater interest of his chosen vocation. It was strange to think of him as a doctor, living a life of arduous toil and terrible risk. Into what savage and lonely places must he go to wrestle with the pain and suffering he sought to alleviate. El Hakim—the desert healer! And she, who loved him, would have no knowledge of his achievements, would never know the final happening that would terminate that life of noble and self-sacrificing endeavour. In the pitiless years that stretched so barrenly ahead she would have only a memory to cling to, a memory that would be at once her consolation and her pain. Into the tender, brooding eyes fixed on him there came a look of mingled pride and anguish. He would never know, thank God he would never know! But if he had cared, if she had brought sorrow to him—she caught her trembling lip fiercely between her teeth and began with fumbling haste to draw on the long gloves he had laid on the sofa between them.

"Oughtn't we to be going back to the other room?"

He turned his head slowly.

"There's plenty of time," he said lazily, "they are still dancing."

"But your desert friends—"

"—can wait," he said succinctly. And dreading the noisy ballroom, too tired and too utterly indifferent at the moment to care if she was outraging the proprieties Marny did not press the matter. The quiet conservatory, the restfulness and courage she seemed to derive from the mere presence of the man beside her were giving her strength to meet the ordeal that still lay before her, the ugly scene that invariably terminated Geradine's so-called nights of amusement. It would happen tonight, as it always happened, and she would have to go through with it. For how many more years? She thrust the thought from her and turned again to Carew. But before she could speak the peaceful little winter garden was invaded. Not a dancing couple seeking for a solitary spot in which to continue a flirtation begun in the ballroom but two men who, deeming the place empty, did not trouble to modulate their voices as they took possession of a wicker seat a few feet away from the fern-hidden sofa.

"And this *soi-disant countess*—this copper-haired goddess you are raving about—" the words were uttered in fluent French but with a rough Slavonic accent.

"*Soi-disant!* I have it from her own lips," interrupted an indignant voice that Carew recognised as belonging to Patrice Lemaire.

"Possibly," was the caustic rejoinder, "but not necessarily correct for all that. An Austrian, you say, from Vienna? The wife of a Count Sach who held a court appointment, and who abused her infamously—and now, since his death, a lady of independent means who travels through Europe trying to forget her unhappy past?"

"That is what I said. Do you doubt it?"

"Your word, no. But the lady's—yes."

"Why?"

"You forget, my friend, that I am also of Vienna. I have no recollection of a Count Sach who held a court appointment, or of the lady who styles herself Countess Sach. And she is no more Austrian than you are, Lemaire. From her accent I should judge her to be English."

"English? Bah! She doesn't speak a word of the language."

"She was speaking it very fluently half-an-hour ago with the *grand Anglais* who is drinking himself tipsy in the buffet."

"With Geradine—that *beast*! *Bon Dieu*, she said the very sight of him revolted her!"

"She will probably find the contents of his pocketbook less revolting, my credulous young friend. *Une femme de moeurs légères*, or I'm very much mistaken."

And listening to the cynical laugh that followed, Marny wondered bitterly what more of shame and humiliation was yet in store for her. At the first mention of her husband she had been startled into a quick involuntary movement but a strong arm had held her back in her seat and cool, steady fingers had closed warningly over her ice-cold hands. Wrestling with her own misery, she was scarcely conscious of Lemaire's furious protest or of the stormy altercation that ensued, and when at last the sound of the men's angry voices died away as they took their dispute elsewhere it was some time before she realised that her hands still lay in Carew's firm grasp. She disengaged them silently. There was nothing to say, nothing that either of them could say. They had overheard what was not intended for them to hear. And the Austrian's insinuations were very likely true. Geradine had spoken more than once of the beautiful Viennese who had recently dawned on Algiers society with no introductions but with an audacity of manner that had served her amply instead. That his acquaintance had probably developed into a more intimate relationship was no matter for surprise to the wife who was fully aware of his flagrant infidelities. It was only one more insult added to the many indignities he had put upon her, one more humiliation to bear—and ignore.

But if she was to retain any kind of hold over herself she must end at once the brief companionship that had given her so much happiness. The proximity of the man beside her, the sense of his unspoken sympathy, the sudden realisation of the sensuous appeal of her surroundings with its dim obscurity and intoxicating odour of languorous-scented flowers was filling her with an overwhelming fear of herself. She dared not stay with him, dared not give way to the emotion which, growing momentarily greater, seemed to be robbing her of all strength. The exalted feeling that before had made her glad that only she should suffer was weakening in the natural, human longing for the love that would never be hers. If she could but tell him, could feel if only for once the clasp of his arms around her, the touch of his lips on hers! She shivered. What was she thinking—what shameless thing had she become? And trembling with the very madness of her own wild thoughts she rose quickly to her feet, her face coldly set, her voice tuned to level indifference.

"I am quite rested now, Sir Gervas. Shall we go back to the ballroom?" Moving away as she spoke she gave him no option but to follow her, and an incoming stream of people put a period to anything but trivial speech between them.

In the central hall, crowded so as to make progress almost an impossibility, an artillery colonel caught at Carew's arm in passing. "When you have time, *mon cher*," he said hurriedly. "His Excellency is asking for you. He is in the White Salon with Sanois and the chief of the Ben Ezra."

Marny glanced contritely at her escort. How long since he had taken her out of the crowded ballroom, how long had she trespassed on his time?

"I am afraid I have monopolised you very selfishly," she murmured shyly, "You must have so many friends."

But her faltering words seemed to be lost in the din of voices, for he made no answer and his attention appeared to be wholly engaged in fending from her the jostling press which surged around them. And five minutes later he had left her with the British Consul's wife and was retracing his steps to join the informal conference that was taking place in the White Salon.

He did not go back to the public rooms and the end of the evening found him still sitting in the Governor's study with Sanois and a few of the more Gallicized chiefs. And for some time after the sheiks had retired he lingered chatting with the general, delaying as long as possible the moment when he must face alone the shattering self-understanding that had come to him.

The chiming of a deep-toned clock warned him at length of the lateness of the hour and he had risen reluctantly to his feet when Patrice Lemaire burst into the room. The boy's usually smiling face was flushed with anger and he flung himself into a chair with an explosion of wrath that did not tend to make more comprehensible the rambling sentences he let fall. That somebody had gone home early and defrauded him of the dances she had promised; that somebody else, name witheld, was a vile calumniator; and that there had been a "beastly scene," which he did not particularise, was all he would vouchsafe. And unable to get anything more definite from him the elder man soon left him to nurse his grievances in solitude.

There were still a few guests wandering about the hall waiting for carriages that were delayed, and a harassed attache seized upon Carew to beg a lift for an elderly Frenchman who was forlornly contemplating a weary walk back to his hotel at Mustapha.

Only when he had dropped his talkative companion was Carew able to give full sway to his own thoughts, and when he reached the villa he walked up the flagged path too absorbed to notice the shafts of light filtering through the closed jalousies of the big front room which, though kept in scrupulous orderliness, had never been used since his mother's death.

He passed into the Mauresque hall and was moving slowly in the direction of his own rooms when Hosein, emerging from a shadowy corner, glided forward to intercept him.

"The *lalla*," he murmured hesitatingly, his hands sweeping upward to his forehead in a quick salaam.

His master faced him swiftly.

"The lalla—?" he repeated sharply.

The big Arab nodded.

"The *lalla* who awaits my lord," he said softly.

For a moment Carew's heart seemed to stand still and under the deep tan his face went suddenly white. She had come to him—God in heaven, she had come to him! Hosein's tall figure was wavering curiously before him as he forced a question in a voice he did not recognise for his own.

"Where?"

"In the salon, lord," replied Hosein and gave way with another deep salaam. And the whispering swish-swish of his robes had died away before Carew moved.

"In the salon—" He started violently. She had come to him—and he—. His face was rigid as he went towards the painted door.

It yielded to his touch and swung to noiselessly behind him, too noiselessly to be heard by her who, at the further end of the room, was standing before the portrait from which she had stripped the curtains that had veiled it for so many years. She was humming a little song, a frankly indecent song of the boulevards, her copper-crowned head thrown back, her gleaming shoulders twitching from time to time with a petulant movement of impatience.

And behind her, leaning against the portiere in which his hands were clenched, Carew stood as if turned to stone staring—staring—not at the slender, girlish form he had hoped and yet dreaded to see, but at the tall sinuously graceful figure of the woman who had been his wife. His wife—that brazen thing of shame, half naked in a dress whose audacity revolted him! Fool, fool to have thought his own mad longing possible!—to have thought that *she*—He wrenched his thoughts from her. And the other? Why had he not guessed, why had nothing warned him when he sat listening in the little winter garden to the angry protests of Patrice Lemaire and the caustic comments of the Austrian who "was also of Vienna!" And yet, how could he have known, how imagine that she could ever come into his life again. And why had she come? To dupe him once more, to try and make of him again the same besotted fool who had loved her with the blind ardour of a man's first passion? That love was dead, killed by her own duplicity. Between them was an unbridgeable gulf—and the memory of a tiny fragile child abandoned with callous indifference. A rush of cold rage filled him and with blazing eyes he swept across the room.

His soft-booted feet made no sound on the thick rugs and still unconscious of his presence the woman broke off her song with a yawn and a flippant remark addressed to the portrait, and turned to find him at her elbow. For what seemed an eternity they stared at each other, her eyes but little below the level of his, then she turned away with an odd little strangled sound that might have been either a sob or a laugh.

"Why are you here?" His deep voice was hard as steel and she raised her head slowly and looked at him, a look in which there was latent admiration, wonder, and an underlying suggestion of cunning curiously blended. "I saw you at the ball. They told me you were going back to the desert. I had to come," she faltered.

"Why?" His face was devoid of all expression as he flung the single word at her. With a lithe, almost feline movement of her graceful body that was undisguisedly alluring she swayed nearer, her eyes all languorous appeal, her hands outstretched towards him. "I came because I could not stay away," she whispered, her voice a subtle caress, "because—because—oh, Gervas, can't you understand? I had to come—because—I—love you, because I have always loved you—in spite of what I did. And I didn't know what I was doing. I didn't think, I didn't realise, he swept me off my feet. And then when it was too late—too late"—her arms were round his neck, her palpitating limbs pressed close to his—"can you guess what I suffered, can you guess what my life has been! Gervas, you loved me once, for the sake of that love forgive me now, forgive—"

Throughout her amazing declaration he had stood like a rock, his face averted. But as her voice died away in a trembling whisper he turned his head quickly, too quickly for the comfort of the woman who clung to him with passionate fervidness for in the eyes that dropped almost instantly under his searching gaze he read, not the love and contrition her words implied, but a look of hard, eager cupidity. The look of a gambler who watches a last and desperate throw. It was not a tardy desire for his forgiveness but some other motive which as yet he did not understand that had driven her to seek a reconciliation with the man who had once been clay in her hands. Though his heart was dead to her, almost he had pitied her, almost he had believed her. The sobbing pleading voice, the absolute abandon with which she had flung herself upon him had been a wonderful piece of acting. She played her part with a skill and eloquence that, but for that last fatal slip, had almost convinced him. But self-convicted she stood for what she was, a consummate mistress of deceit—a liar as she had always been. To how many others had she made that same glib appeal? To how many others had she tendered the charms she so lavishly displayed? The hateful thought leaped unbidden to his mind as he looked at her with a kind of horror, fastidiously conscious of the deterioration that was so visibly apparent in her. The beautiful face so close to his was exquisite as he remembered it, but he seemed to see it suddenly with new eyes—the face of a woman lost to every sense of morality. To what had she sunk during the years since she had left him? What had she become—she who had been his wife, who had been the mother of his son! "*Une femme de moeurs légères.*" The Austrian's sneering voice seemed to echo hideously through the silent room and with a shudder he unclasped her fingers and put her from him.

"I could have forgiven you—anything," he said slowly, "but the child—" his voice broke despite him and a look of bitter pain convulsed his face—"the child you left to die alone—and you knew he was dying—"

"It's a lie," she cried shrilly. "I didn't know."

He raised his hand with a gesture that silenced her.

"It is the truth," he said with accusing sternness. "Do you think there was nobody to tell me? The doctor, the nurses, everybody but you, his mother, knew that he couldn't live. And you left him. My God, you left him!"

She flung him a glance of furious anger, "You always cared for him more than me," she sneered, and for a moment she braved him audaciously with heaving bosom and quivering lips. Then she flinched under his steady eyes and shrinking from him flung herself face downwards on a sofa and broke into a storm of tears. Tears of rage and mortification. With a feeling of suffocation he turned away, not troubling to refute the taunt she knew as well as he to be untrue. The room that was redolent with memories of the noble woman who had lived in it seemed suddenly fouled and contaminated. And heartsick and shaken by the scene he had gone through he crossed to a window and flinging back the jalousies, leant against the framework, staring unseeingly out into the night, struggling to regain the self-control that had almost left him. He was all at sea, striving to solve the problem of the woman who lay sobbing on the sofa behind him. That the life she had chosen had ended in disaster was beyond all question. What she had become was too obvious to be mistaken. It was written plainly on her face for all to see. But what had brought her to such a pass, what had induced the moral *débâcle* that was so apparent? What desperate strait had driven her to the course she had adopted tonight? It was not for love of him she had taken such a step nor did she want his love. What then did she want that she had come to him like any common courtesan seeking by purely physical enticement to regain the old ascendancy she had had over him? There seemed only one possible solution. And yet, remembering the liberal settlement he had made on her, he wondered how even that was possible. With a deep sigh he pulled himself together and went slowly back to her.

"Why did you come to me tonight, Elinor?"

She was still lying prone among the silken cushions, but at the sound of his voice she sat up, shivering as though the room were cold, her hands clutching at the soft pillows of the sofa.

"I told you," she said sullenly.

He made a gesture of impatience.

"Oh, for God's sake don't tell me any lies," he said wearily. "You never cared for me, you don't care for me now. Tell me the truth. For only the truth will help either of us tonight. Why did you come?"

For a second her eyes met his then she looked away and a wave of burning colour swamped the delicate pink and white of her painted cheeks. "Because I'm at the end of my tether—because I'm broke," she said with a reckless laugh that made him wince.

"And the money I settled on you?" he said slowly, hating the necessity that forced him to speak of it.

"Gone—long since. Did you think I could live on that?" she flashed contemptuously.

With an effort he restrained himself. What use to point out to her that what she regarded as a pittance would have kept an ordinary family in luxury.

"Then what you want is money—just money?" he said, his voice as contemptuous as her own.

"I must live," she retorted.

"And how have you lived?" he said heavily. The colour rose again to her face. "What is that to you?" she muttered.

"Nothing—in one sense. If I am to finance you again—everything," he said curtly. "But I must have details. Without them I will do nothing." He paused for a minute, fighting his abhorrence of the whole situation.

"You call yourself the Countess Sach. It is not the name of the man for whom you left me. Is he dead?"

"I don't know—I left him," she answered, very low.

"Why?"

"We quarrelled. I left him," she repeated monotonously.

"Did he marry you?"

"No. I—I told you. We quarrelled," there was a touch of asperity in her fretful voice.

"Did he want to marry you? Was the rupture your fault or his?" For a long time there was no answer then a whispered "Mine" came to him almost inaudibly.

"And the Count Sach?"

"There is no Count Sach."

He turned away with a shrug of hopeless perplexity. He had learned all he cared to know. To force from her the whole story of those sordid years was beyond him. It would do no good to either. She had followed of her own free will the broad path that leads to destruction and she had proved to him again tonight her utter unworthiness. Heartless and without shame, she wanted nothing from him but the means of continuing the life she had deliberately chosen. He had provided for her once, by no argument or reasoning was she entitled to his further bounty. In no sense was he responsible for her. In no sense? With his black brows drawn together in the heavy scowl that was so characteristic, he paced from end to end of the long room, wrestling with himself. And on the sofa where she sat immovable the woman watched the passing and repassing of the tall, stately figure, with glittering eyes that were hard with doubt and fear. What would he do? And gradually the thought came to her that if she could ever have loved any one, she might have loved this man. Not as he was in those old days at Royal Carew, but as he was now. How he had changed! And as she looked at the stern set face that was so different from what she remembered, a sudden feeling of fear ran through her. If he would only speak, only stop that monotonous pacing, only do something to end this horrible waiting.

He came to her at last and she stumbled to her feet to meet him. He spoke swiftly, in a voice that was hoarse and strained. He would settle nothing on her, but because she had been his wife, because of the child she had borne him, he would make her an allowance to be paid quarterly through his solicitors. He made no conditions but he warned her that under no circumstances would the allowance ever be increased.

With averted head and tightly compressed lips she listened to him in silence and when he finished speaking she made no comment and gave him no thanks. And no further word was spoken between them until she left the villa in his carriage, driven by Hosein whose silent tongue could be depended upon. And as the sound of the wheels died away, Carew went back into the house. His face was drawn and gray and his usually elastic step dragged as he passed slowly through the empty halls and across the moonlit courtyard to his own rooms at the back of the house and from there out on to the verandah. For an instant he stood, his haggard eyes upraised to the starry brilliance of the sky, then with a groan that seemed to almost burst his heart, he dropped into a chair and buried his face in his hands.

IX

The first pale streaks of dawn were stealing across the sky before Carew stirred from the chair into which he had dropped two hours before to face the knowledge that had come to him in that tense moment of self-understanding in the little winter garden at the Palace. Stunned by the realisation of his own feelings, racked by the painful scene following his return to the villa, at first concrete thought had been impossible. His whole ability to will and do, his whole mental and physical being seemed crushed under a weight of sorrow that for the time was paralysing. He felt numbed, conscious only of the suffering that, clogging his brain, reacted on his body leaving him inert and lifeless.

But gradually his mind cleared and he was able to think more calmly. He loved. For the second time in his life he loved. And yet it seemed to him that only now did he know the depths of his own heart, only now did he comprehend what true devotion could really mean. The love of his early manhood, the love he had given the woman who had been his wife, was not comparable with this overmastering passion that had come to him in his maturity. If he had loved then as he loved now not even the tragedy of twelve years ago could kill that love. And the greater, deeper, more wonderful emotion he had only just realised was as the dust of ashes in his mouth. There was no joy, no hope in this new love. There was only the pain of renunciation and the bitter knowledge that he had brought sorrow to her for whose sake he would gladly die rather than even a shadow should cross her path. For that she also loved him he knew beyond all doubt. He had read it in her eyes, he had heard it in the anguished tones of her voice when the thought of his peril had driven her to self betrayal as she listened to his story of the finish of Abdul el Dhib. The pain that was his was hers also. The thought was torment. Had she not already enough to bear without this additional burden of a love that could never be satisfied, that would bring her only grief and the torturing remembrance of what might have been? What did his own suffering matter compared with the fact that because of him she too must suffer? It would have been better, a thousand times better, if he had never returned from that last hazardous expedition that had ended in the meeting in the deserted village by Blidah. And yet, to his fatalistic reasoning, that same meeting had seemed a thing ordained;

but for his coming she must have experienced a fate too horrible even to contemplate. It was almost as if he had been deliberately guided in the choice of road he had taken, as if he had been led to her by some inscrutable ruling of providence. And though at the time he had raged at the necessity that had forced him to help her, though his whole soul had revolted from his self-imposed task, he knew now that love had leaped into being when he had carried her to his camp, and that it was love struggling for recognition that had caused the misery and mental upheaval of the succeeding weeks. But only tonight had he realised it, only tonight had he awakened to a full understanding of the almost unbelievable thing that had happened to him. And how or when during their brief meetings she had come to care for him he did not know, nor would he ever know. He only knew that for some strange inexplicable reason she had given him her love, that though she would never be his he would carry through life the knowledge that her heart was in his keeping. And the knowledge humbled him. How could she care! What could she see in him, a man nearly twice her age who, until tonight, had treated her with scant civility, that she should stoop to bestow on him the priceless treasure of her love. But what did it matter—enough that she did care and that he would have to be content with just the fact of her caring. Content! Good God, was the intolerable ache that filled him, the mad longing that possessed him, contentment! He would never be content. The mere knowledge of their love was not enough. He wanted her, above his very hope of heaven he wanted her. The barriers of defense he had raised about himself were torn away at last. The dead heart that had lain cold and lifeless within him was alive once more. Passion swept, and seething with jealousy he made no effort to stem the elemental impulses that seemed suddenly let loose and for a time only the primitive man in him existed urging his desperate need until even murder seemed justifiable to obtain her—the murder of the one who stood between him and what he wanted. Geradine! His fingers curled and tightened as though they were about the throat of the man he hated with all the force of his being. That strange hatred was no longer incomprehensible, and the thought that had so appalled him the night at the opera he viewed now with cold dispassion. What was the life of such a brute compared with her happiness and well-being! Was it murder to rid the earth of such scum, to free her from the tyranny that was killing her, body and soul? Murder! A terrible smile flitted across his face. For her sake he could do even that. Nothing mattered but her necessity. Beside that justice, honour, the man-made laws of society seemed to fade into utter insignificance. And the laws of God—was he to trample them under foot as well? If it must be. He was willing to risk even his soul to save her from further suffering. But was there need for such a drastic measure—was there no easier way to follow? Was there not the way that others had taken—the way that would free her from a life of bondage, that would give him his heart's desire? What was scruple to stand between them? They had only one life to live—and she loved him. She would come to him—*if* he made her. And for her own sake he would make her—for her sake, or for the sake of his own lust?

"But I say unto you that whosoever looketh on a woman to lust after her hath committed adultery with her already in his heart!"

He started to his feet with a smothered groan. It was as if he saw the words in letters of fire, blazing accusingly before his tired eyes. A shudder passed over him and something seemed to snap suddenly in his brain dispelling the madness of the last few moments and leaving him aghast at the horror of his own thoughts. She was not for him to covet. He had no right to love her, no right to think of her as he was thinking now—yearning for her, desiring her with all the strength of his manhood. Strength! What strength was left to him who had foresworn himself, who had turned from his lofty ideals and yielded to a passion that was ignoble! Conscience-smitten he saw himself as he was, fallen from his high estate, crashed from his pinnacle of self-righteous exaltation. It was repetition of history wherein his rôle was horribly reversed. He was no better in intention than the man he had reviled twelve years ago. The sin he had condemned was now his sin. He craved another man's wife, craved her with an intensity that had almost swamped his sense of right and wrong. And she? A dull flush crept over his tanned face. In his mind he had degraded and abased her, had dragged her down to the sordid level of his own carnal desires. Was his love so vile that he must think only of his bodily need? Was physical possession merely the dominating factor of that love? Had the years spent in the desert, the years of self-imposed abstinence, brutalised him so completely that he was incapable of higher, purer sentiment? Did she mean so little to him? Deep down in his heart he knew that she did not, knew that his love was a greater, finer thing than that. It was only the passionate impulse of the moment, the crushing sense of abnegation that made him weak, that made him want her as he was wanting her now—for his own, for that wonderful mating of soul and body that might have been theirs. To take her from the life she loathed to the freer, wilder life he had made his own; to know her safe and happy in his love; to watch the awakening of new hope and peace that would chase the sorrow from her tragic eyes; to be to her what she would be to him—comrade and helper, lover and friend, a partnership made perfect by their mutual love. It was what might have been. But now only a dream of joy that was unattainable, a vision of heaven that made the bitter certainty of its unfulfilment a foretaste of hell. God, how he longed for her! Marny, Marny! With a strangled sob he buried his face in his hands. . .

It was long before he stirred to move slowly with cramped limbs and aching head to the edge of the verandah where he leant wearily against the pillar that supported the green tiled roof, staring with haggard eyes across the garden at the brightening dawn—a dawn that for once gave him no pleasure.

It was over and done with—the wonderful glimpse of happiness that could never be. There was only one road to follow, the lonely road that had been his for so many years, but lonelier, more desolate now than it ever had been. For her sake and for the sake of what honour was left to him he must go, and go at once. Back to the desert, back to the work he had chosen. Alone—and he must go without seeing her again. He dared not see her. His confidence in himself was gone. And yet how could he go, how could he leave her knowing what her life would be, knowing what she must still endure and suffer at the hands of the drunken bully who possessed her. Geradine, whose name was a by-word, whose brutality and viciousness was discussed by all Algiers, whose behaviour to his girl wife was openly hinted at! Was he to leave her at the mercy of such a man? Even that he must do. She was not his—she was Geradine's wife. Geradine's wife—God help her. And his daily, hourly torment would be to know her so. Far from her, powerless to help her, he would have to live with the thought of her continual agony and sorrow. Merciful God, would he be able to bear it!

Made almost tangible by his longing she seemed to come to him where he stood, as once before he had seemed to see her in a strip of brilliant moonlight, and he stretched out his arms hungrily, whispering her name with shaking lips till the mental picture faded and, muffling his face in this thick burnous, he yielded to an agony that was greater than he had ever known. The sky was aflame, the garden resounding with the early songs of birds when he at last regained self-control. But he was blind and deaf to the beauty and harmony about him as he lingered for a few moments striving to bring something like order into the chaos of his thoughts. He was going back to the camp near Blidah, a camp that would be poignantly painful to him with the recollections it would induce. He would see her at every turn, the big tent that had sheltered her would be a perpetual reminder, dominated by the memory of her presence. Even the locality would be hateful to him, but to go further was impossible while Sanois' arrangements were still incomplete. There was no other course for him to take, no other way by which he could effectually prevent any further meeting between them. With a little shiver he turned and went heavily into the house. The study was rank with the fumes of the lamps that had burnt out during the night, and he passed quickly through to his bedroom beyond.

As he entered it the door on the further side of the room opened and Hosein came in with his usual noiseless tread. He offered no explanation for his appearance at an unusual hour and Carew asked for none, but knowing the man he was positive that the big Arab, on his return to the villa, had spent the remainder of the night in the adjoining dressing room watching and waiting for his master's coming. Though his gloomy face was, if possible, more gloomy than usual, his mere presence was a relief, and the customary stolidity with which he received his unexpected orders made the giving of them easier. Only a quicker service, a gentler handling of the garments tossed to him denoted an understanding that was more profound than Carew even guessed at. He was packing suit cases and holdalls with methodical deftness when Carew came back from his bath. Taught by years of experience, he knew even better than his master what was required for the protracted journeys in the desert which were to him infinitely preferable to the life in Algiers, and he took a certain pride in his work which was this morning especially noticeable. His face had lightened somewhat and he was patently pleased to be preparing for the road again. Of necessity Hosein was fully aware of the political significance of the forthcoming expedition, he knew also that it was the General Sanois who was responsible for the delay that had kept them so long in Algiers, and watching him as he moved swiftly and silently about the room Carew wondered in what degree his servant connected his hasty departure with the episode of last night. Distasteful as was the thought it was better so than that even Hosein should have an inkling of the real truth.

The valet had already acquainted the household with the altered arrangements and in the study, besides the coffee and rolls that were waiting for him, Carew found Derar full of importance and weighed down with account books and the necessary business devolving on himself that his master's absence would entail. And while he ate, Carew wrestled with his elderly servitor's endless questions and reiterated demands for instructions with the patience he had learned in dealing with the native mind. It was useless to remind Derar that the orders he gave were in every particular similar to those given many times before, that there was to be no departure from established precedent but that the villa was to be run on the same lines that always prevailed while he was away.

Pessimistically inclined, Derar, as always, prepared for the worst. And Carew, by this time writing cheques and orders at his desk, found himself constrained to smile more than once at the gloomy anticipations that were pronounced with melancholy fervour and interlarded with lengthy passages from the Koran. He listened quietly to the old man's garrulous outpourings in which lamentations on his departure and pious invocations for his welfare were inextricably jumbled with household needs and requirements.

But the strain on his already overstrained nerves was greater than he expected and when at last Derar, still somewhat tearful but armed with plenary powers that made him swell with pride, finally salaamed himself out of the room, Carew scribbled a few lines to General Sanois and then leant back in his chair with a feeling of mental exhaustion. His mind made up to leave Algiers the time that must elapse before his actual departure hung heavily upon him. He glanced at the clock on his desk. It would be half-an-hour or more before his men would be ready and, depressed and restless as he was, the minutes seemed to drag with maddening slowness.

To relieve the tedium of waiting he went out into the garden. Some little distance from the house, amongst a grove of orange trees, he found Saba. Squatting on the ground, his nervous little body clad only in a gay striped gandhera, a fez perched rakishly on his small sleek head, the boy was chattering eagerly to a tiny monkey that was clinging to his shoulder. He was too absorbed in his newly acquired pet to notice Carew's almost noiseless approach and it was the monkey that twittering shrilly with alarm made him realise he was no longer alone. He scrambled to his feet, his blind eyes turning uncertainly from side to side until Carew called to him when he darted forward, loosening his hold on the monkey which fled dismayed up into the branches of the nearest tree.

The confidant of all the servants, Saba was already in full possession of the new orders given to the household, and before Carew could speak he was assailed with a torrent of excited questions that were hurled at him to an accompaniment of joyous squeaks and prancings. The child's pleasure was so obvious that Carew almost wavered in his decision to leave him at the villa with Hosein who was remaining a few days longer in Algiers to finish the preparations for the journey into the desert. But his crying need for solitude made the thought of even Saba's companionship unendurable, and very gently he explained his wishes. The boy's radiant little face clouded as he listened, but trained to obedience he did not voice his disappointment and very soon he was laughing again, childishly eager at the prospect of the journey and speculating on the probable number of days Hosein would require to complete his arrangements. And at the end of half-an-hour Carew left him playing contentedly with his recovered monkey and happy in the assurance that the separation should be a brief one.

The score of men who had come into Algiers from the camp were already collected when Carew returned to the house, and the narrow road that ran past the villa was blocked with horses whose riders, still dismounted, were exchanging raucous and voluble badinage with the small army of household servants assembled to watch the departure. Standing a little apart from the noisy throng, reserved and taciturn as was his wont, Hosein was holding Suliman, restraining with difficulty the spirited animal's manifest impatience.

Carew's appearance occasioned a sudden silence among his followers and the escort leapt to their horses while he himself mounted with less haste and lingered for a few moments to give Hosein some final directions. The actual moment come he would have given all he possessed to be able to remain in the town he had been longing weeks to leave. It took all his resolution to persevere in the course he had determined and give the men the signal for which they were waiting. At the head of his little troop he rode away with unaccustomed slowness and with a feeling of reluctance that grew momentarily greater as each stride of the big bay carried him further from the villa. He knew now what the house wanted, why it had seemed so empty and desolate, and the knowledge was an added pang to the bitterness that filled him. If his dream had been possible; if he could have seen her in reality, as he visualised her in his mind, the mistress of his home bringing life and happiness to the chill and formal rooms her presence would enrich and beautify; if the end of the journey he contemplated could have meant a return to her—Was it strength or weakness that was driving him from her now? Again he wrestled with the temptation of a few hours ago, a temptation that was fiercer, more gripping even that it had been before. Her pitiful helplessness seemed to make his flight the act of a craven. Of what use were the physical powers with which he was endowed if his strength could not save her from the life of misery to which she was condemned. Geradine's lack of control, the almost demoniacal rages that resulted from his intemperance, was common talk. Thick drops of moisture gathered on his face as he remembered the man's huge bulk and pictured her in the grip of those coarse, ape-like hands. To what lengths had he gone in the past—what devilish torture would he yet inflict on the tender little body Carew yearned to hold in his arms. His face was drawn with agony as he swept the cold sweat from his forehead.

The road he was following led past de Granier's villa and ran parallel with the densely wooded hillside that shadowed its grounds. A sudden impulse came to him to look on the house that held the woman he loved—an impulse that was a species of subtle self-torture which even to himself seemed incomprehensible and to which tie yielded with a feeling of contempt. Pulling Suliman up sharply he swung to the ground and flinging the reins to the Arab he beckoned forward bade his escort ride on and wait for him beyond the villa. Standing where he had dismounted he watched them pass, and the last couple were some distance from him before he turned to the hillside where a tiny path wound upward between the close growing trees. A few minutes' stiff climb and then the path curved abruptly to the left from whence it extended more or less levelly in the same direction as the road that lay some fifty or sixty feet below. His pace slackened as he neared the crossway track that led down to the garden entrance of the Villa des Ombres, and in a revulsion of feeling he cursed the weakness that had brought him there. But having come thus far he was unwilling to retrace his steps and, jerking his shoulders back with a characteristic gesture of impatience, he moved slowly forward with noiseless tread along the winding path that curved and twisted round the boles of the big trees. Their great girth obstructed anything but a limited view beyond them and made only a few yards of the way visible at a time.

It was still very early. Save for the birds twittering amongst the trees and the long strings of woolly caterpillars joined one behind the other pursuing their patient and meandering course over the rough ground, the hillside appeared to be deserted. But as Carew rounded the trunk of an exceptionally large tree, the jutting roots of which made necessary a more than usually wide detour, he came to a sudden halt with a quick intake of the breath that was almost a groan. With clenching hands and madly racing heart he stared at the girlish figure lying huddled amongst the undergrowth almost at his feet. Her face was hidden and she lay very still, so still that a terrible thought came to him parching his mouth and blanching his face under the deep tan. He tried to whisper her name but no sound issued from his stiff lips and unable to speak, unable to move, time was a thing forgotten while he struggled with the paralysing fear that held him motionless.

He never knew how long it was before she stirred, before the faint echo of a smothered sob allayed the dread that had taken hold of him and lessened the strangling grip that seemed clutching at his throat. But still he did not move. He would not go. He had tried to play the game—and the game had turned against him. He had wrestled with himself to no purpose. Fate had played into his hand and the meeting he had sought to escape was now unavoidable. The sight of her prostrate in an abandonment of grief had shattered all his strength—he could not leave her like this. Not trusting himself to touch her he waited with an almost bursting heart for her to realise his presence—and as once before in the opera house, so now did she seem gradually to become aware of the steady stare fixed on her. With a shuddering sigh she sat up slowly, turning her head towards him. And the deathly pallor of her face, the look of frozen misery in her tragic black-rimmed eyes sent a rush of savage rage through him that almost choked him. God, what must she have suffered to look like that! He sought for words but his own suffering held him speechless.

It was she who spoke first. She had looked at him almost unknowingly, then a wave of colour rushed into her pale cheeks to recede as quickly leaving them whiter than before. Stumbling to her feet she stood before him, swaying like a reed, struggling to regain her composure, striving to formulate the conventional greeting her trembling lips could scarcely utter. "Sir Gervas—" He guessed rather than heard the fluttering whisper. But before he could answer, before he could wrench his gaze from the pain-filled eyes that were wavering under his, he saw her stiffen suddenly and shrink from him with a backward glance of fearful apprehension. "What—who—" she muttered hoarsely. And, listening, he too heard the sound that had startled her—the deep murmur of men's voices raised in heated altercation that came echoing up the hillside from the roadway beneath them. The voices of his own men, as he knew. But what did she think? And the anger and hatred that was seething within him flamed anew into all but uncontrollable fury as he watched her leaning white-lipped and shivering against the trunk of the giant cork tree and wondered how long it would be before that delicate organism and highly strung nervous system finally succumbed to the brutal treatment that was slowly but steadily reducing her to a physical and mental wreck. His hands clenched with the horrible pain of his own helplessness. But with a supreme effort he mastered himself, stifling the words that sprang to his lips and forcing his voice to naturalness as he answered her reassuringly. "It's only my men—arguing as usual, the noisy devils."

She looked at him strangely.

"Your men—" she repeated dully. And pulling herself erect she turned abruptly and walked unsteadily to the edge of the steep descent. Through the intervening trees she could see them clustered at the foot of the hill. His men—the lucky ones who were fortunate enough to share his life! A feeling of bitter envy came to her and she watched them through a mist of tears. Picked men, men chosen for their loyalty and endurance. Fierce sons of the desert these—differing altogether, even to her unpractised eyes, from the Arabs she had seen lounging about Algiers—and mounted on magnificent horses which they sat superbly. A fit escort for the man who would lead them. What did this unusual following portend? In Algiers, for she had seen him many more times than he knew, he always rode alone. Was this the end at last, the time she had looked forward to with dread—the time when he would ride out of her life forever? Her lips quivered. Never to see him again, never to hear the beloved voice whose low, soft intonations would ring in her ears while life lasted, never to know again the restfulness and strength his presence brought her! How could she bear it, oh, dear God, how could she bear the desolation and misery that would be hers! Her trembling hands crept upward to her breast, clenching convulsively over the heart that was aching and throbbing with a pain that was intolerable. She must know, though knowledge meant the agony of death.

Shuddering she turned and went slowly back to him. A cigarette between his lips, he was leaning against the tree where she had leant, his face an impassive mask that baffled her. Was the fleeting glimpse of a totally different expression she had seemed to see in his eyes a few minutes ago only the effect of her own overstrained imagination? Was she such a fool that she could have thought for one moment of wild sweet happiness, that her love and longing could have begotten his love? His indifference seemed complete—the parting was nothing to him. How could it be otherwise—it was only she who cared, only she whose heart was breaking, only she who would be left comfortless and alone.

The restraint she imposed on herself made her voice cold and hard as she uttered the question she nerved herself to ask.

"You are going away?"

"Yes."

Despite herself she winced at the brief syllable of assent that was voiced in a tone as cold and as hard as her own.

"Back to the desert?"

"Yes."

"For good?"

"For good," he answered firmly. She turned from him quickly to hide the tears that blinded her. But a strangled sob she had not the strength to restrain betrayed her. Almost inaudible it was but he heard it.

"*Marny!*" The cry was wrung from him. And the next moment she was in his arms, clinging to him despairingly, weeping as he had not believed it possible for a woman to weep. Unmanned by her sudden breakdown, aghast at the terrible sobs that seemed to be tearing the slender little body to pieces, he strained her to him with passionate strength. "Marny, Marny, for God's sake—don't cry like that. Your tears are torturing me." But conscious only of the shelter of his arms, too weak to struggle against the feelings she had so long suppressed, she was powerless to check the storm of emotion that overwhelmed her. Lying inert against him, her face hidden in his robes, she sobbed her heart out on his till the violence of her grief terrified him and he caught her closer, bending his tall head till his cheek was resting on her tumbled hair, whispering words of love and entreaty.

"Have pity on me, child, you are breaking my heart. Do you think I can bear to see you weep—Marny, my love, my love."

Her arm slid up and round his neck. "Oh, let me cry," she moaned, "for five years I've had to be a thing of stone. If I don't cry now I shall go mad." A spasm swept across his face and his own eyes were dim as he ceased to urge her, waiting patiently till the tempest of her tears should pass. And gradually the tearing sobs ceased and she regained control of herself. Exhausted and ashamed, not daring to meet his eyes, almost dreading the sound of his voice, she clung to him in silence, wishing passionately that her life could end, thus, in his arms.

And to Carew the close contact of her trembling limbs was a mingled rapture and pain that was agony. His face buried in her fragrant hair, he prayed desperately for strength to leave her, for strength to meet the parting that must come.

Still holding her he raised her head with gentle force. Her eyes were closed, the thick, dark lashes lying wet on her tear-stained cheek, and the hungry longing to touch them with his lips was almost more than he could withstand.

"Won't you look at me, Marny? Am I never to see your dear eyes again?" he murmured huskily.

A tremor passed through her and for a moment she did not respond. Then the dusky lashes fluttered faintly and slowly the heavy lids unclosed. For long they looked, staring as though into each other's souls, and against her tender breasts she felt the violent beating of his heart.

A quivering sigh escaped her. "Gervas—oh, Gervas, Gervas," she whispered, and lifted her face to his. The sadness in his eyes deepened into anguish and his firm mouth trembled as he shook his head.

"I mustn't kiss you, dear. Your lips are his—not mine, God help me. I haven't even the right to touch you. I'm a cur to hold you in my arms like this, but I can't let you go—not yet, not yet, my darling." His voice broke, and insensibly his arm tightened round her, crushing her to him with a force of which he was unaware. She turned her head with a little sob. "How could we know that this would come to us—how could we know that we would care," she cried. "I never thought you loved me. I thought it was only I who—who—" She clenched her teeth on her lip, fighting the sobs that were rising in her throat. "Oh, why was it you that came that night near Blidah!" she burst out passionately. "What did my life matter? And I—I who would die for you, I've brought you unhappiness. Gervas, why don't you hate me!"

"I thought I did—once," he answered with a twisted smile, and brushed the shining hair tenderly from off her forehead.

Physical pain had been forgotten in the mental agony that swamped her but now, remembering, too late she tried to stop him and he had seen the ugly wound on her white brow before her flying hand reached his. A sharp exclamation broke from him. "What have you done to yourself? *My God, has he dared*—" His face was ghastly and the look in his blazing eyes terrified her. Fearful of the consequences of his anger, fearful of she knew not what, she lied to shield the husband who had struck her.

"No—no—" she panted. "I slipped—I slipped in my room last night."

Love and intuition told him that she was lying and he put her from him with a groan of helpless misery. And free of his supporting arm she slid to the ground for her limbs were trembling under her. He sat down near her, staring gloomily before him, wondering how he could bring himself to leave her, tortured with what he had seen and cursing the man whom, more than ever, he longed to kill.

Her sorrowful eyes never left his stern, set face and at last she could bear the silence no longer. Her hand stole out timidly and touched his. "What are we going to do?" She waited long for his answer, so long that she wondered if he had heard the faint whisper, and her trembling fingers tightened on his arm. "Gervas, speak to me," she entreated.

"What is there for me to say," he answered, and his voice was harsh with the effort speech cost him. "There is nothing to do but the one hard thing that is left to us. We have got to forget that this morning has ever been. We have got to forget everything but the fact that you are bound, that you are not free to come to me. If there was some other way, if I could have taken you—" He tore his eyes from her face and leaped to his feet. "But there is no other way," he cried with sudden violence. "I can't take you. You've got to forget, and forgive me—if you can."

She buried her face in her hands.

"Forget!" she wailed. "Will you forget?"

"Not in this life nor in the life to come," he whispered swiftly.

With a sob that wrung his heart she flung out her arms appealing. "I can't bear it, Gervas, I can't live without you."

He caught the outstretched hands in his and drew her to her feet.

"Don't make it harder for me, dear. God knows it's hard enough," he said unsteadily. "I love you. I want you—more than anything in heaven and earth I want you—but I've got to leave you. Help me to do the right thing, Marny. Help me to go, now, while I have the strength." But with a broken little cry she clung to him, her eyes beseeching.

"I can't, I can't! I'm not strong like you. I can't let you go yet—not altogether—not back to the desert. Stay—only stay till we leave," she pleaded, "it won't be long, only a few weeks—"

"My dear, what help will it be if I do stay?" he said wearily. "It will only make it harder for both of us." But frantically she urged him. "Please, please," she entreated. "Oh, I can't explain—I don't know what I feel myself—but there seems to be something awful coming nearer and nearer to me and I'm frightened—*I'm frightened*. If I could know you were in Algiers it would make it easier—I shouldn't feel so—alone. Gervas, if you love me stay till we go."

If he loved her! He clenched his hands to keep them from her and turned away with a heavy sigh. "Must I prove my love?" he said sadly. A sob broke from her. Did he think she doubted? Why was she such a coward as to ask this thing of him! Humbly she went to him begging his forgiveness but with a quick gesture of distress he stopped her.

"There is nothing to forgive," he said gently, "there can be no misunderstanding possible between us, dear. If it will help you, if my being in Algiers will make it easier for you, I will stay until you go. But more I cannot do. This has got to be the end, Marny. We've got to say goodbye to each other. I mustn't see you again—I daren't see you again."

A deadly faintness came over her. Numbly she felt him take her hands and hold them crushed against his face. And through the surging in her ears she heard his voice, far off and muffled as though coming from some great distance.

"My dear, my dear—God keep you, now and always."

And then she knew that he was gone. She struggled to move, to conquer the inertia that seemed rooting her to the ground. Only to see him again—to catch one last glimpse—

Tears were raining down her face as she stumbled to the edge of the little path and, screened by the trees, looked down on the roadway beneath. With her hands pressed over her lips to stifle the sobs that were choking her she watched him standing beside his men till the little troop vanished in a cloud of dust along the Blidah road and, left alone, he leaped on to his own horse and sent him at a reckless gallop in the opposite direction. Then a merciful blackness came over her and she fell senseless amongst the tangled ferns.

THERE FOLLOWED A WEEK THAT for Carew was a period of uninterrupted suffering, suffering that seemed to grow more acute, more unbearable with each succeeding day. With nothing to look forward to, with no hope to ease the burden of his loneliness and longing, with the bitter knowledge burning into him that barely half-a-mile away in her prison house of misery she too was suffering, he struggled through days that seemed endless and nights that were torment.

Seeking for distraction, for anything that would occupy his enforced leisure and turn the trend of his thoughts, he offered his services to Morel and toiled in the scientist's laboratory from early morning till late in the evening, endeavouring by hard work to deaden the pain that never left him. During the long hours of self-imposed labour he strove to banish her from his mind, to concentrate solely on the experiments that at any other time would have claimed his whole attention. But the remembrance of her was with him continually. While he carried out Morel's instructions with mechanical precision he seemed to feel her presence close beside him, to see clearly before his eyes the piteous tear-stained face that would always haunt him, and through the stillness of the silent workroom he could almost hear the sobbing tones of her anguished voice. "Gervas, I can't live without you!" And he had left her, left her to Geradine's mercy. If, in the grip of this tremendous passion that had come to him so strangely, he had sought to entice her from a husband who cared, or from one who—though indifferent—still treated her with ordinary decency and respect, he would have known his offence to be unforgivable. But chained as she was to a beast like Geradine, the marks of whose brutality he had himself seen on her delicate face, was there not excuse for his love, for the raging temptation that still assailed him to take her from a life of martyrdom and give her the happiness that was her youth's prerogative? How had she come to be the wife of that drunken, hectoring bully—what unthinkable ordering could have linked her life with his? Impossible that she could ever have loved him. Surely the mere brute strength of the man could not have attracted her, inducing her to a step she had lived to rue. Five years, she had said. Five years ago she must have been only a child—she was little more now. What circumstances or what tragedy had thrust an immature girl into the keeping of such a profligate! And what had those five years meant to her! As the days dragged slowly by and he applied himself to the work to which he forced his wandering attention he wrestled with a problem he could not hope to solve, racking himself with the thought of what she must have endured and would still have to endure.

But it was the nights he dreaded most. The nights when, waking from fitful sleep that, dream-haunted, gave him no rest, he stared wide-eyed into the darkness murmuring her name, aching for her, till the pain of it drove him out into the garden there to tramp the dark tree-bordered alleys and star-lit stretches of grass until bodily fatigue brought him back to the house to toss wakefully and watch for the dawn when he could start for the early morning rides that were his only alleviation. It was in the lonely hours of the night that the thought of her suffering was strongest with him. It was then that his fevered mind, unchecked in his solitude, became the prey of ghastly imaginings until, half mad with his own thoughts, he almost yielded to the temptings of the insidious inward voice that bade him forego honor and take the happiness he had sacrificed. Was he to stand aside while her youth and health were wrecked? Was she to be offered up on the altar of his conscience? Must she be the victim of his scruple? "She would have gone with you—she would have gone with you that morning—" Night after night the mocking voice rang in his ears, and night after night he fought the same fight in anguish of soul, battling with the promptings of his heart.

Then came a day when a telephone message from Morel, who had received an urgent summons to Paris, put a stop to the work at the laboratory and left him to face inactivity he viewed with dismay. In no mood for the society of either General Sanois or the officers at the barracks, resolved to run no chance of a further meeting with the woman he had determined never to see again, he passed the long hours of the morning, sitting on the verandah with a medical book in his hand which he did not read, and in restless wandering about the lovely garden whose loveliness was lost on him.

Utterly weary of himself, for the first time in days, he would have welcomed the companionship of Saba. But the blind boy was at the camp near Blidah whither he had been despatched when Carew had decided to remain on in Algiers. The day seemed interminable.

Worn out with sleepless nights he slept heavily for the greater part of the afternoon and was awakened with difficulty by Hosein in time for the solitary dinner he thought would never end. Afterwards, ordering coffee to be brought to him, he strolled through the silent halls and empty rooms back to the verandah where he had spent most of the day.

The night was singularly dark but the darkness agreed with his own gloomy thoughts and after he had finished his coffee he extinguished the reading lamp on the table near him and sat for a long time staring fixedly into blackness.

Inaction became at last impossible. He had sat for two hours and his limbs were cramped and his head throbbing for need of physical exercise. Two more hours and he would be ready to blow his brains out, he reflected with a dreary laugh. Going to his bedroom he changed quickly into Arab dress and left the house unseen.

Beyond the door in the wall he hesitated frowning. Then with a shrug and a muttered oath he turned in the direction of de Granier's villa. To torture himself by gazing on the house was not to see her, he argued. By no reasoning could he be said to be breaking the resolution he had made. The road was free to him as to any other. And what chance was there of seeing her at this time of night! Jerking his heavy cloak back he stopped to light a cigarette and then strode on with the slow step to which flowing robes had accustomed him.

For a time it appeared as if no other midnight wanderers were abroad, but as he neared the high enclosing wall of the Villa des Ombres his quick ears caught the sound of hurrying, stumbling feet and the raucous intonations of a voice he recognised. Instinctively he shrank into the deeper shadow of the wall as Tanner, the English groom, reeled past him with words that seemed to turn the blood in his veins to ice. "The swine, the swine—the blasted swine! 'E'll do 'er in, by Gawd, 'e will! *Christ*, 'ow she screamed—and the damned door locked so as I couldn't get in! And 'im mad drunk—the beast! My Gawd, my Gawd, what'll I do? I'll 'ear them screams till I die!" And sobbing and blaspheming in impotent rage the little man tore on and vanished into the night.

But towards the house from which the groom had fled, Carew was racing with a deadly fear knocking at his heart. The gates were open and, panic-driven, he dashed along the carriage drive and up the steps of the villa hurling himself against the door which, unbarred, gave way before him. In the dimly-lit entrance hall he stumbled and almost fell headlong over the prostrate figure of an Arab who moaned and writhed on the marble floor. Callous to everything but the one ghastly fear that gripped him, Carew kicked his feet clear of the man's robes and shook him roughly. But the fiercely uttered question died on his lips as a piercing shriek rang through the silent house. A shriek that was followed by others so terrible, so frenzied, that for a moment he reeled under the horror of them. And with the agonizing screams was mingled the sound of a man's raving and other more pregnant sounds that drove Carew to the verge of madness. With a groan he leaped to the door of the room where was the woman he loved, but, locked from within, it resisted his furious onslaught and, as well acquainted with the villa as he was with his own, he knew that to force in was impossible. Desperately he wrenched at the handle, then a sudden thought came that sent him flying down the corridor. There was another door leading into the drawing room, a secret door that, flush with the wall and hidden by curtains, was possibly unknown to the tenants who had rented the house. Reaching the ante-room with which it communicated and tearing aside the embroidered hangings he flung his whole weight against the fragile panels, crashing through into the room beyond. One sweeping glance sufficed him. Dragging his eyes from the battered little body stretched almost at his feet he crouched for an instant, stiffening like a wild beast preparing to spring, his face the face of a madman.

And startled by his sudden appearance, too blind with passion to recognise the man who had gone through the sandstorm with him, Geradine saw in the tall, robed figure facing him only an unknown Arab who had dared to force a violent entrance into his house and he flung forward with a savage snarl, brandishing the heavy hunting crop with which he had flogged his wife into insensibility.

"You damned nigger," he bellowed. "What the hell—"

But with the sound of his voice Carew sprang, his clenched fist driving straight at the other's mouth. For a second Geradine staggered, then with a roar of mingled pain and fury he slashed with the crop at Carew's face. But the blow fell short and the next moment two powerful arms closed round him. Though strong above the average, his life of intemperance had unfitted him for any protracted struggle and tonight, wearied already by his outburst of savagery and not sober enough to use with advantage what strength he had, he was helpless in the grip of the muscular hands that seemed to be crushing the life out of him. Choked with the strangling hold on his throat he was almost unconscious when the clutching fingers slid suddenly to his arm and he was forced to his knees.

And with the whip that was still wet with her blood Carew avenged the woman who lay so deathly still beside him. Maddened with the thought of her suffering, he wielded the heavy weapon till Geradine's coat and shirt were torn to ribbons, crimson stained and sticky, till his moans became fainter and finally died away, till his own arm grew tired with the punishment he inflicted. Only then did he fling the whip from him. Scarcely glancing at the inert figure sprawled face downwards on the floor, indifferent whether he had killed him or not, he turned slowly to that other pitiful little figure and, hardly conscious

E.M. HULL

of what he did, tore the burnous from his shoulders, and wrapping it round her lifted her into his arms and carried her away.

The hall was empty as he passed through it. But he was oblivious of the apparently deserted house, oblivious of everything but the slight burden he held. As if in a dream, his mind almost a blank, he followed mechanically the road by which he had come half an hour before. And not until he had reached his own villa, until, led by instinct rather than definite reasoning, he found himself in his own bedroom, did the dream-like feelings pass and he awoke to realize what he had done. But that could wait. At the moment only she mattered.

Laying her on the bed he stripped the blood-wet silken rags from her lacerated shoulders, wincing in agony as they clung to the delicate broken flesh his trembling lips covered with passionate kisses. But he was doctor as well as lover and, forcing his shaking fingers to steadiness, he bathed the cruel wounds with tender skill, doing all that was possible for her comfort before he dropped to his knees to wait till she should regain consciousness. And when at last she stirred it was some time before recognition dawned in the dazed eyes that were gazing blankly into his. But the sudden joy that filled them faded swiftly into a look of terrible fear.

With a cry that greyed his face she flung herself into his arms.

"Don't let him get me! Don't—let—him—get me," she shrieked, again and again, till the horror of it was more than he could bear and he crushed her face against him to stifle the sounds he knew would ring in his ears while life lasted.

"Hush, hush," he whispered, almost fiercely. "It's done—it's finished. He will never touch you again. You need never see him again. Lie still and rest. There's not a soul who knows where you are but me." And even in the extremity of her terror his voice had power to soothe her and she relaxed in his arms with a shuddering sob. For a long time he held her silently, fighting the biggest battle of his life, striving to subdue self, to think only for her. But her nearness made thought impossible and at last, in despair, he sought to rise. She clung to him with a murmur of entreaty.

"Let me go, dear," he muttered. "I've got to think—I've got to think what is best to do." And tenderly he put aside her trembling hands.

Fear fled back into her eyes as she watched him cross the room to the open window, and slipping from the bed she waited for what seemed an eternity, shaking with weakness, afraid to question him, afraid for the moment of the man himself.

And when at length he spoke, in a voice that was almost unrecognisable, he did not look at her. "I can get you out of Algiers—that is easy. But to whom shall I take you? Where are your people?"

For a moment she stared in dazed unbelief, then with a pitiful sob, she staggered nearer to him. "Gervas, don't you love me—don't you want me?"

His face was anguished as he flung towards her. "Want you? *My God!*" he groaned, "but it's not what I want that matters. It is you I am thinking of. You are Geradine's wife—I can't take you. I can't dishonour you. I can't drag you through the mud—"

"Mud!" she echoed, with a terrible laugh, "what mud could you drag me through that would be worse than the mud that has choked me for five ghastly years? Gervas, Gervas, I've come to the end. I can't fight any more. I can't bear any more. I've no one to turn to—no people—no friends. There's nobody in all the world who can help me—but you. If you won't save me I will kill myself. I swear it. Oh, Gervas, have pity! Take me away. I'm safe only with you. I'll be your servant—your slave—anything you will—only save me, save me! If I see him again I shall go mad—*mad*—" She was at his feet, clasping his knees, her upturned face wild and distorted with terror. And as he swept her up into his arms with a gasp of horrified protest and looked into her frenzied eyes, he knew that she was very near to madness now. But still he hesitated.

"You know what it will mean if I take you with me into the desert?"

"I know, I know," she sobbed, "it will mean heaven and rest and joy unspeakable. And I—who have lived in *hell*! Oh, Gervas, give me the chance of happiness!"

It was not what he meant, but he saw that she was past understanding. Only by keeping her could he avert the mental breakdown which was imminent. To save her reason he must do that for which his heart was clamouring, that which he had determined never to do.

And in the light that leaped involuntarily to his eyes she read his answer even before he stooped his lips to her trembling mouth.

E.M. HULL

X

Very early in the morning, in the dark hour that precedes the dawn, Marny Geradine rode out from Algiers in the guise of an Arab boy, her slender figure concealed in the voluminous folds of a long white burnous, her fair face hidden by the haick that was pulled far forward over her brow. Beside her Hosein was riding with a wary eye on her horse, ready at any moment to catch the bridle should the nervous strength that was supporting her fail suddenly. A few paces ahead of them, Carew, in the dark blue burnous he affected, was hardly distinguishable in the gloom. Trembling with bodily weakness and the still lingering fear she could not conquer, she strained her eyes to keep him in sight. Only with him near her was she safe. On him and on his strength she was utterly dependent, for she had no longer any strength of her own. The courageous spirit that had sustained her for so long was broken at last, and spent in mind and body her only hope was in him. He had sworn that she was safe, that he had passed unrecognised through the Villa des Ombres, that he had brought her unseen to his own house. But the words that had soothed her as he held her in his strong embrace seemed to lose power when he was absent. He had been obliged to leave her almost at once and the touch of his first kiss was still warm on her lips when he had hurried away to make the arrangements for which so little time was available. He had bade her rest, but nerve racked and overwrought, rest had been impossible as she lay starting and shivering at every noise that echoed through the strange house. Like a terrified child that requires repeated and audible consolation, she longed for the sound of his voice, for the tangible comfort of his shielding arms.

And now as she rode through the deserted streets of the sleeping suburb, fear for herself was mingled with a new and terrible fear for him. She had as yet no knowledge of what had passed in the Villa des Ombres after she had lost consciousness and she was obsessed with the thought of her husband. She saw him in every shadow, the very sound of the horses' feet seemed to her excited fancy like hurrying pursuing footsteps. She hated herself for her want of confidence. At the bottom of her heart she knew that her trust in Carew was implicit, that it was only her overstrained nerves that made her shiver with dread, that turned her sick each time her horse quickened his pace or swerved from some object that only he could see. She tried to fight against her weakness, to believe that her disguise was complete, but she knew that she would have no peace until the town was left behind, until, the open country reached, she could abandon the rôle of attendant and ride beside the man to whom she had given herself and gain fresh strength and courage from his nearness. And from time to time unconsciously she strove to lessen the distance between them, checking her horse again with a sharp little sigh as she heard Hosein's voice "*Doucement, doucement*" repeated warningly.

The way seemed never ending.

To avoid passing the Villa des Ombres a wide detour was necessary and Marny began to think they would never win clear of the tree-lined avenues and succession of silent villas that appeared to extend indefinitely.

There were few abroad at this early hour, but the occasional passing of some chance pedestrian made her shrink within the folds of the enveloping burnous, wild eyed with apprehension and faint with the heavy beating of her tired heart. And once the sound of galloping hoofs behind them came near to shattering what little self-control was left to her and with a choking cry she drove her horse against Hosein's, clutching frantically at the man's arm and reeling weakly in the saddle. But it was only an Arab, wraith-like in the darkness and immersed in his own concerns, who tore by at breakneck speed on a raking chestnut that squealed an angry defiance at the other horses as he clattered past. She recovered herself with a feeling of shame for her own cowardice, wondering miserably if she would ever regain the strength and nerve that five years of crushing experience had slowly sapped from her. Once she had not known what it meant to be tired or afraid. Weariness and pain to her had been merely terms, without meaning, without significance. But in those five years she had learnt a bitter lesson. Physically and mentally she had suffered until suffering had become the dominant factor in her existence, until she had wondered how far endurance went, how long before her burden would become heavier than she could bear. And now, still dazed with the horror of the last few hours, she could hardly believe in the fact of her deliverance. Was it really over, the life of pain that had transformed her from a happy carefree child into a sorrowful disillusioned woman who had prayed for death to release her from bondage that was intolerable. And death had been very near to her last night. She had realised it when, seeking to prevent what she knew to be an injustice, she had thrown herself between her husband and the wretched Arab valet and Geradine, mad with drink and rage, had turned to wreak on her the same punishment he had inflicted on his servant. His face had been the face of a devil, distorted almost beyond recognition, and in his glittering red flecked eyes she had read her fate. Temporarily insane he was past knowing what he did and, helpless against his strength, she was well aware now that but for the coming of Carew the ghastly scene must have ended in tragedy, that body or brain must have succumbed to the fury of his passion. Never while she lived would she forget. Still close to hers she seemed to see that savage bestial face, the staring bloodshot eyes blazing with merciless ferocity, her lacerated shoulders still quivered as if they shrank again under the cruel blows that had rained on her till consciousness fled. The brutality of years had reached culmination when, with words whose foulness had scorched her soul, he had beaten her like a dog. That was what she had been! His dog—kicked or caressed as the mood took him. A thing of no account. His chattel—sold to him like a slave in an eastern market, taken by him merely to satisfy his basest instincts. Shudderingly she tried to banish thought, to put him from her mind, but her shaken brain was beyond control and over and over again she lived through the cruelty of the years that were past until every nerve in her aching body seemed strained to breaking point.

Trembling from head to foot and bathed in perspiration she wondered if the horror of it would ever leave her, if all her remaining life was to be a nightmare of hideous recollection.

Drooping with fatigue, her wet hands slipping on the bridle she grasped mechanically, she prayed desperately for the open country that meant freedom and happiness. And gradually, yielding to the physical pain that was swamping all other feeling, she ceased to notice the locality through which they were passing and she had almost drifted into unconsciousness when the sound of the voice she had longed for roused her to the fact that at last the town was left behind. Slowly she raised her head to meet the grave eyes that looked searchingly into hers. And at sight of her face Carew reined nearer, and she felt his cool strong fingers close with practised touch about her wrist.

"Can you hold out a bit longer, dear? We're rather close to Algiers yet," he said. And the tender anxiety of his voice made her set her teeth to keep back the sob that rose in her throat, a sob of joy and wonder at the consideration to which she was so unused. She drew herself straighter in the saddle and smiled at him bravely.

"I'm all right," she gasped, "if—if I can ride beside you," she added, faintly. His lips tightened as he eyed her doubtfully. Then without answering he wheeled Suliman towards the south.

The movements of her horse were easy, and away from the metalled roads the slow canter at which they rode was less jarring, but it took all her resolution to maintain the upright carriage she had adopted and hide from him the weakness that was steadily overcoming her. The nervous strength that had upheld her at first was slipping from her fast now that the immediate fear of discovery was past, and in the reaction of relief she feared the collapse that was threatening momentarily. She pulled the haick closer about her face that he might not see the moisture lying thick on her forehead and rode on with compressed lips fighting the spells of faintness that made her head reel and the surrounding landscape appear to waver in curious undulations before her eyes.

The dawn was brightening. Already it was light enough to see distinctly, and despite her fatigue, Marny looked with interest on a district that was new to her.

For some time still their way led past farms and fruit gardens, but of human life they saw little. And the few field workers and goatherds they met were absorbed in their own affairs and paid no heed to their passing, or at most bestowed on them a perfunctory salaam that was due to Carew's supposed rank. He looked like a chief, she thought with a strange new feeling of pride. It was difficult seeing him thus to remember that he was an Englishman. To her he would always be an Arab, a man of the open, a desert dweller. And in the sandy wastes of the great wilderness towards which her thoughts had turned so longingly she would live with him the wild free life of her dreams, a life that might prove hard and dangerous but a life that would be made sweet by his love and companionship. If only she need not have come to him like this! If only he had found her in the time of her unfettered girlhood when he could have taken her unstained and without dishonour! But over their love now hung the shadow of disgrace. And it was for her sake that he had done what would be held up to him as a reproach. For her sake—He heard the strangled sob she tried to smother and winced, his eyes sweeping the horizon impatiently. He knew that she had almost reached the limit of her endurance and his arms were aching to hold her, to ease the pain of her weary little body against his own strong limbs, but while the scattered farms still stretched about them he dared not risk the chance of passing observation. Neither, because of

E. M. HULL

her weakness, did he dare to quicken their slow pace—an unaccustomed pace at which Suliman was fretting and protesting, rearing from time to time as he tried to break into the usual gallop.

But at length the last outlying vineyard was passed, and screened by the rising ground of the foothills they were approaching, precaution was no longer necessary. With a sigh of relief Carew swung his horse close to hers and, bending sideways, lifted her easily out of the saddle. She yielded without demur, relaxing against him with a moan of utter exhaustion. He knew that she was crying, but he knew also that the tears which hurt him so poignantly were necessary to relieve the excited brain that had gone so perilously near to destruction and he made no attempt to check them. Tightening his arm about her he gave Suliman his head. And with a snort of pleasure the big bay leaped forward, free to go his own pace at last, galloping as he had galloped when once before he had carried double. The memory of that midnight ride came to Carew as he glanced down at the girl he held before him. With what different feelings he had carried her then! How he had revolted at her proximity, hating the slight burden that was now so precious. Every moment had been torture. Now, in the ecstasy that filled him, he wished that the way were longer, that the moment might never come when he would have to waken from his dream ride of almost unbelievable happiness and face the stern realities of the difficult course that lay before them. For an instant his sombre eyes grew stern and brooding, then he thrust the thought of the future from him. There was time, and enough to think of that. Now he could only think of her. His face grew very tender, very pitiful as he looked at her. Poor little tired child, bruised and broken with appalling experience—would even his love, great as it was, compensate for the suffering that had wrecked her young life? All that was best in him rose up as he caught her closer with a stifled whisper. That he might never fail her, that she might never regret the step she had taken, never regret the faith she had in him, was the prayer that burst from his innermost soul—a prayer that was deeper, more fervent than any he had ever uttered in his life.

But as the bay tore on with long swinging strides that were the perfection of movement, Carew put from him everything but the joy of the moment. After the enforced stay in a town he had come to loathe, after the tedious days of comparative inactivity made hideous by mental struggle, he felt like a man released from prison. Behind him lay all he wished to forget. Before him lay a new life, new happiness, new hope. He could hardly realise yet what it meant to him. No longer alone, with something more than his work to live for, he seemed to see the world suddenly with new eyes—a world of new wonder, a world transformed and beautified. Eagerly he looked at the brightening sky. The dawn had almost come, a dawn that was to him symbolical.

A feeling of exultation came over him. The wild rush through the air, the cool wind blowing against his face, was like an intoxicant stirring him as it always stirred him, and today more powerfully than ever before. For did he not hold in his arms his heart's desire—was not the woman he had craved his at last! With a quick fierce laugh he drove his knees into Suliman's ribs and swung him round to face the open hillside. Gallantly the horse attacked the steep incline, but the gradient was punishing and gradually his pace slackened till it dropped to a walk and, picking his steps carefully amongst the scrub and boulders, he wound his way laboriously up the twisting track till he reached the summit to stand with heaving sides and wide distended nostrils.

And at the same moment the sun rose clear of the banking clouds of gold and crimson, and the full light came with startling suddenness revealing all the wild beauty of the desolate hills. A scene of more than ordinary grandeur, or so it seemed to the man whose heart was throbbing with a passion that almost frightened him and whose whole sensitive being was thrilling and responding to the radiant glory of this most marvellous sunrise he had ever witnessed. Behind them Hosein was on his knees absorbed in rapt devotion, and alone with her he viewed the advent of the new day, the new life that they would live together. The reins dropped loose on Suliman's neck as he raised her high in his arms till their lips met and her shy eyes fell under the ardour of his burning kiss. A kiss that with its hungry passion, its complete possessiveness awoke her to a fuller realisation of the step she had taken.

She was trembling when at last he released her, her quivering face scarlet with shame. Miserably she stared at him, struggling to free herself.

"Let me go," she moaned. "I hadn't any right to ask you—I hadn't any right to make it difficult for you." But in her piteous eyes he read the despair that gave the lie to her stumbling sobbing words.

"You *want* to go—back to him?" he said, slowly. And he was answered in the sharp cry that burst from her as she shuddered closer into his arms, clinging to him with all her feeble strength. With a soft little laugh of triumph he kissed her again and turned in the saddle to shout to Hosein

E.M. HULL

who had finished his prayers and was waiting discreetly in the background with no sign of his inward astonishment visible in his imperturbable face. That the master he worshipped had been stricken with sudden madness was to him the only possible explanation for the departure from established principle, that in his years of service he had become thoroughly acquainted with. Shrewdly observant he had seen and wondered at the gradual change that had come over Carew since the night when he had amazed his retainers by bringing a woman to the camp from which women had always been religiously excluded. And now that same woman was lying across his saddle, a willing captive to the man who was bending over her with a face that was transfigured. That his master had no right to her, that she was the wife of the foreign Sidi who had made himself so notorious in Algiers, were matters of indifference to Hosein. It was no business of his. If his lord had at last found happiness—who was he to judge him! He had been mad with that same madness himself once—

As he ranged alongside leading the spare horse, Marny tried to raise herself.

"I'm rested now—let me ride," she murmured. But Carew saw her face contract with the pain that movement caused her, and shook his head. "You are not fit to ride. Lie still and rest," he said, decisively.

"But you can't carry me all the way, I'm so heavy—" she objected, faintly.

"Heavy!" he laughed, "about as heavy as an extra carbine."

And following his swift glance she noticed for the first time the leathern holster that projected beyond his knee. The sight of it reminded her of the hazardous life that would be hers and made her rebel against the weakness that seemed to make her so unfit a companion for him.

"Let me try," she pleaded. But he shook his head again.

"Do as you're told my dear," he said, with a smile that softened the peremptoriness of his tone. "You're worn out, and you are on the highroad to fever unless you take things easily. I can't have you knocking up out in the desert. You'll want all your strength where we're going."

Where were they going? She wondered without caring. She knew nothing of his plans. She was content to go where he took her, content to follow where he led. She had given her life into his keeping, she was satisfied to leave to him the ordering of that life. With a tired sigh she dropped her head on his breast, thankful for the support of the strong arm crooked about her, yielding to the strength that was so strangely gentle.

A drowsiness she did not attempt to combat stole over her as she lay with closed eyes listening to the murmur of the two men's voices. They were speaking in Arabic which she did not understand, but it seemed to her that Carew was giving certain orders to which his servant responded with his usual brevity. Then there was silence and dreamily she became aware that Hosein had left them and that they were alone on the top of the sun warmed hill. Dead with sleep she felt Carew's arm tighten round her, heard without fully comprehending his explanation that he had sent the Arab on to prepare the camp for their coming, and slept as his lips touched hers.

IT WAS LATE IN THE afternoon when she woke. Still heavy and confused with sleep, at first she was conscious only of the feeling of bodily comfort that enveloped her. Her tired limbs were at rest and she lay propped against soft cushions that eased the dull ache of her wounded shoulders. With a little sigh of physical content, she nestled deeper into the silken pillows, inhaling the faint oriental perfume that clung about them, wondering vaguely when Ann would come to waken her. Ann? Ann would never come to her again! Ann was gone, the victim of petty spite and tyranny. And she—With a strangled cry she started up, trembling violently, staring around her in bewilderment. Then remembrance came with a rush, and sobbing with relief she sank back on the cushions of the wide divan where once before she had slept with such curious confidence.

Wonderingly she looked about the room, at the simple but costly Arab furnishings, at the well stocked gun rack that stood near the couch on which she was lying, at the litter of masculine belongings that with their suggestion of intimacy served to bring home to her even more fully than before the significance of what she had done. His room! The hot blood flamed into her cheeks and she hid her face in the pillows, whispering his name, shivering with a new sweet fear and joy that made her long for him and yet shrink from even the thought of his coming.

How long since he had brought her here? How long since she had fallen asleep in his arms on the top of the sun-bathed hill? The room was perceptibly darker when at last she raised her head and sat up, listening for some sound to penetrate from the adjoining room that should assure her of his nearness. But she heard only the distant hum of the scattered camp—the shrill squeal of an angry stallion, the doleful long-drawn bray of a donkey and, near at hand, the monotonous creak and whine of some unknown piece of mechanism whose use she could not guess. Strange, unfamiliar noises that yet seemed so oddly familiar, like the faint echoes of a far-off memory urging the remembrance of another long forgotten life when she had lived and loved in close proximity to the sounds that now thrilled her with vague wonderings. Did love ever die—was this passion that had overwhelmed her so suddenly only the reawakening of a love that had been born in bygone ages? Had she loved him then! Had he too lived in that remote past that seemed struggling for recognition? Had their wandering souls, long desolate and alone triumphed over the barrier that separated them to converge once more and know again the transient rapture of earthly happiness?

With a tremulous smile she slipped from the couch and went slowly to the little dressing table at the further end of the room. Curiously she stared at herself in the tiny mirror, frowning at the weary white face she saw reflected.

The close-drawn haick had been removed and, tumbled by the heavy head-dress, her hair lay loose in curling waves about her shoulders. The colour crept into her cheeks again as she strove to roll it up into something approaching order. And as she wrestled with the few pins that remained to her, two hands placed suddenly on her shoulders made her start violently. "Must you hide it all away? It was very pretty as it was." There was a new note in his voice, a new hint of definite ownership in his manner as he coolly unloosened the soft coils she had hastily bound up and drew her to him. But she dared not meet his look and, surrendering to his arms, she hid her face against him in an agony of shyness.

With a tender word of expostulation he slipped his hand under her chin and raised her head. His ardent love was crying out for expression but the shamed piteousness of her eyes checked the passionate words that rushed to his lips. What was his love worth if self came before consideration? He stooped his cheek to hers.

"Do you think I don't understand," he murmured, "do you think I don't realise how—strange it is? But you can't be shy with me, dear. Only remember that I love you, that I'd give my life to keep you happy. I'll do all I can to make it easy for you—" But even as he spoke the restraint he imposed on himself slipped for a moment and he crushed her to him conclusively. "Child, child, if you knew how I have longed for you! If you knew what it means to me to hold you in my arms—*here*—to know that you are mine, mine, utterly. Marny—" He pulled himself up sharply with a gesture of compunction, his hands dropping to his sides.

"Forgive me, dear," he said, gently, "I didn't mean to be rough with you—I wouldn't hurt you for the world."

The tears that were so near the surface welled into her eyes and she looked at him strangely.

"Rough?" she whispered, slowly. "I wonder if you know what roughness means—I wonder if you could hurt me if you tried!" Then her face contracted suddenly and her hands went out to him in shuddering appeal. "Keep me from remembering!" she cried, wildly, "help me to blot out the past. I can't tell even you. I want to forget—everything—everything but your love. Oh, my Desert Healer, you heal others, heal me too! Make me strong again—strong and fit to share your life, to be your helper—Don't let me think! Oh, Gervas, don't—let—me—think!"

The look he had dreaded to see again was back in her eyes and her whole body was shaking as she clung to him with all her shyness forgotten in the greater mental distress that made her seek his help and consolation. With almost womanly tenderness he soothed her, holding her till the nervous trembling passed and she lay still in his arms.

"It's over," he said, at last, "over and done with. It's a new life we've begun together, dearest. A new life that will bring you health and strength and, God helping me, a greater joy than we have ever known. The desert will heal you, Marny, as it healed me years ago. Shut your mind to the past. Think only of the future—and of our happiness."

A bitter sob escaped her.

"We haven't any right to be happy," she moaned. He did not answer but she felt him stiffen suddenly and her eyes leaped to his with a new fear dawning in them.

"Gervas—" she gasped, "what will you do—if he won't divorce me? Oh, you don't know him as I do, you don't know of what he is capable. He would do it just to feel that his power was over me still, just to keep me bound, just to hurt us. Gervas, if I can never be free, if I can never be your wife—what then?"

A shadow passed over his face as he looked down at her.

"Will the price of our happiness be too big for you to pay, Marny—or is it me that you doubt?" he asked, slowly.

"*Gervas*—" But his kisses stopped her frantic protestations and there was only love and pity in his eyes as he gathered her closer. "You will always be my wife—as you are my wife to me, now. Nothing can ever alter that. Nothing shall ever come between us. God knows how you've suffered, and He can judge me for what I have done when the time comes. But while I live you're mine and no power on earth shall take you from me." His deep voice was vibrant with passion and for a moment the fierce pressure of his arms was pain. Then as if ashamed of his own display of feeling he put her from him.

"I'm a brute," he exclaimed, remorsefully. "Come and eat, you pale child. I hadn't the heart to wake you before, you were sleeping so soundly."

Shyness fell on her again as he led her into the adjoining room. And throughout the meal that followed she was very silent, eating mechanically what was put before her and studiously avoiding his eyes as from time to time she glanced with furtive curiosity about the big tent.

His heart ached for her as he watched her with an intentness he was careful to conceal. He was longing to help her, longing to make easier the difficult situation which he knew she was only now realising in its entirety, fearful of augmenting her constraint by any word or gesture that should emphasise the new relationship between them. Love made it easy for him to guess her thoughts. With fine intuition he understood perfectly the struggle that complete realisation must have awakened in her mind. Though she loved him, though she had given herself to him, still he knew that she must be shrinking sensitively from the consequences of her own act. His arms had been a refuge she had turned to in her need, but they were the arms of the man who loved her and here, in his tent, she must be facing the hard fact of her obligation, facing the payment of her freedom—a payment that only love could make endurable. More than ever did his own love clamour for utterance but he gripped himself resolutely, playing the part of impassive host with almost cold courtesy while he attended to her wants and keeping the conversation strictly to trivialities, and trivial conversation was not easy. They knew so little the one of the other. He had as yet no knowledge of her tastes, no knowledge of her interests. In spite of the love that had swept them both off their feet they were, to all intents and purposes, strangers to each other, and further hindered by her shy reserve a common meeting ground was difficult to find.

But when the short twilight had faded and the lamps were lit in the tent, when Hosein had come and gone for the last time leaving them alone, he found it impossible to maintain the detached attitude he had adopted, impossible to avoid reference to certain subjects that must of necessity be discussed between them. The sense of their aloneness, the intimacy of the moment, was stirring him deeply and the sight of her lying amongst the heaped up cushions of the divan, lovelier than he had ever seen her, infinitely pathetic as she seemed in her utter dependence on him, was an appeal that was too strong to be resisted and his heart was beating furiously as he went to her.

And affected no less than he, her breath came fast and her shy eyes met his for only a moment as she moved to make place for him. Sitting down beside her he caught her slim hands up to his lips. Then, still holding them in his firm grasp, he crashed through the faint barrier that had risen between them and spoke with unreserved frankness of the future and the life that they would share together. And afterwards, because he believed that only by mutual confidence and trust could their love be perfected, he broke the silence of years and told her the story of his life, the tragedy that had wrecked his early manhood and driven him to a self-imposed exile, and of the consolation he had found in the work that had become so dear to him. And his own confidence ended, he drew from her, bit by bit, the history of her girlhood and pitiful marriage. But of what she had suffered at the hands of the brute to whom her brother had sold her she would say nothing.

"You know," she whispered, with quivering lips, "you saw—the morning after the Governor's ball. I can't speak of it. It hurts me." For a moment he held her closely, his eyes blazing as once before she had seen them blaze, then he rose abruptly and striding across the room flung back the closed entrance flap and stood in the open doorway staring out into the night.

She twisted on the divan to watch him, wondering what chain of thought her words had set in motion, wondering if he was vexed at her reticence. But he gave no explanation of his hasty movement, and after a time he came back slowly, his face inscrutable as she had ever known it, and squatted, Arab fashion, on a pile of cushions near her. Lighting a cigarette, for a while he talked fitfully, his brief remarks punctuated by lengthy silences she did not know how to break. And as the evening wore on he grew more and more distrait until finally he ceased to speak at all, sitting motionless with his eyes fixed on the rug, smoking cigarette after cigarette.

She knew that it was late. The tom-toms and pipes, that earlier in the evening had resounded from the men's quarters, had long since died away. She was conscious of a silence that could be almost felt, she found herself straining her ears to catch some sound that should moderate the deep quiet that was reminiscent of long ago nights in Ireland. But for once there was peace amongst the picketed horses and not even the wail of a jackal came to break the intense stillness. It was as if all the world slept and only she was awake—she and the man to whom she must soon yield the final proof of her love and surrender. She slid her arm across her burning face and shrank closer against the silken pillows, shivering uncontrollably, torn with the conflict that raged within her. She loved him, with her whole being she loved him— madly, utterly. To give him all he demanded would be joy beyond expression—but, oh, dear God, why must their love be stained with sin! Last night he had loved her well enough to let her go—and her coward body had driven her to plead with him until his renunciation became impossible. It was she who was responsible. It was her sin, not his—and let her be the only one to pay. Passionately she prayed it, clenching her teeth to smother the sounds of agony that rose in her throat. Weak with emotion, vaguely frightened by his continued abstraction, she was aching for the clasp of his arms, hungering for his kisses, longing for the comfort and reassurance of his voice. Of what was he thinking as he sat motionless, scowling heavily as he stared into space, no longer even smoking. Was it the remembrance of the early sorrow of which he had told her that made his face so stern and sad? A swift spasm of jealousy shook her. But she crushed it down, her tender brooding eyes growing misty with tears. What need had she to be jealous! The past was over—and his love was hers. He had proved it beyond all doubt. And he had done so much already, it was foolish to expect that every moment of his time could be given to her. He had other matters beside herself to engage his attention, matters that now, because of her, must necessarily have become more complex. It was only natural that he should be pre-occupied and silent. She must be content to wait. He would turn to her again in his own good time.

And when at last he stirred and rose with swift noiselessness to his feet, she was lying so still that he thought she was asleep. For a moment he bent over her, his hands reaching out to the little recumbent body, his strong limbs shaking with the fierce tide of emotion that was pouring over him, his passionate eyes aflame with love and longing. Hungrily he gazed at the woman he had taken for his own. Why did he hesitate? Was she not his, his of her own free will, his to give him all he asked! Of what use to refrain? Who, after what he had done, would believe that he had spared her! And if her fears were justified, if she failed to win release—what would either of them have gained? If not tonight—then sooner or later, for he would never let her go. Wife or mistress, whichever it was to be, he would keep her while the breath of life was in him. Lower and lower he bent till the warm sweet nearness of her, the faint intoxicating perfume of her fragrant hair, and his own desperate need combining shattered the last remnant of his self-control and he swept her up into his arms, straining her to his heaving chest, raining kisses on her lips, her eyes, her palpitating throat, till, panting and exhausted with the force of his ardent embrace, her head fell back against his shoulder and he carried her white-lipped and trembling towards the inner room. But as he reached the screening curtains that barred his impetuous way he came to a sudden halt and the quivering eagerness of his face gave way to a look of doubt and bitter misery. Yearningly he stared into her frightened eyes, then with a gasping sob he slid her slowly to her feet and pushed her gently through the silken hangings. "Go—for God's sake go," he muttered, and wrenched the curtain into place.

Not yet! Not while there still remained a chance that he might take her without dishonour. What the world would not believe was yet possible to him who loved her. Until he was sure, beyond all doubt, that she could never be legally free to marry him he would hold her unscathed, unsoiled by his passion. And, Merciful God, how long would that be? How long would he be able to hold out! He was pledged to Sanois and he had sworn to take her with him. Was he strong enough to withstand the temptation of long months spent in close proximity, riding day after day at her side under the burning sun, sleeping night after night with only a frail curtain between them? He did not know. He only knew that tonight his strength was gone and that he dared not stay beside her. The calm radiance of the star-lit sky, the deep stillness of the night mocked his as he fled from the tent he did not trust himself to look back on. A night of mystical beauty, redolent with the subtle odours of the east, languorous and heavy scented—a night for love and the fulfillment of desire.

With a groan he swept his hand across his eyes, wrestling with physical agony that was intolerable, cursing the scruple that kept him from her, cursing the man who stood between them. The blood was beating in his ears and his brain was on fire as he stumbled through the shadowy darkness of the little valley, striving to subdue the longing that possessed him, striving to banish the torturing thought of her nearness. Blind to the road he was taking, he saw only the sweet pale face that had flushed to the touch of his burning kisses, saw only the tempting beauty of the slender loveliness he craved. Was she asleep, as he prayed with all his soul she might be—or was she too awake, longing for him as he was longing for her, suffering as he was suffering? Just now she had trembled in his arms and he had seen the fear that leaped to her flickering eyes, but she had made no effort to repulse him, had made no plea for release. Instead she had clung to him. And it seemed to him that he could still feel the touch of her fingers, ice-cold and shaking against his, still feel the rapid beating of her heart, the tumultuous rise and fall of her delicate bosom as he carried her swiftly across the room. She had been willing, and he—He flung out his hands with a bitter cry and dropped like a log, burying his head in his arms.

Hour after hour he lay motionless on the soft warm sand, too passion swept to sleep, till at last the raging fever that consumed him abated, and he knew that, for the time being, his victory over himself was complete.

But there was no peace in his mind. There was another decision that had to be made before the stars faded and the sun rose on a new day—a decision he knew in his heart was already determined. By acceding to the frenzied appeal of the woman he loved, in his endeavour to save her from further suffering, he had done a thing unpardonable. That did not trouble him. He did not regret it, he would never regret it. Her happiness was the only thing that weighed with him. Last night her need, and only her need, had been his sole consideration. Mad with fear she had implored him to take her from Algiers and, trembling for her reason, he had consented. But tonight his thoughts were centered on the husband from whom he had taken her. He would never give her up—but he would steal no man's wife in secret. He was going back to Algiers—going back to face the man he had wronged. And what would be the outcome of that interview? No matter what Geradine had done—she was his wife. No matter what she had suffered at his hands— he was her husband. No extenuating circumstances could gloss over the hard indisputable fact or lessen his own culpableness.

What would Geradine do?

Carew rose deliberately to his feet with a harsh mirthless laugh. He knew what he would do himself if the position were reversed, what he would unhesitatingly have done twelve years ago if the opportunity had been given him. And if Geradine shot him like a dog, as he deserved to be shot, what would become of the girl who trusted to him? To stay—and forfeit his own self-respect. To go—knowing that he might never return. Heavens above, what a choice! But there was no other way thinkable. His mind was fixed, and the rest lay with Geradine. Would the cur who had stooped to strike a woman fight to regain possession of her, fight to avenge his honour? If he only would—by God, if he only would! The breath hissed through Carew's set teeth and his strong hands clenched in fierce anticipation as his mind leaped forward to the coming meeting. The primitive man in him was uppermost as he thought with curious pleasure of Geradine's huge proportions and powerful limbs. There was not much to choose between them. True he had thrashed him last night, but the man had been drunk. Heaven send that he was sober this time!

With a strange smile he swung on his heel and strode back to the sleeping camp.

But as he neared the tent his swift pace lessened and his sombre eyes were dull with pain as he passed under the lance-propped awning into the empty living room. How could he leave her to wait alone until he came again—or did not come! What would be the effect of those long-drawn hours of suspense on the nervous brain that was already dangerously overstrained and excited? His stern lips quivered as he parted the curtains and felt his way to the long low couch that was only dimly visible.

His tentative whisper was answered by a stifled sob, and out of the darkness two soft bare arms came tremblingly to close about his neck and drew his head down to the pillow that was wet with her tears. That she had wept bitterly was evident, and shaken by the distress his resolution almost failed. But he crushed the momentary weakness that came over him. "My dear, my dear," he murmured, huskily, "have I made you weep so soon? Have I failed you tonight of all nights when you needed me most? Did you think I didn't care—that I didn't want you! Do you think it was easy for me to go from the heaven of your arms to a hell of loneliness under those cursed stars? God knows it was hard—as hard as it is for me to say what I've got to say to you now." And with characteristic directness he told her plainly the course he had decided.

At first she did not seem to understand, then as she grasped the meaning of his words a cry of terror burst from her. "You can't go— you can't, you can't. Oh, Gervas, stay with me, don't leave me! If you go you'll never come back and I—" she shuddered, horribly, and her frenzied voice sank to an agonised whisper. "He'll kill you. *Gervas, he'll kill you!*"

"Pray God, I don't kill him," he retorted, grimly, and with gentle force he unloosened the tightly clasped arms that were locked about his neck. "I've got to go, dear," he said, steadily, "it's the only thing I can do." And unable to bear the sound of her passionate weeping he turned away. But with a wail of anguish she leaped to her feet, striving with all her strength to hold him.

"Gervas, Gervas, don't leave me like that—tell me you love me, tell me you'll come back to me—"

For a long moment his lips clung to hers, then he laid her on the bed. "You know I love you, Marny," he answered, "it is because I love you that I am going back to Algiers." There was a note of intense sadness in his voice that made her bury her face in the pillow to stifle the sobs that were fast growing beyond control, but there was also in it a ring of finality that made further pleading impossible. Nothing she could say would move him. His will was stronger than hers and she knew that, despite the love and consideration that henceforward would make possession so different, she had but exchanged one master for another.

When she raised her head again she was alone and she started up, trembling with dread, listening till her ears ached that she might hear the last sound of his voice. But there was only silence in the adjoining room and, driven by an irresistible impulse, she fled through the communicating curtains. The loose entrance flap was only partially closed and, screened by the looped-back draperies she waited scarcely breathing, straining her eyes through the gloom, praying that she might see him once more.

And when he came it was only a momentary glimpse, a fleeting impression of two shadowy horsemen who flashed past the tent to vanish in the darkness beyond as though they had never been, and sobbingly she stumbled back to the inner room, flinging herself in a passion of tears on the bed where she had wept throughout the lonely hours of the night. She did not question his action, it was enough for her that he had done what he thought best. And there was no bitterness in her grief. Selfless, she did not think of herself. It was only of him she was thinking, only for him she was agonising. The brutal strength she knew by terrible experience, the savage unbridled nature she had learned so thoroughly—what would he do? What ghastly tragedy would ensue from the meeting of these two men so strangely opposite, so strangely linked by a common desire? Tortured by horrible imaginings, mad with fear, she writhed in mental anguish that took from her all power of reasoning, and tossing to and fro on the soft bed that still gave no rest to her aching limbs, she wept until she had no more tears, until exhausted she fell asleep.

It was mid-day before she woke. The room was filled with light, hot with the vertical rays of the sun blazing down on the roof of the tent. Slipping from the bed she stood for a moment holding her throbbing head between her hands, then moved languidly towards the dressing table. At the further end of the room she found a little bathroom, Spartan-like in its appointments but containing all that was needful and half-an-hour later, bathed and refreshed, she went listlessly into the living room.

As she came through the curtain, Hosein, who was squatting on his heels by the doorway, rose to his feet with a deep salaam. And listening to his low-voiced inquiry whether it was her pleasure to eat, she wondered how long he had been waiting there, wondered what lay behind his inscrutable face and suave deferential manner. She had learned from Carew last night of his Arab servant's devotion, and of the confidence that existed between them, and his presence now gave her a curious feeling of reassurance. She knew without being told that Carew must have left her in his keeping, knew also that Hosein must be perfectly aware of the reason of his master's absence, and his calm demeanour and untroubled expression seemed insensibly to soothe her own agitation of mind. But when the meal which had appeared with almost magical quickness was finished, when Hosein had gone again and she was alone once more, the temporary courage that had come to her faded as new doubts and fears crowded in upon her more overwhelmingly than before. How could she rest! How could she bear the torture of long hours of waiting—waiting that might never end!

And mingling with the present agony came the memory of past suffering. Why had the way of life been made so difficult for her? To what end the misery she had endured? Was it that through sorrow and pain she might attain to a greater perfection hereafter? Her lips quivered. The goal had been too high for her endeavour. Her faith had not been strong enough to trust only in the Divine Comforter. In her despair she had turned to earthly consolation, and the clamouring of her starved heart had driven her into the arms of the man who loved her. And stronger than she, he had striven to save her from the consequences of her weakness. But she had tempted him—tempted him with her fear, tempted him with her threat of suicide. Why didn't he hate her for the vile despicable thing she was! Gervas! Gervas! Cold and shivering, tortured with suspense, unconscious of the passing hours, she huddled on the divan, hoping, despairing, until concrete thought became at last impossible, until all her senses seemed merged into one dominant perception as she lay listening, listening for the soft thud of galloping hoofs.

And in the end, it was no actual sound that roused her, but an instinctive intuition, an indefinite something penetrating to her brain that sent her flying with shaking limbs and palpitating heart to the open doorway.

The sun was setting and every detail of the rosy-tinged landscape stood out in sharp and clear relief. But her wild dilated eyes saw nothing of the peaceful beauty of her surroundings as she waited, sick with apprehension for the moment that should determine her fate.

The camp was curiously silent. There was no sign of life, nothing to impede her view except the odd blur that came over her eyes at intervals. How long she stood there she never knew. One thought only held her motionless, one question that her pallid lips repeated monotonously. Which—which?

And then, quite suddenly, she *knew*—knew even before the three swift moving horses swept into sight from behind the angle of jutting rocks that framed the entrance to the little valley. Faint with the shock of relief she clung to the curtains for support, watching them gallop towards the tent as though the hounds of hell were at their heels. Why were there three? Only one attendant had gone with him. And the horseman who rode so closely behind was no Arab. Her heart seemed to miss a beat as she recognised the slim little figure whose crouching seat in the saddle was so familiar to her. Oh, God, what had happened! Why was Tanner with him!

But she had no time for reflection. She saw the foam flecked black horse, savage and intractable still in spite of the punishing ride, race to the very entrance of the tent; saw his rider drag him, screaming and fighting, to a standstill. Then as Carew leaped to the ground, an overmastering panic seized her and she shrank back into the room wide eyed and trembling.

He came through the doorway slowly, reeling slightly as he walked, and took her into his arms without a word. His face was grey with dust and fatigue and there was a strangeness in his manner that forced utterance from her.

"Geradine—" The fearful whisper was barely audible, but he heard it and his arms tightened round her with a quick convulsive movement.

"Dead," he said tensely.

She did not flinch from him but her face went ghastly and a terrible shudder passed through her.

"Not you, oh, Gervas, not you?" she breathed, imploringly.

His tired eyes looked into hers with infinite tenderness, infinite understanding.

"No, thank God, it was not I," he said quietly. "Malec killed him. They killed each other. Tanner found them when he went back to the house early the next morning. The other servants had cleared out—the place was empty. I can't tell you any more, dear. It's too—beastly."

She was leaning weakly against him, her face hidden in his robes, shivering from head to foot. And as he broke off abruptly, she shuddered closer to him, clutching at his burnous with shaking fingers.

"Was it my fault—was it *our* fault?" she gasped, with a ring of horror in her voice.

"No," he answered, almost violently, "it was his own fault. He brought it on himself. But he's dead, poor devil, and God knows I haven't the right to judge him."

He held her silently for a moment, then the strained rigidity of his features relaxed and a great gladness dawned in his eyes as he stooped his tall head to the soft curls lying on his breast.

"Marny," he whispered, impellently, "Marny—my wife!" And with a little cry that was love and trust and joy unutterable, she lifted her tear wet face and yielded her lips to his.

A Note About the Author

E.M. Hull (1880–1947) was an English romance novelist. Born in London, Hull was the daughter of a Canadian mother and a father from New York City. As a girl, Hull visited Algeria with her family, providing the setting for many of her successful novels, including *The Sheikh* (1919), an international bestseller. Notoriously reclusive, Hull settled in Derbyshire with her husband, a civil engineer and pig farmer, with whom she had a daughter, Cecil Winstanley Hull. *The Sheikh* served as source material for a popular 1921 silent film of the same name by Paramount, leading to the sale of millions of copies of Hull's novel.

A Note from the Publisher

Spanning many genres, from non-fiction essays to literature classics to children's books and lyric poetry, Mint Edition books showcase the master works of our time in a modern new package. The text is freshly typeset, is clean and easy to read, and features a new note about the author in each volume. Many books also include exclusive new introductory material. Every book boasts a striking new cover, which makes it as appropriate for collecting as it is for gift giving. Mint Edition books are only printed when a reader orders them, so natural resources are not wasted. We're proud that our books are never manufactured in excess and exist only in the exact quantity they need to be read and enjoyed.

bookfinity™

Discover more of your favorite classics with Bookfinity™.

- Track your reading with custom book lists.
- Get great book recommendations for your personalized Reader Type.
- Add reviews for your favorite books.
- AND MUCH MORE!

Visit **bookfinity.com** and take the fun Reader Type quiz to get started.

Enjoy our classic and modern companion pairings!

Classic & Modern

9 781513 277448